THE ROM COM MOVIE CLUB

THE ROM COM MOVIE CLUB

BOOK ONE

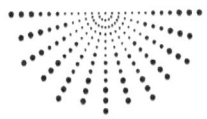

BERNADETTE MARIE

5 PRINCE PUBLISHING

Published by 5 PRINCE PUBLISHING & BOOKS, LLC

PO Box 865, Arvada, CO 80001

www.5PrinceBooks.com

ISBN digital: 978-1-63112-296-5

ISBN print: 978-1-63112-297-2

Cover Credit: Marianne Nowicki

For Stan,
First date as a couple.
A dream come true.
A life of rom com style fun.
I love you!

"Some dreams come true; some don't. But, keep on dreaming. This is Hollywood. Always time to dream, so keep on dreaming." ~Pretty Woman, 1990

ACKNOWLEDGMENTS

Special thanks goes out to my Mother, Sister, Husband, T, N, G, S, & J for always allowing me the chuckle, eye roll, and shared love of my beloved rom coms.

"Love is patient, love is kind, love means slowly losing your mind." ~*27 Dresses*

For Cate who puts up with dissecting my gibberish.

"I like you very much. Just as you are." ~*Bridget Jones's Diary*

For Megan Hammond, Lindsey Haggerty, Daisy Salgado Pham, and Carrie Winfield. Thank you for making me look good.

"I gave her my heart and she gave me a pen." ~*Say Anything*

For my loyal readers—Thank you for coming back time and time again.

"They say nothing lasts forever; dreams change, trends come and go, but friendships never go out of style." ~*Carrie Bradshaw, Sex and the City the Movie*

OTHER TITLES BY

THE ROM COM MOVIE CLUB

The Rom Com Movie Club - Book One

The Rom Com Movie Club - Book Two

The Rom Com Movie Club - Book Three

FUNERALS AND WEDDINGS SERIES

Something Lost

Something Discovered

Something Found

Something Forbidden

Something New

THE DEVEREAUX FAMILY SERIES

Kennedy Devereaux

Chase Devereaux

Max Devereaux

Paige Devereaux

STAND ALONE TITLES

The Happily Ever After Bookstore

THE MATCHMAKER SERIES

Matchmakers

Encore

Finding Hope

THE THREE MRS. MONROES TRILOGY

Amelia

Penelope

Vivian

THE ASPEN CREEK SERIES

First Kiss

Unexpected Admirer

On Thin Ice

Indomitable Spirit

THE DENVER BRIDE SERIES

Cart Before the Horse

Never Saw it Coming

Candy Kisses

ROMANTIC SUSPENSE

Chasing Shadows

PARANORMAL ROMANCES

The Tea Shop

The Last Goodbye

HOLIDAY FAVORITES

Corporate Christmas

Tropical Christmas

Date for Hire

THE ROM COM MOVIE CLUB

CHAPTER ONE

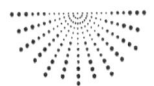

THERE WAS A RITUAL, AND NO ONE STRAYED FROM THE RITUAL.

Pajama pants. Check.

College T-shirts. Check.

No makeup so that a face mask, acquired by the hostess, could be worn at some time during the evening. Check.

Popcorn. M&Ms. Diet soda. Wine. Pizza.

Check. Check. Check. Check. And check.

Lisa looked around the small living room right off the even tinier kitchen, and decided she had everything in order. It was only four in the afternoon and she looked as if she were staying in for a slumber party, but that was what Rom Com Movie Night was all about.

They'd created the monthly viewing "club" after having watched *Grease* in the dorms, and Lisa mentioning that she'd never had, or been to, a slumber party. And though it was never intended to be a slumber party, sometimes it just happened.

Usually, movie night was the second Saturday of the month, but Tina's sister had planned Tina's bridal shower for that afternoon, and Lisa couldn't help but wonder if that was on purpose. Cicely was a wonderful woman, she really was. A younger sister to them all, but there had always been some resentment toward Tina's besties. Cicely didn't have a core base of friends like her sister did, and that was too bad, she could have used her own posse.

So, without a word about it, Rom Com Movie Night was simply moved to the first Saturday in May.

Lisa never much cared for being the hostess, and luckily it was only once every four months. Her condo was the smallest of all the houses where the besties lived.

Ruby's apartment was also a two bedroom, but with a bigger floor plan, and she usually had a roommate. Though, she didn't tend to keep any one roommate for long.

Mindy had a house with a yard, a gazebo, and a fountain. It had been her grandmother's house and she'd inherited it after college graduation. Everyone agreed that they'd be happy to do movie night there every month, even though the house was extremely outdated, but fair was fair, and they all took their turns.

Tina was currently living with her future in-laws because weddings were freaking expensive. As soon as she and Aaron were married, they were moving out—or so she'd said.

Lisa turned on the oven for the pizzas. She'd premade the pizzas and created a video for her YouTube channel, which was all about food. She thought homemade was better than someone running out in the middle of the movie to get them or risk some eighteen-year-old college kid toking up in his car with their pizza in the passenger seat.

The doorbell rang just after four. There was no surprise in finding Tina standing at the door, a bottle of wine in hand, and her favorite Snoopy pajama pants on.

She had her blonde hair pulled up into two ponytails, like Chrissy from *Three's Company*, a sitcom Lisa used to watch reruns of after school with Mama Rose.

"I'm going to drink this entire bottle of wine by myself. Put my name on it," Tina growled through gritted teeth.

Lisa took the bottle and smiled at her friend who barely stood five feet tall. "Future in-law drama?"

Tina groaned as she walked into Lisa's condo and plopped right down on the sofa. She had on a T-shirt from the first college her fiancé attended, the University of Maryland, and she'd worn fuzzy slippers instead of shoes.

"His mother wants those stupid almonds on the tables at the reception. Seriously? Do you know my mother broke her tooth on one of those once? It's a liability and a cost I don't want to have. And, now her best-friend's sister wants to come to the wedding. I don't know that woman. We have all the invitations out and RSVPs coming back. This is my wedding."

Lisa took the corkscrew she'd laid out on the counter, and opened the bottle of wine that Tina had brought. Filling one of the wine glasses she'd had at the ready, Lisa poured Tina a full glass of wine and carried it to her as Tina scooped up a handful of M&Ms and began to pop them into her mouth one by one.

"What does Aaron say to all of this?" Lisa asked.

Tina took the wine glass and sipped. "He thinks I should just be calm. His mother has a lot going on right now."

"And you don't?"

Tina's eyes went wide at the validation. "Right?" She sipped again. "They went from empty nesters to us moving in. Temporarily," she demanded. "And now Aaron's brother has moved back in because the company he worked for just sold and there are like a thousand employees being moved around the country or getting laid off."

Lisa sat on the arm of the sofa. "And which is he?"

"Undecided. They have an office here in Denver, but he's not sure."

"I've never met his brother. What's his name?"

"Ryan." Tina finished the M&Ms in her hand, set down the

glass of wine, and pulled her phone from where she'd tucked it in her bra. She scrolled through her Facebook feed and then handed Lisa the phone.

"Where has he been hiding?" Lisa swooned.

Tina's brow rose as she picked up her glass of wine. "In Illinois."

"But he's coming here?"

Tina laughed. "I warn you against him."

"Why?"

"Because I live with his mother too."

Lisa laughed, but she couldn't help but let her finger scroll over the pictures on his Facebook feed. Tall, dark, handsome—he fit the bill.

In a photo with Aaron, he stood at least four inches taller than his brother. And in a photo on a boat—fishing—he was a well-defined specimen of man.

Lisa's mouth went dry. "Is he seeing anyone?"

Tina was mid sip of wine as she looked up at Lisa. "No. He used to date some woman in Chicago, but they've been off again more than they were on."

"Tragedy."

"You're not hooking up with my new brother-in-law."

"Who said hooking up? I'm thinking I could fall in love with this guy and keep him."

Tina snorted out a laugh. "Keep dreaming."

Lisa thought she just might keep dreaming. And to think, Mr. Tall-Dark-Handsome would be around a lot soon. They'd be at dinners together. Rehearsals. Parties. Weddings. Receptions. Oh, yes. Ryan Blair was in her sights now.

When the doorbell rang, Lisa stood, Tina's phone still in her hand.

On the front step, Ruby and Mindy stood in pajama bottoms and college T-shirts, bare-faced, hair up, and each of them had something to drink in their hands.

"What are we watching?" Ruby asked as she strolled into the condo.

"*While You Were Sleeping*," Lisa replied.

Mindy's eyes went wide. "Bill Pullman. Yummy."

Ruby turned back to her and winced. "Over Peter Gallagher?"

"Too many eyebrows," Mindy snorted a laugh and then looked at the phone in Lisa's hand. "Who is that?"

Lisa looked down at the picture she'd landed on of Ryan in ski gear. "The future Mr. Palmer, of course," she teased and Tina groaned.

"It's my future brother-in-law, and Lisa's horny," Tina called out from the couch.

Ruby laughed a thunderous laugh, while Mindy blushed at the comment.

Ruby shrugged. "Just think. You and Tina could compare notes."

"Oh-my-God!" Tina took a large sip of her wine and handed her glass back to Lisa. "More. I'm going to need a lot more."

CHAPTER TWO

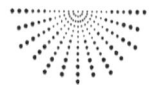

Moving boxes lined the walls of the garage. Ryan's boxes took up one side and Aaron and Tina's the other side. There was enough room to walk down the middle of the garage, sideways, to get into the house.

To humor themselves, Aaron and Ryan had each uncovered their sofas and set them facing one another with a cooler in between as a table.

Ryan twisted the top from his beer and kicked his feet up on the cooler, mimicking his brother.

"You're getting married," Ryan groaned into his beer. "That's the most fricking grown-up thing ever."

Aaron snorted a laugh. "No, that would be having kids. But this would be the next biggest."

"I thought I was hot shit living in Chicago, out from under Mom and Dad."

"You were hot shit. Now you're just shit, living in their spare bedroom with all your crap in their garage."

That hit home just right, Ryan thought as he sipped his beer. "This can't last long. I'll lose my mind."

"What's not to love? You come home to dinner on the table. She washes our clothes, though Tina hates that."

"Seriously, maybe Tina should rethink marrying you if you're that happy being here."

"Nah, she loves me too much," Aaron laughed as he took a long pull from his beer. "So what are we doing for my bachelor party?"

"I have to plan that?"

"You're my best man."

"Shit."

"And no couples crap," Aaron protested. "And I don't need something stupid like strippers or clubs. But maybe we could go axe throwing or go-cart racing."

Ryan laughed. "You're nothing but a big child."

"A big child who gets homemade chocolate chip cookies on Wednesdays."

Ryan shook his head. "She still does that?"

"It's like a religion."

"Okay, I'll stick around for that," he teased. "Where is Tina tonight?"

"It's Rom Com Movie Club night."

Ryan raised a brow as he lifted his beer to his lips. "What the hell is that?"

Aaron pulled his phone from his pocket and scrolled. He stopped on a photo with four women in pajamas, his fiancée among the women laughing, each with a glass of wine in their hands.

"Who are they?" Ryan asked.

Aaron pointed to the brunette at the end of the photo. "Mindy, she was Tina's roommate freshman year. You know Tina. This is Ruby," he pointed to the chesty redhead with her hair piled into a messy bun on top of her head. "And this is Lisa."

Ryan took his brother's phone from him and studied the photo. Lisa was the tallest of the four women, and by build,

7

looked the most athletic, according to the arms she boasted in the tank top with the *Fighting Irish* written on it.

"This is a real club?" Ryan asked zooming in on Lisa's face.

"It is to them. They've done it once a month since college."

Ryan nodded slowly. "Slumber party?"

Aaron shrugged. "Sometimes. It depends on how much wine they drink," he said taking his phone back from his brother and scrolling through more photos. "This was them going to the theater. A little more put together."

Ryan looked at the photo of the same four women, standing in the same formation as the last photo.

They were all dressed up in dresses of different lengths. Though he thought maybe Lisa and Ruby had on the very same dress, the length of Lisa's legs, in heels, made the dress look drastically different than it did on Ruby.

"Which of these gals are married?"

Aaron shook his head. "You're not shopping, are you?"

"Just window shopping," Ryan promised.

"Tina is the first to get married."

Ryan let out a low hum. "Very nice."

"You're a pig," Aaron took back his phone.

"Just a lonely out-of-sorts bachelor drinking beer on his couch in his parents' garage. I seriously don't see anything wrong with me at all."

They both laughed at that and finished their beers.

"You're not too many down, are you?" Their mother's voice rang out from the house, over the boxes.

"Just one," Aaron said.

"Tina was going to take this box of cookies with her and she forgot them."

Ryan stood. "I'll eat them."

"Like hell you will," their mother's voice grew near as she appeared from between the boxes. "Head over there and give them to her." She handed the box to Aaron.

Ryan set his empty beer bottle on the top of the cooler and took the box from his brother. "I'll take shotgun. You can drive my truck."

Aaron nodded his acceptance of the plan. "We'll pick this up later," he assured their mother before they both kissed her on the cheek and headed toward Ryan's Ford Bronco, with the new tags still on it.

"I can't believe you're going to let me drive this," Aaron said as he jumped into the driver's seat and had to move the seat closer to the steering wheel.

"It's worth it. You're taking me, and this box of cookies, minus one," he said opening the box and taking one out, "to a pajama party where there are women drinking wine. I'm going to walk in with a box of gold. I'll be a god."

"My earlier statement stands. You're a pig."

"And you're happy I'm home. Admit it."

Aaron shifted a glance in Ryan's direction, as Ryan bit into the stolen cookie. "I hate it when you're right."

CHAPTER THREE

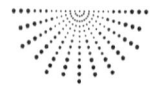

ALL FOUR WOMEN HUDDLED ON THE SOFA WITH AVOCADO MASKS covering their faces. Their four wine glasses waited for them on the counter, each designated with the special charms that went from one house to another each month and signified whose glass was whose.

"How the hell do you get a man of that size off the train tracks?" Ruby asked as they watched Sandra Bullock's character, Lucy, try to wake up Peter Callaghan, who was in danger of being run over by a train.

"That's why it cuts right to the hospital. It doesn't show them having to lift him and throw him in an ambulance," Lisa said. "There is nothing sexy about the EMT version of this story."

Ruby snorted out a laugh at that. "Rom coms are deliciously stupid."

Lisa nodded, but she wasn't so sure. Hadn't they all gone to the opera, and sat in a box, just to experience what Julia Roberts had in *Pretty Woman*? How many times had they each giggled when one of them would say, "Oh, look! There's a band."

And somewhere in that same night, they walked down a set of steep stairs and waved like beauty contestants in their very best

Agent Hart impression from *Miss Congeniality*, which had also sparked a Vegas trip to Treasure Island after they'd seen the second movie. Of course, they'd planned the trip to fall on April 25th, because in the movie, when Cheryl, Miss Rhode Island, was asked to explain her perfect date, she'd misinterpreted the question, and instead of defining a date out on the town, she declared that April 25th was a perfect date.

And on a trip to New York, they'd eaten at Gray's Papaya just because Hanks and Ryan ate there in *You've Got Mail*, and Matthew Perry went on about it in *Fools Rush In*. Though none of them were impressed with the food, it was an epic adventure, and that's what counted.

Sure, the movies were certainly not based in reality, but who wanted that?

Though Lisa thought it would be wonderful to have a family like Peter and Jack Callaghan's, in the movie they were watching. A mom, a dad, and even a grandmother under one roof. Siblings that seemed to know each other well, yet appeared to be generations different in age, that cherished everyone. Heck, there was even a dear old family friend.

No, she understood Sandra Bullock's character Lucy more than she understood the Callaghans.

A tear broke through and dampened the mask that was hardening on her face. She hoped it would dry. One of them always seemed compelled to sob over something during movie night.

She wiggled her freshly-painted pink toes, which matched everyone else's. If these nights ever stopped, Lisa would be devastated.

When the doorbell rang, all four women turned collectively to look at the door.

"You're making pizza, right?" Mindy asked.

"Yup," Lisa replied

"Did you hire a stripper?" Ruby snorted a laugh.

"As if." Lisa stood, and walking on her heels, keeping her toes up, she looked out of the peep hole. "Shit! It's your fiancé and his brother," she directed the comment to Tina.

"The box of cookies I forgot," Tina said, realizing why they'd shown up.

Mindy was the first off the couch, running down the hallway to remove the green mask that had hardened and begun to crack. Tina followed her down the hall.

Ruby shook her head. "Pansies," she said as she jumped over the back of the couch and pulled the door open before Lisa could even consider running after the other two women to remove the pulp from her face.

"Delivery for me? You shouldn't have," Ruby's voice boomed as she stood there in her pajamas, wet toes, and cracking facial mask.

Lisa heard Aaron's laugh. "Looking good, Ruby."

Ruby twirled in front of the men. "I'm always on game. Come in. If you stay, you must wear a facial mask and the color of the night is Pink Lemonade for your toes."

She stepped back and the two men entered the dimly lit condo.

Lisa watched as Aaron smiled at her, but then she got her first real-life look at his brother Ryan, and she was officially petrified right where she stood.

"Hey, Lisa," Aaron said, but all she could do was stand there like a green and pink tree. "Mask a little too tight?"

She nodded and headed down the hallway where the other two had already made a wet mess trying to get the masks off their faces.

RYAN PULLED IN HIS LIPS SO HE WOULDN'T SMILE. THE PICTURES were nothing compared to what he'd just witnessed.

Ruby wasn't a girl who gave a shit about opinions, and he liked that. She'd taken on the pajama theme seriously, right down to not even having on a bra, but she didn't seem to mind that even in front of a stranger.

Ruby was already in the kitchen opening the refrigerator. "She has a few beers, no doubt a stale bottle of Coke, or we have wine. Lots of wine."

Aaron shook his head. "I'm fine."

But Ryan had a pull to stay for a moment. "I'll take a beer."

His brother shot him a look as if he wanted to get out of there the moment he talked to Tina, but Ryan was all in. He had no intent on wearing a mask or painting his toes, but crashing a girls' slumber party, that had always been on his list of things to do. He just didn't think he'd be thirty by the time he did it.

Tina appeared from the bathroom. Her face was damp with traces of green still lingering on her cheek and forehead.

"What are you two doing here?" she asked as she walked straight to Aaron.

"Mom wanted us to bring you the cookies you forgot."

She blew a stray hair from her face. "It wasn't that important."

Aaron shrugged. "It seemed to be, or we wouldn't be here."

Her lips had gone into a straight line. She looked at Ryan. "Ryan, this is Ruby," she introduced him to the redhead who was getting him a beer.

He gave her a nod.

"This is Mindy," she said, signaling to the woman who continued dry her face with a towel.

Mindy gave him a small wave.

"And that's Lisa, our host," she said as the blonde walked out of the bathroom, her face fresh and red from scrubbing the mask off.

She wore a UCLA T-shirt, and he wondered if that was generic or if there was a connection to UCLA

"It's nice to meet you," Ryan said as Lisa neared them.

"Nice to meet you too." She looked past him to his brother. "Aaron, nice to see you."

CHAPTER FOUR

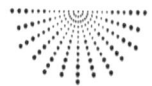

RUBY TWISTED THE TOP OFF THE BEER IN HER HAND, AND HANDED it to Ryan, serving it with a wink. Admittedly, that irritated Lisa, but she wasn't sure why. Was it that the men were in her home on a Rom Com Movie Club night? Was it the wink that Ruby gave to Ryan, a man they all just met? Or was it irritating that Ruby was freely giving away Lisa's beer?

"So, whose place is this?" Ryan asked as he sipped his beer.

"Mine," Lisa said, looking toward him.

He nodded and took a pull from his beer. "It's nice. I have to think about getting a place. Now I need to decide if I want a condo, a house, a townhome, a tent."

Aaron snorted out a laugh. "Only in Colorado are they all an option. Show him around, Lisa. It's a nice place."

Lisa's eyes went wide, and Tina smacked Aaron on the arm. "You can't just invite someone into someone's house and then tell them to show them around."

"It's fine," Lisa said, pausing the movie. "Well, this is the kitchen and living room."

Ryan nodded and looked around. "Cozy but plenty of room," he said, setting his beer on the counter.

He followed her down the hall to the first bedroom. "I use this room for an office," she said, and Ryan stepped into the room with her.

"Nice set-up," he said looking around at the pink and gray walls. Reaching out, he touched one of the ring lights near her computer. "What do you do?"

Lisa tucked a stray piece of hair behind her ear. "I'm a food blogger."

Ryan lifted a brow. "That's your job?"

She nodded. "Is that so strange?"

"I didn't think people did that for real. I mean, I didn't think they made money on it," he said as he turned and saw the YouTube Creator Award on her wall. "Holy cow. They don't just give these things out. You're the real deal, huh?"

"Like I said, I make my living doing it."

"I'm impressed," he said looking around the room. "I'll have to look you up."

Lisa swallowed hard as Ryan's dark eyes settled on her and he smiled. "*Lisa Does Dishes, a Culinary Adventure.*"

Ryan blinked. "Oh, that's the name of the channel?"

"Yes."

"Got it," he said smiling. "And you cook the dishes?"

"Of course."

His smile widened. "Maybe I could come over and you could cook me something."

"Oh, well..."

"I'm forward. Or that's what Tina says. But, hey, I'm thirty. I've learned that if I want to know about something, or someone, I have to ask, right?"

"Right," Lisa said. "I could cook for you."

The corner of his mouth lifted even higher, and Lisa's heart hammered a little faster.

"I'd love that. Next Saturday?"

Lisa blinked hard. "Sure," she agreed and then waved her

hands. "No."

"No?"

"Bridal shower," was all she managed.

"I think I heard something about that. Are you throwing that?"

Lisa shook her head. "Her sister is."

"But you're in the wedding?"

"Yes."

"I've seen pictures of the bridesmaids' dresses. I'll bet you'll be stunning."

He was right, she thought. He was forward. It was a bit refreshing, she had to admit, but it certainly threw her off her game—especially since she was standing in front of him fresh faced, with her hair piled atop her head and wearing a pair of pajamas.

Lisa stepped out of the room and Ryan followed.

"There's a bathroom," she pointed out. "And this is my room."

He didn't step into her bedroom, she noticed. Ryan took it all in from the doorway.

"I like your decorating style. The grays and browns. Very modern."

"Thank you."

"Yeah, this is a nice place," he said looking around as if he were touring with a realtor. "Anything would be nice that wasn't my parents' house."

"You live with your parents?" she asked, even though she knew that.

That smile was back, and Lisa noticed when he smiled with only half of his mouth, it twisted her up a bit.

"Just moved in. So, the house is full with Tina and Aaron there too. My job got moved, or downsized, or relocated. I guess it depends on how you look at it. But we have a branch in Denver, so I'm considering putting in for the position here."

"What do you do?" Lisa asked.

Ryan leaned his back against the door jamb, tucking his hands into his front pockets. "I'm a web designer for a company that develops technology for other companies."

Lisa lifted her brows. "That sounds deep."

Ryan smiled. "It's a very minute part of a company that is worldwide. So, they closed my office in Chicago, and said we could all apply at a different location."

"That seems a little cold."

Ryan shrugged. "That's corporate America."

"Maybe I should have you look at my website. You could give me feedback."

"I could do that." Ryan scanned a look over her. "So, UCLA?"

For a moment Lisa wasn't sure what he was talking about, or why he'd changed the subject so suddenly. Then she remembered that was the shirt she was wearing.

"We wear collegiate T-Shirts with our pajama bottoms for movie night."

"You went to UCLA?"

Lisa shook her head. "No. I bought it at an airport."

Ryan shifted, still leaning against the doorjamb, he crossed his arms in front of him. "So where did you go to college?"

Lisa chewed her bottom lip and crossed her arms in front of her, mimicking Ryan's stance. "I didn't go to college."

"Oh, for some reason I thought you were all college friends."

"We were—are," she amended. "I lived near campus and worked at a coffee shop. The girls seemed to embrace me and pulled me into their circle. I spent time in their dorms, went to parties, and vacationed with them. I'm still part of their clique."

"It seems as if you got the better deal. All the good parts of college and no finals."

She tried to laugh, but she'd have given anything to be part of the classes and take those finals. But that wasn't in the stars for Lisa. She was just lucky enough to have a job, a roof over her head, and to find friends that changed her life.

CHAPTER FIVE

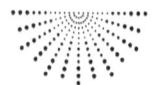

Ryan stood in front of Lisa, still leaned against the doorjamb. He lowered his arms, and again tucked his hands into the front pockets of his pants.

"I think I have an entire box of T-shirts from college," he said.

Lisa's brows rose. "Are you looking for an invitation to Rom Com Movie Club?"

"Is that an option?" he asked, smiling down at her.

"No. It's an exclusive club," she said, and her lips twitched into a smile.

"Well then, I guess you'd have to wear my T-shirts to represent."

Lisa sucked in a breath, and that stirred something in his chest. Okay, he was flirting, but there was something about this girl.

"And what school would I be representing?"

"NYU."

"No kidding?"

"No kidding. Took off for New York at eighteen. Came back after graduation just long enough to settle back in Denver and then I got a job in Chicago. Now I'm back."

"I'm envious. I've never been anywhere. Well, the girls and I have taken vacations, but that's it."

Ryan shifted, moving from leaning his back against the door jamb to resting his hand against the wall next to Lisa. "You've never lived somewhere else?"

"Oh, I've lived lots of places. They just were all in the Denver metro area."

"And you've only vacationed with the girls?"

"Yes."

"No Disneyland when you were little?"

Something flashed in her eyes, sadness maybe. Ryan was suddenly sorry he'd asked.

"No."

"And where would you go if skies were the limit?"

Lisa worried her lip. "Iceland to see the Northern Lights."

"Okay, I like it. Nothing tropical for you, huh?"

She shrugged. "Tropical vacations for single women are only to pick up men, right?"

"And if you weren't single?"

Her mouth opened slightly. "I'm always single."

"But if you weren't?"

She swallowed hard and he watched her throat move. "What's wrong with cold locations for couples? More reason to snuggle, right?"

Ryan grinned. "You have a point. I've never been to Iceland."

"It's not a spring break hot spot."

He deserved that. "Maybe we can discuss vacation plans when you make me dinner."

She laughed, and the sound of it sent chills over his skin.

"You are forward. I agree with Tina."

Now he laughed. "I'm harmless."

"Dude, can we go?" Aaron's voice had them both looking up to see him standing only a few feet from them.

Ryan looked back down at Lisa. "Brothers are such pains in the ass." Ryan eased back. "I haven't finished my beer yet."

Lisa stood still, watching Ryan walk away.

Aaron shook his head. "I'm sorry about him."

"Why?"

"Because this looked cozy, which means he was turning on his charm and he was uninvited."

"It's not a problem."

Lisa moved past Aaron.

The movie was still paused. Ruby was filling wine glasses and Ryan was drinking his beer.

"What movie are you watching?" he asked.

"*While You Were Sleeping,*" Ruby replied as she sipped from her wine glass.

"I love that one," Ryan said. "Where are we in the movie?"

Tina's eyes went wide. "You're not staying."

"You're boring," Ryan came back at her, but laughed and moved in to kiss the top of her head. "Fine."

He finished his beer and Ruby took the empty bottle and dropped it in the recycle bin.

"Ladies, it was nice to meet you all," Ryan said before settling his eyes on Lisa. "Sunday?"

She noticed all eyes land on her. "Sure. Six?"

"Sounds like a plan." Ryan slapped a hand on Aaron's shoulder. "Okay, bro. Let's leave these nice ladies to their movie."

Aaron shook his head and laughed before kissing Tina gently on the lips. "I'll see you later," he said softly in her ear, but loud enough that everyone could hear.

A moment later the men were gone, and Lisa's friends turned to her.

"Sunday?" Ruby asked.

Mindy shook her head. "You're going to go on a date with him? You just met him."

Tina sipped her wine. "She's not going to date him," she added.

Lisa looked at each of them talking about her while she stood there.

"It's not a date." Lisa moved to pick up her wine glass. "He's interested in what I do for a living. I'm going to cook for him."

"Date," Ruby said.

"Opportunity to get to know someone," Lisa defended.

"Date," Ruby repeated.

Lisa huffed out a breath. "Fine. Date."

Mindy sipped her wine. "At least you could have someone to dance with at the wedding."

Lisa laughed as she sipped her wine again. Wasn't that a funny thought. Some man, that Lisa didn't know an hour ago, walked into her condo and now she had a dinner date. Yes, it would be someone to dance with at the wedding, but Lisa wasn't thinking anything longer term than a dinner on Sunday. Nothing but her friendship with the women in her kitchen had been long term in Lisa's life.

She'd had a new home nearly every year of her life until she was twelve.

She'd gone to thirteen different schools.

She'd lived with at least as many different families.

No, Lisa didn't believe in long term, because people usually gave up on her.

She would go on loving the women who surrounded her because they were the first people to never give up on her. If a man came along, someday, who wanted to stay and be with her, then maybe she'd consider opening her heart to him. But Ryan Blair obviously didn't stay in one location. So, dinner would be it. Besides, it was one more video for her channel.

CHAPTER SIX

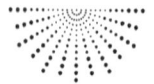

THE ONE THING LISA COULD COUNT ON WAS A WINE HANGOVER THE morning after Rom Com Movie Club.

Stumbling out of bed and down the hall to the bathroom, she made sure to not look in the mirror. Lisa used the bathroom, washed her hands, and then her face. She brushed her teeth and her hair, tying it up in a loose knot on her head, making sure to not pull it tight. Her head already pounded, and her stomach sloshed.

The house was tidy. That was one thing about her girls, they never left anyone's house without tidying up first.

With her eyes still mostly closed, Lisa walked to the kitchen, opened the refrigerator, and pulled out a Gatorade. Electrolytes first—coffee next.

The knock on her door had her wincing from the noise.

Who in the hell was knocking on her door at, she looked at the clock on the microwave, eleven on a Sunday morning?

Okay, she could find the humor in the fact that it was so late in the morning. Opening the bottle, she shut the refrigerator door, and slowly walked to the front door.

Because she was cautious, she peeked through the peephole.

Seriously?

Lisa opened the door to find Ryan standing there, a tray with two coffee cups and a white paper bag in his hand.

Wincing at the sun, Lisa leaned against the door frame. "Hi."

The corner of his mouth turned up into a slight smile, and oh what a smile.

"Hi," he said back. "I brought some coffee and a donut."

Lisa raised a brow. "A donut?"

"It's a big donut."

She nodded. "And why did you bring coffee and a donut?"

Ryan shrugged. "I felt like being friendly. But," he scanned a look over her still in her UCLA T-shirt and the same pajamas she'd had on the night before, "if you're not feeling friendly, I could just leave the coffee."

"But not the donut?"

He shook his head. "Donuts are for friendly people."

Lisa laughed. This guy was much funnier than his brother, whom Lisa found to be a bit stiff, but she wasn't the one in love with him, so it didn't matter.

Stepping back, she opened the door and let him in.

"It doesn't look like you had a party last night," he said as he walked toward the kitchen.

Lisa shut the door. "It wasn't much of a party. You saw us."

"That's as crazy as it gets?"

Shrugging, Lisa set her Gatorade on the counter, climbed up onto one of the bar stools at her counter, and rested her head in the palm of her hand. "That's as crazy as it gets."

"Yet, you're hungover."

"I get hungover with a glass of wine. I had three."

"I'm glad I came with coffee then." He grinned at her again, and that made her already sloshy stomach tighten. "Napkins?"

"I have paper towel behind you."

He turned, pulled off two sheets of paper and turned back to the counter. "Why is it that Taco Bell will set you up with sauce

23

for life when you order one burrito but order a donut and you get nothing. Or," he continued, "you order enough Chinese takeout for six people and they give you three sets of chopsticks and two fortune cookies."

Ryan shrugged as he pulled apart the large, glazed donut he'd taken from the bag. He set one half on her paper towel and the other half on his, before he cocked a hip against the counter.

"You're welcome to sit down. I have another stool," she offered with a nod of her head.

"I'm good to stand. I can see you this way."

Lisa snorted out a laugh. "And it's a sight to behold this morning," she teased.

"It is," he said, and his voice was sincere.

Tearing off a piece of her donut, she popped it into her mouth. She still wasn't sure why he was standing in her kitchen.

"So why are you feeling friendly this morning?" she asked.

"I didn't want to wait a week to see you. When I meet someone who I'd like to get to know, I—"

"Just show up at their house?"

"Well, yes. Is that creepy? I didn't think about it being creepy. I'm not trying to be."

Lisa laughed again. "I'm not creeped out. Aaron is a stellar guy, or we wouldn't be letting Tina marry him. I'm going to give you credit for being a stellar guy too, since you share genes with him. But, if you prove me wrong, I'll wreck their marriage."

"Got it. Aaron had to go through the three of you to get approval to be with Tina?"

"Yeah, that's about the way of it," Lisa agreed.

"So, I'll have to sell myself to Ruby and Mindy to get to you? Since Tina knows me and all."

HER EYES HAD GROWN WIDE, AND RYAN LIFTED HIS COFFEE TO HIS lips and grinned at her from behind it. Lisa intrigued him, and he meant it when he said he couldn't wait a week to see her. If Aaron caught wind of his pop-by, he'd get an earful. No doubt in time he would hear about it, but for now, Ryan was making a friend. He might have grown up there, but he didn't have a list of friends to call and connect with. He'd been gone more than a decade. His friends were in New York and Chicago.

Lisa took another bite of the donut and chewed thoughtfully. Was she unable to say anything? Had he stunned her?

Then she leaned in on her forearms and looked pointedly at him. "You're not here because you're interested in me, right?"

Ryan lifted a brow. "And if I were?"

"I'd think you'd need more time to figure that out. We've spent all of twenty minutes in each other's presence."

"And that's not enough time to decide that I want to get to know you better?"

"I'm just saying, in my experience, well, no."

"Are you hard to get to know? Not easy to like?"

Her lips twitched and she looked down at the donut. "I...well, I'm..."

He wasn't sure what the hiccup in this was, but it seemed to have gotten to her. "Let's just say twenty minutes is enough time for me to make a friend, and I thought you were a worthy enough friend to share a big donut with."

Now she worried her lip before she finally looked up at him. "I appreciate that."

CHAPTER SEVEN

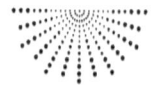

Ryan didn't stick around long, and Lisa was sure it was because she'd made him feel uncomfortable.

After her upbringing, she should relish meeting new people. She'd been doing it since she was six. And, when she met people, it was usually when she'd been dropped off at their house with a trash bag full of her belongings and she was to live in their house.

Not only was she meeting new people, but she was also meeting a new family. A family that she was expected to just be absorbed into. *Here's your new room. Here's your chore list. Here's your place at the table.*

In only a few of the homes was she welcomed in a fashion where she was important enough that they asked her questions as they went through her bag of things.

Picking up a rag that had been draped over the sink, Lisa wiped down the counters. So, Ryan Blair wanted to be her friend. *Her* friend. That was something.

Her phone was on the counter, because before he'd left, they'd exchanged phone numbers. Lisa picked it up and scrolled through her notes file at dinners she'd been wanting to prepare.

It might be wise to do a run through before she cooked for Ryan on Sunday.

Lisa closed out the list and opened her text messages. She started a new one to Ryan.

Hey, it's Lisa.

The bubble with three dots immediately popped up on her screen.

Hey, it's Ryan! he replied, and Lisa laughed as she sat down on one of the bar stools.

Are you allergic to anything? Food wise, that is.

He sent her the face emoji that was thinking with its finger to its temple. *I've never met food that didn't like me. Now, let's talk about spinach.*

Lisa laughed. *You don't like spinach?*

Popeye lied. Not once have I ever choked down spinach and gotten muscles. So, I don't eat it. I refuse! Now he sent the green sick emoji.

Got it. No spinach. Anything else?

Those bubbles popped up again, and then disappeared before his next text came through. *Nah, that's it. Now your turn. What kind of wine do you like? Or do you like beer more? Wine didn't seem to like you.* Again, he sent the green sick emoji.

Lisa sent a beer mug emoji.

Perfect. I like beer too, he replied. *Favorite color?*

Lisa looked at the message, set down her phone, then picked it back up.

Why?

Ryan sent the emoji with one eyebrow raised. *I thought we were conversing. What's your favorite food? What's your favorite drink? What's your favorite color.*

Letting out a long breath, she decided she was rather enjoying his banter. Until she'd met the girls, who she considered sisters, no one had ever given much thought to conversing with her and asking her these kinds of questions.

Blue, she answered.

Do you like baseball?

Lisa laughed out loud, alone in her kitchen.

Um, I suppose?

When her phone rang right in her hand, she stared down at the screen where Ryan's name popped up.

"Hello," she answered.

"Um, I suppose? Is that really an answer?" he teased.

"Of course it was an answer. I don't follow baseball. I suppose I like it."

Ryan let out a low hum. "I suppose that'll do. I have tickets to a Rockies game on Tuesday. Would you like to go?"

Lisa sat, drumming her fingers on the counter. Would she like to go? "Wouldn't your brother like to go? Or your dad?"

Ryan let out another hum. "Well, see, if I ask one of them, then the other will just be mad that I didn't ask them. You see my problem, right?"

"So, if I went with you, it would do you the favor of not making you choose?"

"Exactly."

"And this is all part of your process of getting to know me?"

"You're officially my only friend in town."

This time, it was Lisa that let out the low hum. "You're from here. I know you have friends."

"My friends are mostly in New York and Chicago."

Lisa figured that made sense, but she still didn't understand why he felt she was worthy of knowing.

"What time is the game?" she asked.

"Two o'clock. We can take the train down and enjoy ourselves."

Running her tongue over her teeth, she considered that. What was he expecting from her? Did he think she was some party girl since he'd shown up and she was hung over? Then again, she hated driving downtown for games or concerts, maybe he did too.

"Okay."

"There's a station not far from your place. I'll come over around one."

Lisa thought about her schedule. Tuesday she was creating a charcuterie board to post on her channel. Maybe she could change it into a basket lunch. Oh, that would need a shopping trip tomorrow to get a basket. She needed to iron the picnic cloth.

"Lisa?" Ryan's voice woke her from her thoughts.

"Yeah."

"One o'clock?"

"Can you come at twelve? I'll have lunch ready."

"Well, the best part about being currently unemployed, I can say I'll be there."

Lisa realized she was grinning at the phone.

RYAN KICKED HIS FEET UP ON THE COOLER BETWEEN THE COUCHES in the garage, rested his head back, and grinned up at the rafters. He and Lisa had solidified their plans, and he felt as if he'd just asked out the most popular girl in school.

"What are you doing?" his brother's voice broke through the silence as he cleared the stacks of boxes and sat down on his own couch.

"Enjoying my unemployment," Ryan said lifting his head to look at his brother.

"I don't suppose Mom is going to let us keep her garage like this forever. A job and a house better be in your future," Aaron offered.

"Oh, I think a lot of great things are in my future."

"Such as?"

"A lunch date. A date to the baseball game. A dinner date. And if I play my cards just right, maybe I'll have a date to your wedding."

His brother's eyes narrowed on him. "You've been busy. What, did you stop in at the earring boutique at the mall and stock up on dates?"

"Funny. You're a funny guy," Ryan snapped as he dropped his feet to the ground. "It's all Lisa."

"My Lisa?"

"Your Lisa? I'm sure Tina wouldn't like the way that sounded," Ryan argued.

"You know what the hell I mean."

"Fine. Yes, your Lisa."

"Don't go hitting on her."

"I didn't have to hit. I asked. Now I have three dates."

"She's not just some girl to pick up, use, and leave when you find some job."

Ryan bit the inside of his cheek. "Thanks for the high praise, bro."

"Serious. She deserves something stable. She's never had stable in her entire life, and those girls aren't just going to let you prance in and occupy her mind."

Now Ryan opened the cooler and pulled out a beer. He slammed the lid back down and put his feet back on it, making a point not to offer his brother a beer.

"Screw you. You don't get to say who interests me and who I do or don't get involved with."

Aaron shoved Ryan's feet from the cooler, causing him to readjust on the couch.

"Screw you," Aaron countered opening the cooler and taking out a beer. "Tina doesn't need your shit three weeks before the wedding."

"I'm not offering her any shit."

"If you get involved with Lisa you are."

"I asked her to a ballgame. She asked me to come early for

lunch. We had dinner plans already. It's not like I'm marrying her. I'm not sleeping with her. I'm—hell, I don't know what I'm doing. But I think your misguided anger is pissing me off."

"Just the three dates. Promise me."

"I'm not going to promise," Ryan pulled from his beer. "If Lisa's not interested, she can tell me."

CHAPTER EIGHT

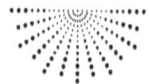

L<small>ISA AND</small> M<small>INDY WANDERED AROUND</small> W<small>ORLD</small> M<small>ARKET LOOKING</small> for the perfect picnic basket.

One of the perks about having three best friends was that they all worked different schedules. And, since Lisa was self-employed, and making a living thanks to YouTube, she could almost do anything she wanted at any time.

As it was, Mindy's work week was Tuesday through Friday. Lisa could always count on her for Monday morning shopping when she was looking for a prop, an ingredient, or even a new shirt.

"Oh, wow," Mindy cooed. "What could you do with this?" she asked holding up a metal vase.

Lisa laughed. "Nothing," she said and then reconsidered. "Though, we could make six gallons of margaritas and pour it in there."

Mindy laughed and set the vase back down just as Lisa's phone rang in her hand. She looked down at the caller ID, and then answered it on speaker so they could both talk to Tina.

"Hey, Tina. What's up?" she sing-songed.

"What are you doing?" There was a bite in Tina's words, but Lisa was sure she'd just heard it wrong.

"Shopping with Mindy," Lisa answered.

"Hey, Tina-bo-bina," Mindy said leaning in toward the phone.

"Get me off speaker, and that's not what I'm talking about." Tina's voice was nearly a low growl now.

Lisa and Mindy exchanged confused glances as Lisa turned off the speaker. Then Mindy held her hands up in surrender and walked toward another eclectic home furnishing.

"Tina, what's wrong?"

"You're not going to date my brother-in-law. That's that. Cancel your plans."

Lisa walked toward the front of the store and stood near the front window. "I beg your pardon?"

"It's not a good idea."

"I think we have some friendly plans. I'm not dating him."

"Lunches, ballgames, dinners—that's dating."

"No, it's hanging out, and it's legal, hon."

Tina grew quiet on the other end. "This is Aaron's time to shine," she whined on the other end of the phone. "Ryan moving home and in on one of my best friends, well, that's a lot."

"For who?"

Lisa could hear her breathing on the other end, and she knew Tina was in for the argument, but running out of ammunition.

"Three weeks. I have three weeks until my wedding. Four until my honeymoon. I just want it all to go smoothly."

"And me having dinner or going to a ballgame is going to steal your thunder? What that really says is you don't think much of me at all."

"Lisa," Tina's voice had softened. "It's not like that."

"Oh, it's like that, or we wouldn't be having this conversation." Lisa looked up when Mindy held up a picnic basket and Lisa nodded. "Listen, I'm all about your wedding, the events leading up to it, and your marriage. I'm happy for you. You're as close to me as I assume any sibling would be. I'm not going to ruin your day."

There was a resigned sigh on the other end of the phone. "I know," Tina said. "I don't think it's you. I think it's their mother. I hate living in her house."

"Then get a place."

"We will. It's just that she dotes on Ryan, and it irritates me."

"He hasn't been home for a long time. It'll run its course. Besides, he'll move out soon too. Then it'll be all up to you to be the one front and center since she'll be wanting grandkids."

Lisa heard Tina inhale. "Shit! That's exactly what she's going to want."

"Of course it is."

"I'm sorry I was nasty to you," Tina said, and this was the part of the conversation Lisa was prepared for. Tina was always the first to jump into a fight with her, and the first to back down.

"I promise to do my part to make your wedding extra special. I'll even poke holes in all the condoms."

That had Tina gasping and then laughing. "I love you. Tell Mindy I love her too."

"Will do."

Lisa shook her head as she disconnected the phone call and Mindy walked toward her with the basket.

"She's freaking out, huh?" Mindy asked handing Lisa the basket.

"Well, she is the one voted among us to be the first to get married and the most likely to be high strung."

Mindy snorted out a laugh. "You are dating her brother-in-law."

"I have plans with her brother-in-law."

"That many plans *is* dating."

Lisa pursed her lips and looked at the basket she was buying just for those plans. "I'm going to have lunch with him tomorrow.

Then, we're going to a ballgame. On Sunday, I'm going to cook a meal and record it to put it on my YouTube channel, with sponsored products that make me money. After that, I might dance with him at the wedding. We'll see how it goes. If it's amazing, maybe I'll make plans with him again."

"And if he's amazing in bed?"

"I don't think I said I was going to bed with him."

Mindy nodded slowly. "Ruby has ten bucks it'll be your second date, though, technically, I think that's dinner at your place."

Lisa groaned. "I'm not dating him."

"I'd say if you don't, I would, but he didn't give me a second look when he crashed our party. He gave you plenty of looks, dropped by for breakfast, and I'll bet his number is in your phone."

Lisa held the basket to her. "So?"

"So, you were in pajamas, and not sexy ones. Your hair was a mess and you still had green on your forehead. A man doesn't move in on that unless he's connected to what's inside. And, he did ask you out to a ballgame after seeing the hungover version the next morning."

Mindy turned and walked toward a stack of plates she'd first seen when they'd walked in the store. Lisa stood right where she was, the basket held to her.

Was that right? Had he not seen the rest of them that night?

She swallowed hard. It was friendly banter and plans. That was it.

Though, she had to admit, she'd been attracted to Ryan the moment she'd seen a picture of him, and then when he'd walked into her house, that thought was confirmed.

Still, they weren't dating. Lisa wasn't someone to keep hold of anyway. No one stuck around for her, so she wasn't going to put stock into it.

But for the moment, she was going to enjoy the plans that

were made with a man she found attractive. It was all she could promise herself anyway. Thinking that there could be more would only lead to serious heart break.

CHAPTER NINE

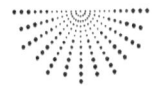

Lisa's doorbell chimed right at noon on Tuesday. At least he was prompt. She'd dated enough men to know that wasn't usually a trait found in anyone that found her interesting. Then again, she reminded herself, they weren't dating.

When Lisa opened the door Ryan held out a bouquet of daisies and handed them to her. "These are for you."

She felt the heat rise in her cheeks immediately. "Why?"

He narrowed his gaze on her and she shook off her comment with her free hand.

"That's a bad habit I have," she admitted. "Thank you. They're lovely."

"And I think you're lovely too, and that's why," Ryan said as he stepped through the door and closed it behind him.

Lisa moved to the kitchen, opening a cupboard, and pulling down a vase. As she went to the sink to fill it, she noticed Ryan was taking in the sight of her kitchen set up.

"So those lights in your office are mobile?"

Lisa laughed as she filled the vase. "Usually this is the norm. My kitchen was in pristine condition since the girls were over."

"You guys don't use the lights and take selfies in your Rom Com Movie Club uniforms?"

Had anyone else said that to her she would have taken it for a diss, but when Ryan said it, Lisa snorted out a laugh. "No, very few selfies come out of movie night."

Ryan sat down at one of the bar stools as Lisa unwrapped the flowers and put them in the vase.

"So you were recording?" he asked pulling the legal pad of notes toward him and looking at them.

"I was. It'll go up in a few weeks."

Ryan's attention moved to the basket on the counter. "That's our lunch? When you said come for lunch, I didn't expect that."

"I create content on Tuesdays. This one was a charcuterie board, so I adjusted it and made it a picnic lunch."

"Charcuterie board?"

Lisa lifted a brow. "Meat and cheese tray."

"Okay, why didn't you just say that?"

She knew she was smiling, and the way he smiled back made her chest tighten. "Because it's more than that. It's breads, jams, olives, nuts, chocolates."

"My mother would love this."

"We could call her," Lisa offered.

"Maybe some other day. As it is, my entire family is on my nerves."

Lisa rested her elbows on the counter and propped her chin up with her fists. "Let me guess. There's a wedding in three weeks and we're going to ruin it with our charcuterie board, ball-game, and dinner."

His smile widened and he leaned in on his elbows, mimicking her with his chin on his fists. "Why yes. How insensitive of us, right?"

"Completely. As if the past six years of them dating haven't solidified their place in time. But me, going out with an attractive man, will ruin it."

His eyes lit. "I'm attractive?"

Lisa swallowed hard. "Well," she began and then wrinkled up her nose. "Shit."

"Oh, you can't back down now. You said it."

"Fine. You're attractive."

"Thanks," he mimicked throwing his hair back, and Lisa laughed. "For the record, you're a smoke show."

Now she wasn't laughing at all, but he was. Did he mean that or was he kidding. She wasn't sure. But whatever the expression on her face, it must have registered badly, because Ryan sat up straight and studied her.

"I meant that as a sincere compliment. I'm sorry if—"

"No. No," she said lightly and desperately wanted to press her hand to her stomach to ward off the butterflies that had taken flight, or were those bees out to sting, she wasn't sure. "Thank you for the compliment."

"I am sorry if my brother is being a dick about all of this."

Lisa picked up the basket. "Tina called me yesterday and let me have her opinion."

"Well, I guess we'll see how lunch and the ballgame go. And dinner on Sunday, of course," he said as he hopped off the bar stool.

"Of course."

"Then after the wedding, we can decide, on our own, if we're dating."

Lisa worried her lip. "Oh. Okay."

He was grinning at her. "I know I really just met you, but for the record, I'm interested."

"I guess we're starting this friendship off with a lot of honesty, huh?"

He nodded slowly. "Friendship. Yep, totally honest."

"I'm interested too," she said and then was sure those were bees in her stomach. "But for the record, since I'm thirty-one and have never had a serious relationship, I'll understand when you're no longer interested."

Ryan watched Lisa carry the basket from the counter, turn off the light in the kitchen, and head to the front door. He followed, taking the basket from her when she turned to lock the door.

Something had flipped inside of her when he'd said he was interested. What had she been told in the past that would make her decide he'd not be interested in her someday?

Then his brother's conversation with him replayed in his head.

She deserves something stable. She's never had stable in her entire life, and those girls aren't just going to let you prance in and occupy her mind.

What did all that mean?

Lisa walked toward the small grassy area past the condo building where there were tables and grills for tenants' use. Ryan followed with the basket.

When he set it on the table she'd chosen, Lisa took the top off, pulled out a tablecloth and spread it out.

He watched as she unpacked the basket with small plates and glass containers. She was in her element, and he suddenly found he wasn't in his.

Ryan had had serious relationships. He'd had his share of them, but he supposed if there were multiple ones, then they weren't very serious. There was even the thought of proposing once. But as he watched Lisa unpack the most elegant picnic he'd ever seen, he realized that he had been caught up in his ex-girl-friends' feelings when he'd considered his proposal. They'd both had friends headed to the altar, and they wanted to be engaged too—and then the relationship had taken a nosedive.

With DeeDee they were too young. He didn't love her, and she just wanted a ring. He'd considered it, but he wasn't ready.

With Courtney, well, he was all in. The ring had been bought. The proposal all figured out. The hotel suite for after, booked. Then there was the business trip that he didn't take because the flights had been canceled. And obviously, Courtney had been too busy with the man she was seeing behind Ryan's back to ask him to leave their bed before Ryan got home.

"Everything okay?" Lisa looked at him, pausing her set up of the picnic.

"Yeah. Ya know what, everything is good."

CHAPTER TEN

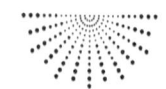

"I PROMISED YOU NO SPINACH, BUT THE SPINACH DIP WAS SO GOOD, I had to bring a little jar. But I'm not offended if you don't have any," Lisa said as she sat down on one of the benches and Ryan sat across from her.

"This is beautiful. It's no wonder you have so many followers. Do you need to take a picture of this?"

Lisa shook her head. "I already did."

She pulled her phone from her pocket, scrolled through her pictures, and held it up for him to see.

She'd been busy with that picnic, he thought. The photo she had was of the picnic laid out on the grass, and she was on the tablecloth in a white dress with a big white hat. Her face was obscured, but he knew it was her.

"This is beautiful," he said lifting his eyes to her.

"Thank you."

"Why'd you change?" he asked as Lisa opened containers.

"Out of the dress?"

"Yes."

She laughed. "I'm not going to a ballgame in a dress. You get sporty-Lisa for today's outing."

He looked at Lisa in her sneakers, shorts, and Rockies T-shirt. Her hair was pulled back into a ponytail, and he'd be disappointed if she didn't have a ball cap that she was going to wear.

"I like sporty-Lisa just fine."

"Thank you," she said again as she spread jam on a cracker and bit into it, then set it on her small plate.

Ryan followed her example. "We just eat with our hands?"

She nodded as she took another cracker and added a slice of cheese and a piece of meat. "Yep. Make any combination you want. It's like a fancy, adult Lunchable."

"Aaron couldn't eat this. He couldn't mix and match some of these things."

Lisa laughed. "That's why he's a good partner for Tina. She's the same. You know, she doesn't let one item on her plate touch another."

"That's crazy."

She was still smiling when he bit into the cracker.

"And what are you like?" Ryan asked.

Lisa's eyes went wide, and she chewed more thoughtfully. "How do you mean?"

He considered as he piled some meats and cheese slices on a cracker. What did he mean?

"What foods are your favorite? I know blue is your favorite color," he said, referring to their texts from the other day.

Lisa let out a small laugh. "I love all food. Therefore, I *love* to take long walks."

"*Love* long walks?" he asked, mimicking her inflection on the word.

"I don't run. I hate to run. I'm only running if someone is chasing me. But, because I work with food, and I love food, I have to walk it off."

"Tina does yoga in the basement at four in the morning," Ryan added.

"And she can keep that schedule to her damn self." She bit

down on a cracker. "She does that when we vacation. Don't get me wrong. We love her. Love her," she restated. "But she's up before God doing yoga. Ruby snores. Mindy talks in her sleep."

Now he was intrigued. "And you?"

She lifted a brow. "Oh, me? I'm a saint."

A laughed burst out of him. "Would that be how this conversation would go if I were talking to Tina?"

She pursed her lips and dragged a cracker through the spinach dip she'd added to the picnic. "I want to say yes, but they say I'm a bed hog."

"You don't say."

Lisa bit into the cracker and chewed. "I'm a bed hog. I steal sheets, and my feet are cold."

"Unacceptable," he teased.

"What about you?"

"Oh, I'm a saint too," he said, and her laugh resonated through him, again.

Okay, he thought, he'd picked the right girl to be his only friend in town.

She pulled the cracker through the dip again. "You don't snore, slobber, talk, kick, or—"

He raised his hand. "I kick."

Lisa covered her mouth to keep her next bite in. "You kick?"

"I've been told I have."

"A woman?"

Why was his body temperature rising? "Yes."

"You must have secretly not liked her."

There were two bottles of lemonade, the kind that she had filled and then sealed with a stopper. He opened one and took a drink. Though the sweet and tart dried up his mouth.

"It should have been a sign," he managed, and took another sip. "That woman in particular played me for a fool."

Lisa set down her small plate, opened her bottle of lemonade, and took a sip. "What happened? I mean, if you want to tell me."

What did he have to lose? They were friend-zoned thanks to his brother and Tina. He might as well utilize the friend part.

"I had a ring. I had a proposal all worked up. I had a honeymoon suite booked so we could celebrate." He sealed the bottle with the clasp, then nervously opened it again. "I had a business meeting the week before, and I headed out of town. But there was a blizzard, so my flight was cancelled. I managed to get home… only to find some other guy in my bed, with her."

"Ryan, that's awful."

"It was. Even worse, it had been going on for nearly a year. And because her true colors came out after that, she had the audacity to blame it on me. I wasn't around. I didn't pay enough attention to her. I didn't like her mother."

Lisa reached a hand over the piles of containers and rested it on his thigh.

The skin under her touch tingled and heated. The odd mix had him lifting his eyes to her.

Her blue eyes sparkled in the sunlight, and there were small freckles on her nose. Long eyelashes batted at him.

"I know I don't know you well, but I'm very sure you treated her like a princess."

Ryan blinked hard. Seriously, he'd given off those kinds of vibes? He'd like to think they were right, but she'd picked up on that?

"I thought I had."

Lisa pulled back her hand, but he'd wished she hadn't.

"Well, if you were married now, we wouldn't be here enjoying this, nor would we be going to the baseball game."

He nodded. "Don't forget dinner on Sunday."

"Couldn't forget that," she agreed.

And then what, he wondered. A dance at the wedding? Then would he slip her mind? Or would Tina and Aaron stop being such shits and let him feel out whatever this was between him and Lisa that had sparked the moment he'd laid eyes on her?

Ryan watched her sip from the bottle and then pop an olive in her mouth, all while letting the sun warm her face.

In that moment, he decided to apply for the job in Denver. He knew he wanted to stay. He wanted to get to know this *friend* better.

CHAPTER ELEVEN

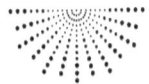

Hot dogs and beer. Popcorn and beer. Candied nuts and beer. Beer, one more beer, and then it was the seventh inning stretch.

Ryan stood for the stretch, and the music played. Fans around them sang, and he looked down at Lisa who winced looking up at him.

"It's law. You have to stand up and sing," he said, noticing that he was loud, and his words slurred a bit.

"I don't wanna."

Ryan reached for her hand and tugged her up to him. She slid in next to him and he wrapped his arms around her. The music played and they began to sing, though neither of them could remember the words.

While he held her up, his arms had slid firmly around her waist. At some point, as she howled out the need for peanuts and Cracker Jack, she'd looped her arms around his neck. And suddenly, Ryan couldn't remember the words to the stupid song at all.

The crowd around them cheered. Some people sat. Others stayed standing as the pitcher took the mound.

Lisa lowered her arms from his neck and turned so that her back was pressed to his chest. His arms easily slipped around her waist and he rested his chin to her shoulder.

"You're swaying," he whispered in her ear.

Lisa licked her lips. "You're keeping me upright just fine."

The thought of keeping her upright was suddenly not what he wanted to do.

Watching the crowd jump up when the player hit the ball toward the Rockpile for a home run, he held her a little tighter. "What do you say we head up those stairs before the end of the game? I'd rather make sure we get to the train before everyone else in this stadium heads out. Especially since we're both a little wobbly."

Her head rolled so that she could look up at him from under the bill of her hat. Those beautiful blue eyes peered up at him through heavy lids.

"The score is a little lopsided," she said. "So I'll take you up on that."

He was glad she agreed. They'd had an amazing afternoon, but with her leaned up against him, his mind wasn't on the ballgame.

If it were any other woman, he'd have made plans around their exit, but since it was Lisa, he just wanted to get her home safe. His brother's irritating warnings kept poking through to him.

That stupid wedding couldn't get here fast enough, Ryan thought. Yeah, things might not work out for him and Lisa. In fact, she might not be interested at all, but he couldn't help but fight the attraction he had for her.

Lisa started to walk, reaching back for his hand, and leading them out while everyone in the row stood. As they slowly walked up the stairs, her hand gripped tighter to his, and their fingers stayed linked until they were clear of the other fans. As they walked toward the exit, Lisa's hand came out from his and she slipped her arm around his waist. Instinctively, Ryan wrapped his around her shoulders, and together they headed toward the train station, laughing as they stumbled along the sidewalk.

Her head rested on his shoulder as the train took them toward the station near her house. Once they reached the station, they started the short walk to her house.

"I'm sorry we left early," Lisa bumped her shoulder into his arm and smiled.

"I'm not. I had an amazing day."

"I can't remember when I've eaten that much junk food."

"That's going to need a long walk tomorrow."

Lisa laughed. "You're right. Ruby is off work tomorrow. I'll drag her ass out with me. If we head to a lake, then I have to walk the whole way around."

Ryan would have offered to walk with her, but then that would be one more thing to hold against them when his brother heard about it.

"How are you going to get home?" she asked as they walked toward her building.

"I'm going to drive," he said, matter-of-factly.

Lisa narrowed her eyes on him. "We drank drink for drink. Though I'm not sloshed, I'm too drunk to drive."

He nodded. "Eventually, I'll drive home?"

She laughed, hooking her arm through his. "I'm glad you moved home. It's fun to have a guy friend," she said, and then reached into her pocket for her key.

Guy friend, he needed to keep that in mind each time she touched him.

"So, you're going to stick around for a little bit, right?" she asked as she fumbled to put the key in the lock on her first try.

"Or I could call my brother?"

She shook her head. "Nah. Stay."

"Okay. For a little bit."

Lisa pushed open the door and they both walked into the

condo. She pulled off her hat the moment she was inside, and then ran her hand over her hair to flatten the stray hairs.

"I'd ask if you'd like a drink, but that's a horrible idea," she laughed and then covered her mouth. "I think the train shook up the beer in my belly. I swear I feel drunker."

"More drunk?"

She dropped her shoulders. "You're seriously not one of those assholes, are you? The kind that corrects grammar."

Ryan laughed now. "No. Trust me, I'm not."

Lisa set her keys and her hat on the counter, then she turned, and Ryan was standing closer to her than he thought.

Looking up at him, she pressed her hands to his chest. "I'm going to go to the bathroom, and I'm going to change. I can smell greasy food all over me." She tapped her fingers on his chest. "The toaster is on the counter. Make us some toast and some coffee. The grounds are next to the maker."

"Toast and coffee? At five-thirty in the afternoon?"

Lisa nodded. "It'll help sober us up. Of course, so would throwing up."

Ryan leaned back from her. "Is that what you're going to do?"

"Nope." She tapped her fingers on his chest again. "I'm going to go change. Then we'll watch a movie. We'll order some pizza when we're hungry. And when you've decided you've had your fill of me, you can call your brother, or if you've sobered up, you can drive home."

She started for her bedroom, but he caught her hand and turned her back. "Why would I have my fill of you?"

Lisa blinked a few times, as if she hadn't remembered saying it. Then she bit down on her lip, hard enough he noticed she'd marked it when she took a breath to talk.

"Because everyone in my life gets tired of me. I'm used to it."

CHAPTER TWELVE

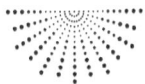

CRINGING AT THE WHEAT BREAD, RYAN DUTIFULLY MADE TOAST while the coffee brewed.

He'd heard Lisa move between the bedroom and the bathroom. The water had run a few times, and he thought maybe he'd heard the shower.

For a moment, he couldn't help but wonder if she'd forgotten he was there. Honestly, he'd taken care of his share of drunk girls, and sometimes they forgot.

Ryan plated the toast, found butter and jelly in the refrigerator, but thought that might not be part of the sobering plan. But he left them on the counter.

There were mugs on a rack near the coffee maker. He chose a Tweety Bird one for her, and because he couldn't help himself, and he thought she was super cute for having it, he took the Oscar the Grouch mug.

Ryan took his coffee black, but he assumed Lisa was a cream and flavor kind of girl. Though there was no evidence of it, he could see her toting around a Starbucks cup each day.

When she finally emerged, she'd changed into a pair of pajama bottoms, and this time she wore a tank top. Thank goodness she'd managed a bra, unlike Ruby the other night. He wasn't sure he could handle it if she'd skipped that part.

The closer she got to him, he noticed the scent. Her hair was wet. She had taken a shower.

"You really meant to clean off that greasy food smell, huh?" he teased, and she looked up at him with red eyes.

"I told you, too much beer and junk food. I was better off throwing up."

He knew he winced. "You did that on purpose?"

She scowled at him. "No." She picked up the Oscar the Grouch mug and sipped from it. He'd wanted to argue, but what was the use?

Ryan picked up the Tweety mug and leaned his hip against the counter.

"I didn't hear you get sick."

"That was the point," she said, picking up a piece of the dry, wheat toast and taking a bite. "Thank you for the toast and coffee."

"My pleasure," Ryan admitted, feeling completely sober. "Let me know when you're ready for pizza. My treat."

"You treated all day."

"Yeah, and it was worth it."

There was a sparkle that flashed in those red-rimmed eyes now, but it faded as quickly as it had arrived. "It's nice to have a guy think that."

Lisa ate the piece of toast and continued to sip her coffee.

"What kind of movies do you like?" she finally asked, once she'd swallowed the last bite of toast.

Ryan gave it some thought. "I'll admit to having an unhealthy attraction to Sandra Bullock. So, those movies you watch, those rom coms, I've seen most of them since that's her schtick."

Lisa laughed easily, and he assumed she'd sobered too. "Which is your favorite?"

Ryan let out a long, loud breath. "Oh, that's a hard one. *While You Were Sleeping*, epic one."

Lisa nodded. "It's still cued up," she teased, and he laughed.

"Let's see, *Miss Congeniality*."

"You can't go wrong with a beauty pageant contestant with a gun."

"Right?" He couldn't help but smile at her. "Oh, and *Demolition Man*."

Lisa crinkled up her nose. "Are you kidding me? That's not rom com."

"Sure it is."

Now she raised a brow. "That has Stallone and Snipes."

"And Bullock and Taco Bell references galore."

"And you consider it a romance?"

"Um, they get together."

Lisa laughed hard now, and when she did, the sound of it sent chills across his skin and he felt lighter in her presence.

Shaking her head, Lisa toasted him with her mug. "I think I forgot that. I will never see it the same way again."

"What about you. What's your favorite?"

"It is *While You Were Sleeping*, that's why I chose it that night."

As if out of instinct, Ryan lifted a finger toward her brow to brush away a strand of lose hair behind her ear. "And why is that one your favorite?"

With the mug cupped between both of her hands, she looked up at him dreamily. "I relate to her as Lucy. She finds a family in the Callaghans, just as I have with the girls. The bonus is she finds true love in Jack."

Ryan leaned on the counter with his forearms and cupped the Tweety mug between his hands, as she'd done earlier with her mug. "She didn't have family, right?" he tried to remember the movie.

"No. She and her father were always going to travel the world and stamp their passports."

"Right," he was remembering. "And how do you relate to her?"

Lisa batted her eyes, sipped from her coffee, and then worried her lip. Finally, she looked up at him with sad eyes. "Neither one of us have a family."

LISA HATED TALKING ABOUT IT, AND SHE COULDN'T BELIEVE SHE'D let Ryan pull that out of her.

"What do you want to watch?" she asked walking toward the TV and picking up the remote. "I've got Hulu and Netflix."

Ryan picked up his mug and followed her.

She sat down on the sofa, and he sat down next to her as she turned on the TV and began to scroll through the channels.

"Oh, *National Treasure* is good," he said.

"Nick Cage romance," she said, setting the remote down and kicking her feet up on the coffee table.

"It's not a romance."

Lisa shifted a look in his direction. "Like you noticed, *Demolition Man* even had a romance plot line. Every movie has a romance plot."

"You didn't think *Demolition Man* had one."

"I didn't think it was a rom com," she corrected. "But, with the number of Taco Bell references, which made it funny, I stand corrected. But I stand firm on the fact that every movie has a romance."

His face hardened. "You're wrong."

"No, I'm not."

Ryan was going to prove her wrong. But every movie he could come up with, there was something in it that had romantic twist. Superman had Lois. James Bond always had a girl. *Natural Born Killers* was the first movie he'd seen with so much blood, yet there was a girl. *The Martian!*

"*The Martian*," he said confidently. "The whole movie is Damon."

"Those two astronauts get together. Remember the very end of the movie?"

Crap! He'd keep thinking. He wasn't done with this game yet.

There had to be a movie where there was no sign of romance or relationship. He'd figure it out, until then, it would give them a conversation to start out with when they were near each other. Not that they needed one at this point, because as she sat back on the couch, he lifted his arm behind her. And before Cage had even lifted the Constitution, Lisa was snuggled up against him. Her head rested on his shoulder, and his arm draped over hers.

CHAPTER THIRTEEN

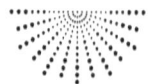

LISA HAD FALLEN ASLEEP AGAINST HIM BEFORE THE TRIO OF Constitution-loving thieves had made it to Ben Gates' father's house. Ryan should have taken that as his exit, but he hadn't wanted to. Instead, he'd kicked his feet up on the coffee table, and somehow over the course of the movie, he'd managed to relax back on the sofa, and Lisa had curled up to him.

Her hand splayed on his chest. Her breath was against his neck, and her legs were tangled with his.

As Gates made his plea to the detective at the end of the movie, Ryan fought the heaviness of his eyelids, while holding on tightly to the weight of her body against his.

They could easily slip into something more than new acquaintances that had been warned not to be together. Ryan could continue to maneuver himself under her. He could carry her to her room. Or he could sit there until every part of his body was numb, and hope that when her eyes fluttered open, she was glad he was still there.

Just as the end credits began to roll, Lisa's eyes opened and she looked up at Ryan, her head still rested on him.

He smiled, brushing a hand over her hair.

"Hey," he said softly as she blinked hard and eased from him.

"Hey," she returned, wiping her mouth as if she might have been drooling. "I'm so sorry."

"Why?"

"I invited you in and fell asleep."

"It didn't hurt my ego," he teased.

Lisa eased back more, moving to the end of the couch. "I shouldn't have kept you here. You have—"

"Nothing more pressing," he admitted, and she nodded. But he figured it was a good time for him to leave. There was no reason to start something. "I should be going."

Lisa stood, and Ryan followed. "I had a wonderful time," she said. "And for the record, I don't drink a lot."

He chuckled. "I didn't accuse you."

"No, but you saw me wine hungover on Sunday, and then lots of beer today. It's not a norm or anything."

He wasn't sure why that was important to tell him, but he could only nod.

"I guess I'll see you on Sunday?" he said as he walked toward the door.

"I'll see you then." Lisa opened the door and leaned up against it as she held it open.

Ryan studied her for a moment.

Her blue eyes were still filled with sleep, and her ponytail slightly mussed. Those pouty pink lips were begging for him to kiss her, but that just wasn't going to happen. Because if he did, he wouldn't want to stop.

"Can I bring anything?" he asked, wanting to stall just a moment longer.

Lisa bit down on her bottom lip before she smiled up at him. "Flowers. We'll add them to the video, and the ones you brought today won't be as fresh," she said smiling.

"Video?"

Now her smile grew wider, and her eyes opened as if she were fully alert now. "Yep, we're going to cook together for my channel."

His stomach clenched uncomfortably. "You're going to record me?"

"Yes."

"Do I have to sign something that says I allow that?"

Lisa puckered her lips. "You wouldn't do that for me? Be in my video?"

Oh, she already had him pulled in, he thought. "Of course I would."

Lisa winked. "Then bring flowers and an appetite. And a lot of time."

"A lot of time?"

"Yeah, it'll take most of the day."

Ryan nodded slowly. "You told me six. So now you want me earlier?"

Her eyes flashed something and then she nodded. "Come at one."

"We're going to start cooking dinner at one?"

"Yep," she said gleefully. "Be here at one."

Ryan couldn't help but trail a finger over her forehead to brush away another strand of hair and tuck it behind her ear. "I'll be here at one."

As he lowered his hand, Lisa caught it in hers.

"One more thing," she said, her voice airy and sexy.

"What's that?"

"I know that Tina and Aaron are—"

"Being assholes," Ryan added his own answer and Lisa laughed.

"Sure. Assholes." She swallowed hard and he watched her throat move. "It's okay if you kiss me goodbye."

Now Ryan's mouth had gone dry. He had to think about moving slowly, because her giving him permission to kiss her had his heart rate kicking up to wild, and she didn't ask him to stay and carry her off. He was treading on uneven ground.

With her still holding on to his hand, he turned it so that their palms were pressed together, and their fingers linked.

A kiss goodbye could be a peck on the cheek, or even the lips, but he didn't assume she meant a peck.

Ryan leaned in and Lisa's eyes closed. He pressed his lips to hers, and her body swayed against his.

Their fingers remained linked at their sides, but because his balance felt compromised, he wrapped his other arm around Lisa's waist.

Immediately, her free hand moved to the nape of his neck, and that little goodnight kiss deepened.

Ryan pulled her against him and when her mouth opened beneath his, he let his tongue slip through to tangle with hers. Her fingers tunneled up into his hair, and she moaned as his thumb brushed a small circle low on her back.

Knowing this goodbye kiss could lead to something else, Ryan eased back, pressing his forehead to Lisa's.

"My brother is an asshole," he whispered, and Lisa laughed.

"Yeah, he is," she teased.

"I'm still okay to come back on Sunday?"

She nodded her forehead against his. "Don't back out on me, okay?"

"I promise," he said, lifting her chin with his finger so that she could look in his eyes. "I mean it."

CHAPTER FOURTEEN

Only the second week of May, and the temperature was stupid hot, Lisa thought as she walked from her car toward Ruby, who was leaned up against her Lexus.

"That car is so bougie," Lisa laughed at her friend's expense.

"I don't have a bod. I don't have a man. But I have a freaking amazing job, so I have a bougie car," Ruby gave the red car, which she'd named Joellen, a tender pat. "How was your date?" Ruby quickly fired off the question as put her foot up on the bumper of her bougie car and stretched.

"Who told you I was—"

"Who do you think?"

"Was she mad?"

"Pissed," Ruby confirmed as she switched legs. "She's damn sure that you're going to take all the shine off her for her wedding."

Lisa blew out a breath. "I'm not going to do that."

"I know that. You know that. But be honest, you don't know Aaron's brother. Maybe he's vindictive and wants the attention."

"I don't think that's true."

Ruby lowered her foot to the ground and rolled her shoulders back. "But you don't know him, really."

"I don't know," Lisa confirmed.

"But how is he?" Ruby asked as they started toward the path that circled the lake.

"He's fine," Lisa answered the question with her own questioning tone.

"God, Lees, I mean, how *is* he?"

Lisa stopped walking. "Do you think I slept with the man?"

"I hope you slept with the man. I saw him. I also saw how he looked at you."

"Shit, Ruby. Does Tina think that too?"

Ruby shrugged and began walking again. "Probably."

"We went to a ballgame."

"And had a sweet picnic lunch."

"Who told her I had a sweet picnic lunch?"

Ruby laughed. "You posted pictures of the picnic you had. You took Mindy shopping with you for the basket. Tina's building her own story."

"The picnic is going up on my channel."

"And we all know that, but Tina's only got wedding brain."

Lisa blew out an irritated breath. "God, if I ever get married, remind me not to be so overprotective of my damned wedding."

Ruby laughed again. "You will be. We all will be." She nudged Lisa as they walked. "Just talk to her. Let her have her shining moment as the princess, and then you can shag the brother."

Lisa shook her head. "You're horrible."

"I'm hopeful. All I have are the stories you girls bring me."

"You've had a love life too."

"Ha!" Ruby snorted out the word and then tightened her ponytail. "I can get the guy at the bar who loses the bet to sleep with the fat chick."

"That's not true."

"It's happened," Ruby countered, and Lisa remembered what

that had done to her sweet friend. "So, I'd rather sit back and live vicariously through all of you."

"All of us? One girl with wedding plans that threatens to uproot friendships. One girl who's so sweet and nearly innocent that she will probably wait to get married before she tells us any details," Lisa and Ruby laughed at poor Mindy's expense. "And then there's me. The one who's so afraid a man will give her some attention and then walk out of her life for no reason."

Ruby shook her head. "I wish you wouldn't think that way."

"How can I not? My entire life was people giving up on me and sending me away. I've never had a relationship that was any different."

"And as one of your dearest friends, I'd like to remind you that after you sleep with a man, you're the one that goes silent. You're the one that pushes them away, probably so that they can't leave you first."

"That's not true," Lisa argued.

Ruby stopped walking again. "Justin," Ruby threw out the name. "You got a new phone number. Blake, you told him you moved away. Ed, you—"

"I get it," Lisa bit out the words. "I get it."

She stared walking again and Ruby caught up.

"I'm not trying to be a shit. I'm trying to get you to see that you deserve love, Lees. You deserve to be loved more than any of us."

"I don't love Aaron's brother."

"Well, maybe you will."

"At what expense? My friendship with Tina?"

Ruby shrugged. "I don't think it would end that way, especially if he's the one."

"I've known him less than a week. How can you consider that he's the one?"

Ruby tucked her hair behind her ear. "It was just something I said."

"I kissed him," Lisa blurted out and Ruby stopped walking again.

"No shit."

"I don't think he'd planned to kiss me, but..."

Ruby held up her hand. "You just moved in under his lips?"

Lisa laughed, and that finally felt good. "I gave him permission."

"So, he asked to kiss you?"

Now Lisa shook her head. "No, I just told him it would be okay."

"You instigated it?"

"I guess I did."

Ruby's grin was infectious. "Just kissed?"

"I told you that."

"I'm desperate for details, so forgive me."

Lisa laughed and they started to walk again. "It was mind blowing."

"How did you stop then?"

"He seems to have a better head on him than I do."

"He stopped and walked out?"

Lisa thought about the exchange. "No. Actually, it was hot and sweet. It was mind-numbing and short," she snorted out a laugh. "And before he left, he pressed his forehead to mine and promised me he wouldn't back out on our dinner on Sunday."

"Because you begged him not to back out. You're so afraid he'll forget you."

"Everyone forgets me," Lisa said matter-of-factly.

Ruby reached for Lisa's hand and lifted it to her lips. She kissed the back of Lisa's hand and gave it a squeeze. "Not everyone leaves you, Lees. And not everyone forgets you."

Lisa's bottom lip began to quiver, and she bit down on it.

Ruby nudged her again. "Let Tina be bitchy and bossy for a few more weeks. And then, feel this thing out with a guy who makes the earth move when he kisses you. You deserve it. You deserve to be loved more than anyone I know." Ruby let go of Lisa's hand. "Besides, we know Aaron is good people. You have to imagine that his brother would be too. They come from a good home."

Lisa linked her arm with Ruby's, resting her head on her shoulder. Her friends understood her. The only dream that had ever eluded her was a good home of her own. Maybe Ruby was right. She did deserve to love someone who could give her that.

CHAPTER FIFTEEN

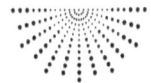

HAPPY BIRTHDAY!

The text had come in at six in the morning, and Lisa stared at it. The letters blurred as her eyes moved in and out of focus.

There were exactly three people who knew when her birthday was, and Mama Rose, Lisa reconsidered. And they all knew she didn't get out of bed until eight in the morning.

But this message wasn't from any one of the three of them. This was from Ryan.

Lisa sat up, rubbed her eyes, and hesitantly turned on the lamp on the nightstand.

Who told you that? She sent the text and then realized it came across as crabby as she felt. *And thank you.* She added as the little bubbles appeared, alerting her that he was texting back.

Really? Was his response.

Because her brain was still foggy, Lisa had to sit for a moment to put all the pieces together.

Right, he *lived* with Tina.

Tina, who wouldn't even respond to Lisa's texts yesterday.

Tina, who probably was having some epic meltdown, which

Ryan was privy to, and the information came out on a curse instead of as simple information.

Oh, yeah, your roommate. Lisa sent the text with the smiley face emoji whose tongue was sticking out.

You didn't tell me it was your birthday week. I would have made it special.

Lisa swallowed the lump that had formed in her throat. She hadn't been out with a man in over a year, and she'd had daily communication with this one since Saturday. How could he possibly have made her birthday week even better? Besides, they'd shared that goodbye kiss when he'd left her house Tuesday night. She considered that pretty special.

She was afraid to think about it further, especially since she was trying not to lose her best friend over it.

Lisa typed back, *I suppose it slipped my mind. I don't celebrate my birthdays, unless the girls make me.*

And just like the other day, her phone rang in her hand.

"Shit!" she huffed out the curse. "Hello?" Her voice cracked and was low and still full of sleep.

"You have to celebrate birthdays," he said, obviously more awake than she was at six in the morning.

"No, you don't have to celebrate them. But thank you for the very early morning message," she tried to sound menacing, but it was hard to do with the smile that seemed to tug at her cheeks.

"I guess it is early, isn't it? Sorry, I've been up for hours."

"Why?"

"I wanted to hit the gym before I headed to work."

Lisa sat up and adjusted pillows behind her. "First of all, yuck, to the gym," she said, and his warm laugh filtered through the phone. "And you got a job?"

"Yeah. It turned out that the office here didn't have any openings like they said they did. But they knew of a company downtown in need of my skills. So, I applied and interviewed yesterday. Now I'm on the train into the big city," he humored.

"In comparison to New York or Chicago, you probably think our mass transit is a carnival ride."

"I'm not going to lie. They didn't have this stuff when I lived here, and yes, it's a humorous attempt at mass transit."

Lisa laughed, but she wasn't sure why. This guy just brought it out in her.

"So you'll be sticking around, huh?" Her voice was light and flirty, but after she'd asked, she felt her stomach twist.

"Yeah. I think I want to stay around here. Especially since my brother is getting married and settling down. That means in time, I'll have some new family. And, the bonus, this week I made a new friend. I'd like to stick around for that too."

Now that twisting in her stomach threatened to make Lisa sick. "Really?"

Ryan chuckled. "Yeah."

She had sucked in a breath to say something—anything, but nothing came out.

"I have to get off at the next stop, but can I take you out to dinner tomorrow? To celebrate your birthday?"

Lisa winced. Now she knew how he knew it was her birthday. He was in on whatever plans Tina had to *surprise* Lisa for her birthday.

"I don't know. I hear Tina is pretty mad at me, and—"

"And you're thirty-two-years-old today. You can make your own decisions," he said, and Lisa winced.

"Wow, you got all the intel."

"You did tell me how old you were the other day."

"I'm older than you."

"You sure are. I like older women."

That made her snort out a laugh and then cover her mouth when she did so. "I'm not old."

"I didn't say old. I said older. So, what do you say to dinner?"

Lisa blew out a breath. "Seriously, Tina won't even talk to me."

"I promised her that I wouldn't hurt you, and I wouldn't lead you on, and I wouldn't sleep with you, and I wouldn't run off and get married, and I wouldn't hurt you," he said all in one breath.

"You said you wouldn't hurt me multiple times."

"Yeah, well that seemed to be a big selling point for her," he admitted. "We're not off the hook, but I'd like to take you to dinner."

"Okay."

"Awesome. I'll pick you up at six tomorrow?"

"I'll be ready," she said.

"Happy birthday, Lisa. Enjoy it. You deserve to celebrate."

They said goodbye and Lisa held her phone to her chest as she rested back against her pillows.

Since she'd met the girls, they'd made sure to make a big deal of her birthday. They usually played it off as they hadn't even remembered, and then they'd pull out all the stops.

There had been surprise parties, fancy dinners, concerts, and a surprise vacation for her twenty-fifth.

But for a young girl who hadn't had but two birthday parties her entire life, Tina, Mindy, and Ruby had made up for it. Lisa always felt like a princess put on a pedestal.

But with one phone call at six in the morning, Ryan had taken that pedestal her friends always put her on, and he made it feel even taller.

He took the job.

He took the job to be with family.

He took the job to stay near his new friend.

Lisa ran her fingers through her hair and let out a long sigh. No one in her life had ever chosen to stay somewhere she was. Everyone moved on, but Ryan wanted to stay. What did that mean?

Squeezing her eyes tight, she thought about *While You Were Sleeping*, which they had watched at last Rom Com Movie Club. Lisa had always associated with the main character Lucy. Lucy had no one until she accidentally became part of the Callaghan family, all because she was in love with one brother, and then fell in love with the other.

The comparison made Lisa laugh, but she'd spent most of her life comparing herself to characters in movies. She supposed she did that because it was so much better than the reality that surrounded her.

Well, it was a stretch to think that she'd fall in love with the brother, though she wasn't in love with Aaron in the least. But he'd always been like a brother to Lisa, ever since he'd met Tina in a math class when they were in college.

Pressing her fingers to her eyes, she pushed away that entire *fall in love* trope anyway. Ryan said he didn't have any friends in town, so she was fitting that bill. He had a new job. Soon he'd have his own place. In time, he'd have his own friends.

Ballgames and picnics would be a thing of the past, Lisa knew. But for that moment she'd at least have memories of six o'clock phone calls and birthday wishes.

CHAPTER SIXTEEN

Thursdays were social media content creation days, and Lisa could get lost for hours designing posts and scheduling them.

By noon, she'd long forgotten about the six o'clock phone call that had awakened her. She'd turned on the TV in her office and started *Pretty Woman*, not to watch, but to have on as background noise. The movie was one of her favorites, and she knew every single word by heart.

When Vivian began to sing *Kiss* by Prince in a bubble bath, in the penthouse, Lisa lifted her head and smiled at the TV. When Vivian made kissing noises, Lisa puckered up her lips and did the same, finishing the song with her.

She laughed alone in her office and finished working on the post she'd been creating.

The ping of her phone had her directing her attention to the message that had just come through.

Red dress. Hair up. Heels on. Ready to be picked up at six.

Lisa laughed at the cryptic text from Ruby.

The smile remained on her lips as she replied. *Why on earth would I dress like that on a Thursday?*

Ruby sent the emoji of the woman shrugging with her hands up and Lisa laughed as Ruby's next message rolled in.

Happy Birthday, Bish!

There was a lightness in Lisa's chest. She felt special. It was a stark difference from her everyday when she convinced herself that she wasn't. But her friends made sure she was always showered with love, and hadn't her newest friend begun that early that morning?

I suppose I'll be ready, she replied.

A photo popped up on her screen of the four of them on the first birthday she'd shared with her dearest friends. It had been her twenty-first, but the rest of the girls had been only eighteen and nineteen, so bar hopping hadn't been a possibility. That hadn't stopped them from showering her with love like she'd never known.

It was the start of the Rom Com Movie Club, and that night they'd watched *The Princess Bride* because at some point during their first year of friendship, Lisa had mentioned that she'd never seen it.

They had bought her the pajamas she'd worn for that night, and a tiara, which still sat atop her dresser.

Ruby had set up her dorm room with pillows all over the floor and fairy lights hung from the ceiling. Tina and Mindy had picked Lisa up, and they had driven through McDonald's for french fries, Taco Bell for burritos and tacos, Dairy Queen for shakes, and picked up a pizza at the Pizza Hut nearest the college campus.

It had been the most glorious night of Lisa's life, and as she looked down at the picture of the four of them in pajamas, standing among the floor of pillows in Ruby's room, she was reminded how much she was loved by her friends.

They'd been part of her life for a third of it, showering her with love and friendship. Lisa wondered why in times such as birthdays and holidays she still felt that tug of abandonment.

Ruby sent one more text. *I love ya, Lees! See ya soon!*

Lisa blew out a breath and held her phone to her chest, just as she had that morning after she'd talked to Ryan.

She was loved. Maybe it was time to accept that she was worthy of that love.

Her thoughts were pulled from the texts Ruby had sent when her doorbell rang. She stood and looked out the office window, where she could see her front step. A man in a blue shirt stood there with a bouquet of flowers in his hand.

Lisa's lips curled into a smile as she hurried to the front door and opened it.

"Hi," the man said. "I have a delivery for Lisa Palmer."

"That's me," she said, still smiling at the enormous bouquet.

The man handed her the flowers and walked back to his van.

Lisa's heart began to pound in her chest as she set the flowers on the counter and searched for the card. She looked at the bouquet that Ryan had brought her before the ballgame, and she smiled. There had never been so many vases of flowers in her house at one time before.

When she found the card, she ripped it from its tiny envelope. *Happy Birthday, Lisa! We hope you have a wonderful day. Your friends at Mama's Pasta Company.*

Lisa burst into laughter. The company had sent out a questionnaire once, and she thought it was interesting they'd asked for her birthday, that must have been why. She certainly hadn't expected that. A part of her was sure the flowers were from Ryan, but why? He'd called and invited her dinner, flowers would have certainly been overkill, but she just couldn't help but think he'd be the kind of man to go overboard with such a bouquet.

She tucked the card back into the flowers and arranged them in the center of the counter.

Thirty-two seemed to be starting out fairly nicely. As a birthday gift to herself, Lisa promised to remain open-minded and to not let years of emotions ruin the special day, as it usually did.

CHAPTER SEVENTEEN

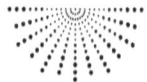

Mom and Dad have game night at the golf club. Want to grab some dinner?

Ryan read the text from his brother and laughed. What had the man done, before Ryan came back home, to bide his time while his fiancée spent time with her friends?

Sure. You buying?

Ryan stepped onto the train that would take him back to his car. He took his seat and noticed that the crowd using the newer mass transit of Denver was larger in the afternoon than it was at six in the morning.

His phone pinged in his hand. *This time. But when you get your first paycheck, you buy.*

Ryan laughed again. *I'll be home in thirty.*

He sat back as the train pulled from the station and thought about how happy he was that he'd made the decision to come home.

When Courtney had broken his heart, and his spirit, he couldn't have imagined that home would have brought him peace. Sure, it had only been a few weeks, but already he felt whole again.

He thought about his date tomorrow night, and he found that he couldn't wait to see Lisa. Opening his Facebook app, he looked up Tina's Facebook friends list and followed the link to Lisa Palmer.

When her face popped up, it was no surprise that her profile was her and her friends, and the cover image was of the picnic basket she'd made for them on Tuesday.

Ryan clicked on the button that would ask her to be his friend, and then he switched right to Instagram and followed her there too.

Obviously, she used that platform for the images she used to promote her YouTube channel.

He scrolled through tempting and seductive food pictures. Damn he couldn't wait until Sunday to get to actually taste something she cooked. His mouth was watering just looking at the pictures.

The notification on his phone told him that Lisa Palmer had followed him on Instagram, and another alert told him she'd accepted his friend request too.

Ryan chuckled. Just knowing they were connected in that way made his body warm.

What are you doing now? The text message came through his notifications, and he left the drool-worthy page filled with Lisa's food photos, and opened his texting app.

Ryan turned on the camera and quickly snapped a selfie of himself on the train, hoping he didn't look stupid. He didn't have the casual calm of selfie taking like the teenage girls he'd seen do it.

He sent the photo and a text, *Riding in luxury, doll.*

How was your first day?

Now it wasn't the picture he'd taken, but he wondered if anyone was looking at the stupid grin, he knew he wore.

It wasn't bad. It's always fun to be the guy who has to ask where the bathrooms are. HAHA

Before she could respond, he sent another text. *What are you doing tonight to celebrate your birthday?*

A photo popped up on his screen, and Ryan immediately sat a little taller, shielding his phone from anyone who might see it.

Lisa stood facing her mirror, the full length one he'd seen in her bedroom. She had on a short, tight, hug all her curves just right, red dress with tiny straps that went over her shoulders.

Her hair was curled and pulled up, and she had on makeup. Well, he thought, he liked both sporty-Lisa and fancy-Lisa.

The heels she wore gave her legs a shapeliness to them that had him reaching for the next button on his shirt and unbuttoning it because it had become much too hard to breathe.

What do you think? she asked.

He wasn't sure what the right response was supposed to be. If he'd been at home, on his couch in the garage, he'd have called her and sat in the stunned silence so she could hear him breathe. But surrounded by strangers, he wasn't sure how he was supposed to relay his thoughts.

The emoji with the wide eyes, the fire emoji, and a heart were what he typed into the text, followed by *O-M-G!!!*

I'll take that as a good sign? she asked.

Um...Yes! he replied, and she sent back a heart. *I feel as if I must admit, I don't think I want you going out looking like that. This interested party is afraid there will be many more interested parties by the end of the night.* He again added the emoji with the wide eyes.

Those annoying dots popped up, disappeared, popped up, and disappeared again. Okay, he might have overstepped a line saying that.

It took her long enough to reply that Ryan's screen had turned off and his phone dinged in his hand as the train pulled up to the station. Moving to exit the train, he looked down at his phone.

This interested party is not looking for other interested parties—other than said interested party.

God, all he wanted to do was drive over to her house and lock the rest of the world out for the night. They could celebrate her birthday alone, and he could appreciate her in that dress all he wanted to.

Be careful tonight, he typed as other hurried commuters walked past him. *Call if you need a ride, or company, or anything.*

Ryan reached his car and unlocked the door before she texted back. *I will, thanks.*

He slid in behind the steering wheel. *Have fun. Happy Birthday.*

Ryan started his car and put it in reverse as her next text came back. There was a picture of a black limousine outside of her house and Tina, Ruby, and Mindy were all dolled up in matching dresses walking toward her.

She was in good hands, he thought. But as he backed out of his parking space, all he could think about was how he wished she were in *his* hands.

CHAPTER EIGHTEEN

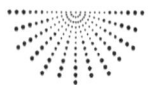

AARON HAD CHECKED HIS PHONE SIX TIMES IN THE FIRST HALF HOUR they'd sat at the bar watching the baseball game on the TV.

"Are you worried about them?" Ryan asked as he lifted his beer to his lips and took a drink, just as their appetizer plate was delivered. "You keep checking your phone."

Aaron shrugged. "I just thought Tina would be checking in, I guess. She's just been in a mood this week."

"You're going to pin that blame on me and Lisa too, aren't you?"

Aaron pulled a cheese stick from the platter and pulled it apart. "Dude, she'll be fine in a few weeks. She just needs to get through her shower on Saturday, final fittings, rehearsal dinner, and the wedding. And I know that living at Mom and Dad's doesn't thrill her either."

"I guess you'd better get a place, huh?"

His brother nodded. "We've looked at a few places. She wants a house, but there are some great condos and townhouses near my work. We just can't commit to a mortgage right now. Not with the student loans we're paying off."

"That's a lot to think about," Ryan agreed, pulling from his beer again. "I don't envy you that."

"And, I'll be honest with you, once we get home from the honeymoon, and she can gush over all the presents and wedding pictures, she'll stop being so hard on Lisa."

Ryan reached for an onion ring, taking a bite, and then pulling it apart. "So where did they go for her birthday?"

Aaron grinned. "To a drag show."

"Seriously?"

"Yep. She doesn't have anyone but them, so every year they plan something elaborate for her. This year there was some drag show beauty pageant."

"And I was worried about Lisa going out in that red dress," Ryan laughed, setting down the onion ring, and lifting his beer to take a sip.

Aaron picked up his beer and took a long pull. "You like her, huh?"

"I really do."

"You haven't even known her a week yet."

Ryan shrugged. "I just think she's worth getting to know. We've had a few nice times. I'm going to take her to dinner tomorrow for her birthday, and she's still cooking for me on Sunday." He took a drink from his beer and then nearly choked on it. "Wait, she's not really cooking *for* me, she said. She's making me help her and we're recording it for her YouTube channel."

Aaron laughed. "Oh, you're in for a long day. I've seen what she puts into getting one of those episodes put together."

"And here I thought I was just scamming a meal."

"You'll work for it."

Ryan sat back on his barstool as his brother took another cheese stick. "You know, you said something the first day you told me to leave her alone."

"I think I've said a lot of things trying to get you to leave her alone."

"Not going to happen. I'm *extremely* interested in her."

"God, just don't make any moves before the wedding."

"I promised Tina," Ryan confirmed. "But you said something about her deserving something stable. What did you mean?"

A deep crease formed between his brother's brows. "Oh, and here I thought you were really moving in on her and would have that intel by now." Aaron studied him. "You don't know what I meant by that?"

"All I know is she keeps telling me she'll understand if someday I'm not interested. Or asking me to promise I won't back out on dinner."

His brother lifted his bottle to his lips and finished down his beer. He let out a long breath as he set the bottle down. "She doesn't have any family."

"Okay, she mentioned something like that. That's why she likes that Sandra Bullock movie they were watching the other night. She relates to the character because neither of them had family."

Aaron nodded. "She's a foster kid. I don't even know how many homes she went through. I don't know why she was in foster care. All I know is she was emancipated when she was sixteen or seventeen. She dropped out of high school and got her GED, and then got a job. She worked near the college when the girls went there, and they scooped her up and she's been one of them for the past decade. They are her family."

Ryan pressed his fingers to his temples. "That makes a lot of sense now."

"Listen, it's probably not my place to tell you that. If you're really interested, then know she comes with a shit ton of baggage."

"We all do," Ryan said.

"Just saying." Aaron motioned to the server to bring them

another round of beers. "She's a nice gal. I like her. But those girls are super protective of her, so watch your step."

And that warning had Ryan wondering at what lengths they would go to keep her from him.

Even Lisa had said she was giving him the benefit of the doubt because he was Aaron's brother, and she thought he was an okay guy. They were mostly cut from the same cloth, Ryan figured. They were brought up the same, and though Aaron played baseball and Ryan played soccer, their moral compass was set to the same direction.

When the server was approaching with their new beers, Ryan quickly finished off his first and handed it to the woman as she set down the new one.

The image of Lisa in that little red dress kept flashing in his head. But it wasn't the dress, though that was a sexy as hell image, it was the smile on her lips and the come hither look in her eye that kept replaying in his head.

And then it was her saying, *Don't back out on me, okay?* that had him gripping his beer bottle a little tighter as he picked it up. When they'd returned home from the baseball game, she'd made a comment about when he'd had his fill of her, he could go. It didn't make sense to him in that moment, but now—he took a long pull from his beer.

When he'd asked her about it, she'd said, *Because everyone in my life gets tired of me. I'm used to it.*

Shit ton of baggage was right.

CHAPTER NINETEEN

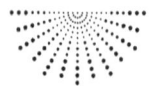

Lisa felt as if she were completely underdressed for the occasion when the emcee pulled her on stage for a "Drag queen birthday celebration," Miss Trudy had said with her hands making a marquee.

Heat had crawled into Lisa's cheeks as her friends cheered from the table. Ruby was standing on a chair, the burly hands of a queen dressed in sequins holding her steady. She whooped and shouted as Lisa was led on stage.

God, she loved those girls. Those girls who had come into that coffee shop on the edge of campus to study for an exam and ended up taking Lisa out for pizza that very night.

Those girls who had celebrated every milestone with her for the past decade and had cried with her when shit just got too hard.

They made her seem worthy and gave her love she'd never had before in her life. They cherished her, and hadn't that done a lot for her?

Without their support, she never would have started her YouTube channel, or sought out sponsorships. Now she made a living working from her spare bedroom and her kitchen. She made charcuterie lunches and planned day-long dinners.

A lump formed in her throat, and she swallowed it down as she was squeezed between two queens, each dressed like J-Lo.

Her friends had given her enough love that a man walked into her life less than a week ago, and she'd spent nearly the entire week with him, and she'd loved every moment.

He'd texted her at six that morning to wish her a happy birthday. He'd brought by a big donut and coffee. He'd let her sleep on his shoulder, well, his chest.

A conga line formed, and a set of hands were on her hips. Lisa hands were then grabbed by the queen in front of her and placed on the queen's hips.

The music was deafening. The cheers and shouts of celebration enveloped everyone in the room. They were all celebrating the very existence of Lisa, and through the smiles and the laughs, tears threatened.

So, the people who gave her life didn't want her—couldn't keep her.

The families that opted to give her a good home, some had better things to do.

The family that did give her a home had to move.

But the women who found her in that coffee shop, they embraced her, loved her, and celebrated this day in the grandest fashion of all. And they celebrated like this every single year.

Those tears fell while she laughed.

Lisa was loved.

When the pageant and celebration at the drag show was over, they climbed back into the limo and headed toward a bar. It was only nine o'clock, and she knew she'd be home and tucked into bed by ten-thirty. Each of the women doting on her had to be at work the next morning, but they'd make sure she celebrated until the very end of the night.

When the limo pulled up in front of the sports bar, Ruby shook her head.

"Which one of you decided to come here?" she asked with a snarled lip.

All eyes turned to Tina, who stuck out a pouty lip. "What?"

"That's Aaron's brother's Bronco in the parking lot," Ruby called her out, and Lisa felt a bubble of anticipation float to her chest, but she kept her face still and tried not to smile. "I saw it when we parked, and the limo picked us up."

"Okay, so maybe it's a coincidence," Tina argued. "Maybe they just happened to be here."

Mindy shook her head. "You were tracking Aaron's phone."

"Fine," Tina resigned. "So I want to see my fiancé."

"Aren't you going home to him in like an hour?"

"Yeah, but…"

Lisa laughed. "Don't bust her chops. This is what true love has done to her."

Ruby raised her brow. "And you're just saying that because the brother must be here if his truck is here."

"I'm just saying y'all owe me a shot, so let's go."

"Holy shit," Aaron said as he looked toward the front door of the bar.

Ryan turned toward his brother, then looking in the direction that had Aaron's attention. The smile that formed on his mouth couldn't have been hidden.

Looking like a four pack of Charlie's Angels, the girls walked through the front door of the bar, all in red dresses with high heels. There wasn't a man that hadn't watched them walk in.

Tina moved directly to Aaron, wrapping her arms tightly

around his neck and his arms went right around her body. She kissed him hard on the mouth.

"Look who's here," she said, and Aaron laughed.

"You were tracking me."

"Don't tell the girls," she teased.

Ruby jumped up on the stool next to Ryan. "Which one is your server? We need shots."

Ryan looked around for the server, but as his eyes passed by Lisa, they stopped. She was absolutely stunning.

"Happy birthday," he said and watched as the corners of Lisa's mouth curled up into that smile that sent chills over his skin.

"Thank you."

Ryan noticed the server walk by and he waved her down. Ruby ordered them all a round of shots, and then pulled Lisa to the stool and made her sit down, while she and Mindy shared the other stool.

"How's your day been?" Ryan leaned in closer to Lisa so she could hear him.

"It's been fantastic. But I've been up since the crack of dawn," she laughed and Ryan leaned in closer to her.

"No kidding? I'll bet you had some insensitive prick texting you."

Lisa leaned in to close the gap. "I wouldn't call him that. It made my day."

"I'm glad to hear that."

The server brought their tray of shots, and Ruby handed them out to everyone.

Ruby lifted hers to the center of the table, and everyone did the same.

"There's no one like her. No one cooks like her. No one makes a fancy cup of coffee like her. No one cries harder when they see a stray dog—"

"Give me a break," Lisa called out and laughed.

"Lees, I know I speak for all of us. Well, all of us girls, when I say, the greatest day was when we met you. I look forward to these celebrations every year, but truly, I love celebrating that you exist."

Lisa batted her eyes, and Ryan could see the tears straining.

"Thank you," Lisa said, making eye contact with everyone at the table. "I love you guys."

"*Salute!*" Ruby shouted and they all clinked their glasses.

"Happy birthday, sweetheart," Ryan said softly, drawing her attention to him. He tapped his glass to Lisa's before shooting it back and breathing out a hot breath.

Lisa laughed, did the same, but instead of huffing out a breath, she put her hand on his thigh and gave it a squeeze.

CHAPTER TWENTY

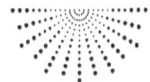

RUBY, WHO DIDN'T HAVE TO GO INTO WORK UNTIL TEN THE NEXT morning opted for another shot. Mindy threw caution to the wind, as did Aaron and Tina.

"I want to see this limo," Ryan said scanning the table and stopping when his eyes met Lisa's.

"It's fancy. Lots of colored lights," she said. "C'mon, I'll show you."

She hopped off her stool and started for the door with Ryan following close behind. She would have reached for his hand, but Tina was giving her some grace, so she didn't want to push it.

But as soon as they were outside, Ryan caught up to her and took her hand. He interlaced their fingers and slowed her walk.

"This was a nice treat," he said as they walked toward the waiting limo. "I didn't think I was going to get to see you on your birthday."

"I didn't either," Lisa admitted as the driver climbed from his seat and hurried to open the door.

"I thought you'd be longer," the man said.

"He wanted to see the limo. Manuel, this is Ryan," she introduced them.

The two men nodded toward one another simultaneously, then Manuel opened the door.

Lisa crawled into the car and Ryan followed.

"This is nice," he drew out the words as he scooted in to sit next to Lisa on the bench seat, and he closed the door.

"There's music, lighting patterns, TV."

"What more could you need?"

Lisa pushed a button above her and the window between them and the cab of the car went up.

She turned to him. "You texted me at six o'clock."

"I think I've apologized for that," he said, very aware that she'd turned her knees so that they nearly touched his.

"I've never been woken up with birthday wishes."

He wanted to argue that, sure that the girls had done that for her at some point, but he didn't want to bring up anything he might have learned about her earlier from his brother. That was for her to tell him.

"So, I gave you a first?" Ryan asked, watching her eyes as they grew darker in the blue hues that lit the limo.

Lisa nodded slowly; her eyelids heavy with something he thought looked a lot like lust. Then, when she licked her lips, he was sure that was what it was.

"You did. It's been the very best birthday," she admitted. "And I say that mostly sober. I only had one drink at the club, and the shot inside."

He couldn't help but reach his fingers to her ear and touch the earring that dangled from her lobe so that it swung slightly.

"The very best," he repeated. "I guess I'll have to think about what I can do to make your birthday dinner tomorrow memorable."

"I was thinking there was one more thing I wanted for my birthday tonight," she said, her voice now low and husky.

"And what would that be?" Ryan asked, letting his voice drop lower too.

Lisa's mouth twitched with a smile. "Remember that kiss we shared on Tuesday?"

"I'll never forget it," he admitted.

She batted her lashes. "I'd like another kiss like that."

Ryan let out a low hum. "Oh, honey, I think we can do better than that."

Lisa's eyes had gone wide when he said that, and he liked that he could do that to her.

Ryan lifted his hands to cup her face, and he lingered to look into those deep blue eyes, which held a bit of need and surprise. For only a moment, he thought about what his brother had told him about her. What had those eyes witnessed in her life?

Lisa's tongue flicked over her lips again, and Ryan felt something stir in his belly that was hot. He'd known her six days. This would be their second kiss. There would be more of them, he knew before he even leaned in. From the moment he'd seen her standing in her living room, her face covered in green, wearing a UCLA T-shirt and a pair of pajama pants, he knew she'd be important to him. Now, only a breath away from her, with everything inside of him stirring to life, he was sure of it.

"Happy birthday, Lisa," he whispered before he leaned in and pressed his lips to hers.

EVEN THOUGH SHE'D BEEN SITTING THERE WAITING FOR THAT KISS, the moment his lips touched hers, heat rose in her from the tips of her toes all the way to the top of her head.

His hands moved from her face and up into her hair as he tilted her head, which deepened the kiss. Lisa parted her lips and Ryan took advantage of that moment to slip his tongue in.

The air in the limo grew thick, and vibrant colors swam behind her eyelids. It was a happy birthday indeed, she thought as she lifted her arms around Ryan's neck and began to ease back on the seat.

His lips moved from hers slightly. "What are you doing?" he whispered, and she opened her eyes expecting to see anger building in his. But there was no anger. There was warmth in his dark eyes—need.

"I...I was..." he didn't let her finish, and she wasn't sure what she would have said.

Ryan moved so that he lowered her under him on the seat. His thigh brushing between her thighs, the weight of his body pressed to hers as he kept one hand at the nape of her neck, and the other at her waist.

He'd keep it a kiss, she knew. This was all too new to make it more, but in this position, there were so many possibilities of what was to come.

Again, his lips moved from hers, only this time they traced the line of her jaw and then traveled to her throat and across her collar bone before traveling to her ear.

"I can't wait until this wedding is over," he said, his voice full of gravel.

"Me either."

"I'm still interested, Lisa," he said easing back so he could look into her eyes. "And not just in the kissing. In you. I like you." He was ginning and she found it extremely cute. Not sexy at all, but cute.

"I like you too."

"Well, happy birthday to me too then," he teased.

CHAPTER TWENTY-ONE

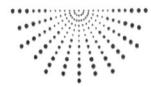

THERE WAS THE UNMISTAKABLE SOUND OF MANY PEOPLE WALKING on gravel, and Ryan eased back, and helped Lisa sit up.

Pulling down the skirt of her dress, she tried to look put together. She knew anyone could see right through it. But in the darkness of the car, perhaps she'd get away without anyone seeing the heat she felt in her cheeks.

Ryan adjusted and opened the door just as the others approached.

"Cool car, girls. Party over?" he asked as he stepped out.

"I have to go to work tomorrow," Mindy whined as she passed by him and crawled into the car.

"At least I get to sleep in for a few hours," Ruby sighed as she too climbed in and sat next to Lisa, where Ryan had just vacated.

"Give me your keys," Aaron said to Ryan. "They're taking the limo back to the house anyway. I'll take Tina, you ride with the girls."

Ryan shifted his head to look at Tina. "Don't you want to ride back with them?"

Lisa could see her cuddle up to Aaron's arm. "Go. I'll ride in your new truck."

Ryan pulled the keys from his pocket with a shrug. "I'd never say no to a limo full of ladies. I'll see you at home."

He ducked back into the car, noticing that Ruby had taken his seat, but she seemed oblivious as she checked her phone. Ryan exchanged smiled with Lisa as he sat next to Mindy.

"This is how my life usually goes," he said as the car began to pull from the lot. "I get the party of girls all to myself when they're done partying."

Ruby laughed first. "When her birthday lands on a weekend, we're more fun."

Mindy nodded. "I say we blow off work next year and take a vacation."

"I'm all for that," Lisa agreed.

Ryan leaned back in his seat. "Do you celebrate all of your birthdays like this?"

Lisa felt the air thicken again as she watched her friends form answers in their heads.

Ruby shook her head. "Lees is the old lady of the group. We celebrate her harder."

That warranted a jab of Lisa's finger into Ruby's arm, and a laugh from Mindy. And with that, the air settled again.

"I hope he doesn't get distracted driving my truck," Ryan said stretching his arms out over the back of the seat, careful not to get too close to Mindy. "I'm in charge of picking up relatives at the airport after work tomorrow."

Lisa blinked hard. "If we need to change plans…"

"Nope. I was promised I wouldn't have to do that," he said firmly. "Besides, I'm good for not being around that first night when everyone sees one another again. I've been *catching up*," he used air quotes, "for two weeks now with just my own family. I'm exhausted. Now my mother is on heightened hostess protocol.

And this is only a few members of the family. I can't imagine what the wedding week is going to be like."

Lisa felt sick in that moment.

Tina was the first of them to get married. She hadn't even considered that marriage meant the blending of two families and those two families were bigger than just immediate family.

Her throat began to constrict and if they didn't get out of that car soon, she wasn't sure she wouldn't get sick.

"How many people are coming in for the shower?" Lisa asked, and when all heads lifted, she knew her voice had wobbled enough to warrant concern.

Ryan seemed to do some calculation in his head. "Five, I guess. I mean that's from our side. I don't know Tina's side at all."

Ruby must have noticed the panic that settled over Lisa, and she took one of the unopened bottles of water from the pocket on the door and handed it to Lisa.

"Thanks," Lisa said, and she could feel Ryan's eyes on her. "It's nice they're coming in for the shower."

"Yeah. Mom is tight with her family."

Lisa drank down the water. Tina was going to kill her when she had a panic attack over meeting their family.

Trauma, this was left over trauma. She needed to work through it. She needed to journal it. She needed to call her therapist over it tomorrow. Already she knew she wasn't going to even crawl out of bed on Sunday. It was going to be too much.

No, she had to crawl out of bed on Sunday. She had a date. She had a full day planned with Ryan.

Damn it! Why hadn't she thought about all this earlier? There was no way she'd be in the mental state to spend all day with him after keeping her wits about her at that bridal shower on Saturday.

They'd reschedule. No problem.

No, it was a problem. Hadn't she all but begged him to not back out on her?

She was in a full-blown panic attack when the limo pulled up in front of Ryan's parents' house.

"Oh, good. He didn't wreck it," Ryan laughed, noticing Aaron and Tina in the driveway.

"C'mon, Lees," Ruby reached for her hand. "Let's get you home."

They climbed from the car and Lisa sucked in the fresh air. Tina hugged her, then Aaron did the same. Mindy kissed Lisa's cheek and gave her hand a squeeze, and in that moment, she knew Mindy had seen the attack come on too.

Ruby started toward her car, and Ryan reached for Lisa as she'd started to follow her.

"Hey, are you okay?" he asked, his hand still on her wrist.

"Yeah. I'm fine."

"I don't know what I said in there to freak you out, but—"

"I'm fine," she said pushing a smile to her lips. "I'm really fine. End of the party. I guess I'm a little sad."

Ryan looked over his shoulder and they both watched as Tina *supervised* their goodbye.

"Yeah," he said. "I'm a little sad too. I'd like to be the one driving you home."

Finally, the smile on her lips wasn't forced. "I'd like that too."

"I'll see you tomorrow."

"If you get caught up with family and can't—"

"I'll be there." He leaned in and kissed her cheek. "We'll finish that kiss tomorrow," he whispered in her ear before he released her wrist and headed toward the house.

Lisa drew in two more long breaths. This was a test, she thought. She was good at tests and making the most of a situation.

Walking to Ruby's car, she drew in one more breath. She wasn't going to let her traumas lose her the guy who was interested. Not this time.

CHAPTER TWENTY-TWO

RUBY HAD FOLLOWED LISA INSIDE THE CONDO UNDER THE GUISE that she had to use the bathroom. But they'd been through this enough times, Lisa knew that Ruby was just making sure Lisa was settled before she drove away.

"I think I want to go to that drag club for my birthday," Ruby said as she walked out of the bathroom and toward the kitchen where Lisa stood already drinking a glass of water and sorting through her mail.

"We could arrange that."

"You had a good night?"

Lisa leaned a hip against the counter and smiled at her friend. "I had the best night. And I mean that."

Ruby rested her forearms on the counter. "Let's make a pact, okay? You let me and Mindy know when you need air during this whole wedding thing. I don't think one of us considered the number of people that would be around at any given time."

Lisa reached for Ruby's hand and gave it a squeeze. "I love you guys. I don't know what I could have done right in the world to have had you all drop in and take me in, but—"

"We feel the same way, Lees. You're our girl. You're one of us. We're family."

And Lisa knew that. No one had ever loved her like those girls did.

Ruby looked at the mail that Lisa had brought in with her. "What's that? It looks like a birthday card."

Lisa plucked it out of the stack and smiled at the return address. She quickly tore it open and pulled out the ornate, hand-made card.

Happy Birthday, our dear, sweet, Lisa. We hope you have a wonderful day. We love and miss you. Love, Mama Rose, John, and family.

Lisa slid it toward Ruby, who also smiled down at it.

"That's very sweet," Ruby said.

Lisa picked up the card and looked at it again, and then pressed it to her chest. Rose and John were the only foster parents that had taken Lisa in and loved her as if she'd been with them since the moment she was born. They'd had two sons, Jason and Ken, and had lost a baby girl at birth. That loss had made them want to give back to kids who hadn't even gotten a chance.

They had put Lisa in soccer and attended every game. They made sure she sang in choir, and they were the ones who taught her to cook. Family vacations included Lisa too. It was with them that she had her only childhood birthday parties.

They'd considered adopting Lisa, but there was so much red tape it never happened. After four years—the four most blissful years of Lisa's life, and the most critical for a teenage girl—the Hughes family got transferred to England for John's job. Lisa was on her own for real.

A tear rolled down her cheek and she quickly brushed it away. The card was meant to send love, not sad memories, and Lisa knew that.

"Who sent you all the flowers?" Ruby distracted her with the question.

Lisa looked up at them. "The daisies were from Ryan before our picnic. The huge bouquet is from a pasta company."

That warranted a snort from Ruby. "You're a lucky girl. A man and a pasta company."

Lisa laughed, God she loved Ruby and her blunt and no-nonsense way.

Ruby turned her attention back to Lisa. "No bullshit either, what were you doing in the limo?" Ruby's brows rose as she waited.

There was heat in Lisa's cheeks again, and that stupid smile was back.

"We were kissing," she admitted, because she could admit anything to Ruby.

"Oh yeah you were." Ruby fist pumped in the air. "That's all?"

"That's all. We weren't out there very long."

"That's Tina's fault. I would have let you be alone all night." Ruby tapped her fingers on the counter. "I would have let him bring you home, but I saw the supervision going on."

"She means well," Lisa said, and Ruby snorted a laugh again.

"She does not. She just doesn't want her wedding disturbed."

"I'm going to try not to do that," Lisa said soberly.

Ruby walked around the counter and pulled Lisa into her. "Mindy and I have your back. None of us have gone through what you have, so we can't pretend to understand it. What we can do is help you through it."

"I love you."

"I love you too, Lees." Ruby said giving Lisa one more big squeeze before pulling back. "And if having that hunky man next to you all day long, with his arms around you, dancing and drinking helps, I'll keep the bride at bay."

Now Lisa laughed. "I can't see how it wouldn't help. I really like him."

"I know. I can see it in your eyes now, and when you saw him when we walked into the bar, yeah, it got hotter in there."

"I don't know how to have a real relationship," Lisa admitted.

"None of us really do. But I'll tell you what I do know," Ruby said picking up her purse from the couch where she'd tossed it when they'd walked in. "The reason Tina is happy is because Aaron loves her so much. And I know he knows how to love because that monster-in-law of Tina's loves them all uncondi-tionally, and that's why she's being so high strung. They're good people, Lees. Good people. Hell, Ryan might not be Mr. Right, but he might be Mr. Right for Now. Let him in a little, when Tina allows," she teased again.

"You think so?"

"He brought you daisies."

And a donut and coffee, Lisa began to make the list in her head.

Ruby moved to her and kissed her on the cheek. "Get some sleep and do what you need to do to steel yourself for Saturday. We're there for you."

"I will."

Ruby let herself out, and Lisa locked the door. She looked at the flowers and the card on her counter. Then, she thought of the six o'clock text message and the kiss. Of course, the night with her girls had been fantastic. Okay, she thought as she walked to her office and pulled her journal from the shelf. She'd journal that first. Then, she'd journal her fears. But she'd end the entry with a detailed description of how Ryan Blair made her feel.

She was even more interested now, she thought of his words to her. She wanted more than a few kisses and dates.

CHAPTER TWENTY-THREE

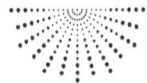

IT WAS THE APPROPRIATE TIME OF EIGHT O'CLOCK ON FRIDAY morning when Lisa rolled out of bed refreshed.

With that kiss from Ryan, and Ruby's help, Lisa had managed to go to bed after journaling about her birthday, and the anxiety had been avoided further. She already had a call into her therapist, so at some point during the day, she'd have to visit her feelings of last night again, but at least she was rested.

When she looked at her phone, she noticed the text message that had come in from Ryan, which she'd missed because she'd already been asleep.

11:59pm and I'm hoping I'm the last person you get to talk to on your birthday. I hope it was magical.

There was another text that had come in just after midnight, and he must have decided that she was asleep.

I can't wait to see you tomorrow night (well, tonight.) We'll finish that kiss we started, and maybe you can have two magical nights.

Text messages from a handsome man did make for a better start to her day than usual. She'd accept that little blessing.

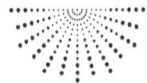

RYAN WAS LIVID AS HE SAT IN THE OUTER LOT JUST BEYOND THE airport. The flight his aunts were on had been delayed, and he'd been sitting outside the airport for over an hour. Aaron had promised to pick up their cousins bright and early the next morning.

Checking his phone, Ryan realized he'd never make it to Lisa by six. He was an hour from her, and he still had to drop his aunts off at his parents' house.

He hated that he'd have to call her. But he wasn't going to cancel. No, he was going to keep his word no matter what.

Ryan pushed the contact for Lisa and the phone rang.

"Hello," her voice came through the speaker and Ryan rested his head back against the seat. Just the sound of her voice stirred him.

"Hey. How was your day?" he asked, working harder than he'd have liked to keep his voice light.

"It's been productive."

"Good."

"But you're not going to be able to make it for dinner, are you?" she asked and a sharp pain pierced his chest.

"Why did you say that?"

"Because you're supposed to be here in an hour, and your voice gives it away."

"Shit," Ryan said readjusting in his seat. "I'm going to be there. I just won't be there at six."

"Honestly, we don't have to—"

"I'll be there," he confirmed. "I want to see you."

"You do?"

"Really interested, remember?"

He heard her sigh. "I'm really interested too, and I want to see you."

"Then, like I said, I'll be there."

Another thirty minutes passed before Ryan received notice that his aunts had landed. It would be another thirty minutes before they got from their gate to the baggage claim. It was going to be nearly eight o'clock before he could possibly get to Lisa.

As soon as his aunts got to the baggage carousel, Ryan drove up to the airport. It was only then that his aunt Janice called to let him know that his aunt Chris' luggage was missing.

Ryan raked his fingers through his hair and let out a curse before he drove out and around to loop back to the lot where he drove around looking for a parking space.

BY THE TIME THEY'D FIGURED OUT WHERE CHRIS' LUGGAGE WAS, another forty minutes had passed. Ryan worked to keep his pleasant demeanor, which must have worked, or his aunt Janice would have called him out on it.

She did ask the question that shook him up. "So how is that girlfriend of yours? Your mama said you were proposing and everything."

Ryan swallowed hard. "How long has it been since you've talked to my mom?"

Janice laughed. "Well, that was a few months ago."

"Quite a few," he let out a little laugh. "We're not together anymore. I'm back here and I left her in Chicago."

His aunts shared a look between them, and Ryan adjusted in his seat.

"I'm sorry to hear that," Janice said. "You're a good-looking kid, you'll have another woman in no time."

Ryan winced. *Good looking kid* was only one of the reasons that sentence crawled under his skin.

Did he dare to tell her that there was a woman? Oh, and what a woman.

No, he didn't dare. Wasn't that what all the hubbub was about? Him upstaging his brother and Lisa upstaging Tina on their special day? Besides, a few kisses in less than a week of meeting did not make for a relationship. There was interest. Hadn't they both said that? But interest didn't mean forever.

Ryan swallowed hard. "Prospects are good," he grinned. "How is Cal?"

Ryan had shifted the conversation to Janice's son, and the rest of the ride was filled with her telling him of all the wondrous things his cousin had managed to do in his short twenty-five years.

Usually, Ryan avoided the topic just so he didn't feel belittled, but under the circumstances, he saw no way around it.

Besides, he wasn't really listening. He was fixated on the clock that shone green in the dark. It was even later than he'd thought.

CHAPTER TWENTY-FOUR

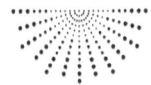

She wasn't mad.

Lisa did everything in her power to not be mad. This wasn't Ryan's fault. They should have rescheduled, but he wanted to take her to dinner. She'd made herself a sandwich when he'd called the first time and said he was going to be late, but that had been hours ago.

When she did feel a spurt of anger, which she now realized was only irritation, she'd gotten out her journal and written about it. That defused it. He wasn't abandoning her. He had a family, and this was the kind of stuff that happened when someone had a family.

Her bottom lip began to tremble.

No. No. No. There was no crying when she was dressed up and had makeup on.

Lisa had a family. And it was because of that family that Ryan was late. Tina was her family.

When she thought of it that way, she laughed.

Tina deserved to have the wedding of her dreams. She'd always talked about being a bride, even before Aaron had happened into her life. Sometimes, Lisa felt sorry for him. Did he have any idea? Not that it would have ever mattered. Aaron Blair was head over heels in love with Tina, and he'd give her anything.

Tina was Lisa's family, and if her date was interrupted because of wedding plans, well, Lisa would just have to live with it. But someday, maybe, Lisa would get married, and she would make sure Tina's schedule was put off in some way.

She chuckled as she turned the channel on the TV and stopped when she came to *Fools Rush In*.

The remote went straight to the couch. She couldn't pass up the classic rom com, no matter how dumb she really thought it was. Perry and Hayek had no chemistry. No matter, the boy meets girl, they get pregnant on a one-night stand, boy marries girl and the family gets involved, it was a trope that was as old as the ages, and a winner in Lisa's book.

Lisa had landed on the scene where they were in the Vegas hotel suite after having gotten married, and Alex, Perry's character, slid his hand over Isabel's stomach—a bonding moment with her and the baby.

For some reason, that part of the movie always moved her.

Maybe because at a time he could have just walked away, he stayed.

Lisa drew in a deep breath. It was fiction, she knew that, but movies like the one she'd landed on had guided her through her life and given her hope. Rom coms were filled with happily ever afters, and that was all that Lisa had ever wanted for herself.

RYAN KNOCKED ON LISA'S DOOR JUST SHY OF NINE O'CLOCK. HE was frazzled and irritated over everything that had happened. His mother pulling him in to conversation with his aunts, holding him up even more, had him nearly snapping at her, but he'd managed to keep his manners intact.

When Lisa opened the door, Ryan sent an appreciative gaze over her.

Her blonde hair in long curls cascaded over her bare shoulders, accentuated by a royal blue halter top. She had on a pair of white pants, and her feet were bare.

As he'd done the other night, Ryan lifted a finger to her ear and tapped her earring.

"You look beautiful," he said.

"And you look tired." Lisa reached a hand toward him, and he took it as she pulled him through the door.

"It just wasn't how I'd planned this evening," he confessed.

When they'd both cleared the door, Lisa closed it, and immediately looped her arms around his neck.

"Maybe this will help," she said as she lifted on her toes to press her lips to his.

Ryan wrapped his arms around her and pulled her in. As her mouth opened to his, Ryan took and let himself sink into the kiss she offered.

Ryan pressed his forehead to hers. "You're right. That helped." He lifted his hands to brush her bare shoulders with his fingertips. "I'm so sorry."

"Don't be. It's not like you didn't keep in touch, at least."

He let his hands slide down her bare arms and capture her hands in his. "You deserve better."

"I deserve what I'm getting. Our timing is a little off. Had we met a few weeks ago..."

Ryan laughed. "Yeah. I suppose it'll be this way for the next few weeks." He kept his head pressed to hers. "I picked a fine time to come home. I should have come home a year ago," he said, and then wished he'd chosen to say something else—anything else.

"Was that when you broke up with..."

"Courtney," he finished her thought. "Yeah."

There was a flash of regret in her eyes for asking. He could see it. But, even though this little thing they were playing with wasn't a relationship, those were conversations that would be had, he supposed.

Ryan gave her hand a squeeze. "Are you still interested in going out?"

"Only if you are. You've had a much busier day than I have."

"I still want to celebrate you. That's what this was all about anyway. You."

Lisa pulled her bottom lip through her teeth, scanning his eyes with her beautiful blue ones. "I appreciate that."

"You deserve more celebration."

Something else flashed in her eyes now, and he recognized it as an annoyance. He'd been with enough women to understand that. But she smiled and moved from him.

As she walked toward the end of the couch, she picked up her shoes, and sat down to slip them on.

Trying to pull himself together, so that he was sure all they would do would be to celebrate her, Ryan walked toward the counter.

"The daisies are holding up," he said, but his eyes were focused on the large bouquet. It irritated him that the sight of them caused there to be a pang of jealousy piercing his chest.

"They are. That's one of the reasons I love them so much. They last longer than roses."

He'd make a note of that.

"It looks like someone was celebrating you," he reached up and touched the petal of one of the roses in the bigger bouquet.

Lisa stood up on a pair of heels that strapped around her ankles. "A pasta company that sponsors me sent them yesterday."

Ryan let out a silent sigh of gratitude that someone else wasn't interested and sending her flowers for her birthday. It was petty, but it was how he felt.

He couldn't help but pick up the card that was on display.

Happy Birthday, our dear, sweet, Lisa. We hope you have a

wonderful day. We love and miss you. Love, Mama Rose, John, and family.

She was standing next to him now as he processed the message. Someone in her life loved her and referred to herself as *Mama Rose.* That seemed like family to him.

CHAPTER TWENTY-FIVE

They ended up at one of Colorado's many microbreweries with a taco truck parked on the street. It had been an easy decision when they'd driven by three other restaurants that had lines out the door.

Standing at one of the tall tables outside the tap room, Lisa took a drink of her chocolate coffee stout. Ryan winced as he watched her.

"I feel as if I need to make clear the fact that I don't drink," she laughed wiping the foam from her lip. "I mean, I drink wine at Rom Com Movie Club, and I might have a beer here or there, but this week, I've had more hangovers than I have in years."

Ryan lifted his much lighter pilsner and tapped his glass to hers. "Here's to a week of celebrations," he said. "Rom coms, baseball games, birthdays, and dinners with a sexy man."

Lisa choked on her sip when he said that.

"You don't think I'm a sexy man?" he asked with his brows raised.

"I just didn't expect you to say it," she laughed. "Wow, nothing like putting me on the spot."

"Let's just say I absolutely admire the view I have," he smiled as he lifted his beer.

"So, you think I'm sexy?"

Ryan puckered his lips. "Now see, this is where I get in trouble. I can joke about me being sexy, but I feel as if I told you I thought you were sexy, I'd be crossing some kind of line."

"What if I give you a pass?"

"As in a pass that if I say it, I won't get in trouble? You won't hold it against me?"

"Exactly."

"I still think it feels weird."

Lisa leaned in on her elbows, propped her chin up on her fists. "Okay, I'll cross the line myself. I think you're sexy. I've seen your Facebook posts and your Instagram pictures."

He was sure color filled in his cheeks, but he liked this game they were playing.

"Red dress, mid-thigh." He closed his eyes. "Strappy heels, and some little purse that sparkled. Hair in curls and a glass of champagne in your hand."

She was studying him when he opened his eyes.

"Wedding for one of the girls that they went to college with," Lisa admitted. "I was Ruby's plus one."

"Sexy." Ryan let out a low hum and lifted his beer, and she followed his lead. "Happy Birthday, Lisa"

"Thank you."

By eleven, they were walking back up the steps to her condo. Lisa carried her shoes, and Ryan kept his hands in his pockets.

"Would you like to come in?" she asked, but he shook his head.

"Yes, but I'm going to decline."

Lisa fished her key from her purse. "Are all of those people staying at your parents' house too?"

"Luckily no. My mom has three sisters, and one lives nearby. So, they're going to stay there."

"I look forward to meeting them tomorrow," Lisa said, and Ryan's eyes went wide.

"For some reason it didn't cross my mind that you'd be meeting them all. Shit."

Lisa unlocked the door and turned back to him. "Why does this sound like a problem?"

Ryan ran his hand over the back of his neck. "I have to admit, it just feels funny. I mean, I feel as if we're starting something here, but really we're just getting to know each other. Tomorrow you're going to meet almost all the women in my family. My mother, grandmother, aunts, cousins."

Lisa smiled. "I've met your mother."

A line formed between his brows. "Oh. That's weird too."

She laughed. "Will I hear anything you don't want me to hear?"

"I don't think so. I'm an open book." But he winced. "You know what? My mother wasn't too forthcoming about my breakup with Courtney." He chewed his bottom lip. "There might be some talk."

"Alright. I'll let them all know you and I are going to be sleeping together, so they can forget about her."

Now his mouth dropped open, and Lisa took great joy in watching his throat work. "Wow. Shit. Wow."

She couldn't help but grin at him. "I'm kidding."

"On which part. That we're going to do that or that you're going to tell them about it?"

Lisa stepped down so that they were eye to eye and looped her arms around his neck, dangling her shoes from her fingers behind his back. "Interested, remember?"

"Oh, I remember."

"And I think it was you telling me right after I met you that you're thirty, so you've learned to be forward and ask for what you want."

Ryan nodded. "I did say that."

"Well, I'm thirty-two. Consider that my asking, and I'm not going to say anything to anyone about us seeing each other," she confirmed.

Lisa watched as he continued to process everything, she just said to him.

"Okay. Again, wow." He wrapped his arms around her. "For the record, when I'm seeing a woman, I don't see other ones."

Lisa tucked her fingers from her free hand into Ryan's hair. "You're a real gentleman, huh?"

"I'm not someone who plays the field."

"I like that." She searched his eyes, and she knew he was true to his word. "I don't usually date at all."

"Does that apply here?"

She tucked her lips between her teeth. "I don't think it does."

"Okay," he said smiling, his mouth now just a breath from hers. "We'll keep this dating status between us for the next few weeks."

"I think that's safe," she admitted.

"But the day after that damn wedding I'm changing my Facebook status."

Now she couldn't help but throw her head back with a laugh. "I'm okay to take it slow too. And when you're ready to move on, I'll understand."

The humor in his eyes died, and a seriousness moved over his face. A muscle twitched in his jaw, and she was sure she'd done something in that moment to make him mad.

"Don't do that," he warned.

"Do what?"

"Don't give me permission to move on. I'm not going to tire

of you or just toss you aside," he reprimanded, and Lisa realized what she'd done. It was habit.

"I didn't mean—"

"I know." He lifted his hands to cup her face. "I'm not like other people in your life. If things don't work out, that'll be a shame, but we'll deal with it like adults." He brushed his thumb over her cheek. "For now, we feel it out. We don't know each other at all, and I can't wait to get to learn about you."

She'd felt herself flinch.

He'd noticed, she knew he did, but he kept smiling at her. "It'll be okay to let me into your life. And tomorrow, if you hear anything about me, ask me. I'll let you know if it's true."

Now she laughed. "I'm a little freaked out about going."

"Because of my family?"

"Family in general."

"You'll be fine. The girls will be with you."

Lisa nodded, and Ryan leaned in and pressed a gentle kiss to her lips.

"And if you just can't handle it, I'll swoop in and pick you up," he said.

"Promise?"

"I do."

CHAPTER TWENTY-SIX

THUD! THUD! THUD! FINGERNAIL DRUMROLL.

Ruby was knocking on Lisa's door, in her coded knock that was specific to Ruby.

Lisa hurried through the condo and pulled open the door, still wrapped in her towel.

"You're like an hour early," Lisa scolded, and hurried back toward the bathroom.

"Yeah, cuz I thought if I didn't come pick your ass up early, you'd back out."

"That's not fair," Lisa said wrapping her hair around the barrel of the curling iron as Ruby leaned against the door jamb to the bathroom.

"It's totally fair. This is going to be a hard day for you, admit it. You're going to act fine. You're going to look fine. But the whole time you're around people who are family and are sharing family stories, you're going to be having an anxiety attack."

Lisa released her hair from the iron and turned to her friend. It was times like this, when she wasn't sure if having friends that knew her so well was blessing or a curse.

"I wish everyone knew I'd be fine," Lisa said picking up her curling iron and making another curl in her hair.

"You will be fine. You won't be fine next week."

And Ruby had hit the nail on the head. Hadn't she already considered staying in bed all day on Sunday?

"I'm prepared," Lisa admitted, pulling the iron from her hair. "I've already decided, I can't spend all day in bed tomorrow because Ryan will be here."

Ruby raised a brow. "As in, he'll wake up here?"

"That's not what I said."

"Again, love, I'm living vicariously through you. And at this point, I'm tired of vicariously living through Tina. When the sex was hot and heavy, and she'd let us in on that, okay. But now, I'm wedding bored."

Lisa laughed at that. Weren't they all? And didn't that feel bad? They should be happy for Tina, which they all were. But they were over it, and there were still two more weeks to go.

CICELY HAD DONE A NICE JOB SELECTING THE VENUE AND SETTING up the shower, Lisa thought, as she and Ruby walked in arm in arm.

When Tina saw them, she rushed them, enveloped them in a hug, and let out what sounded like a cry for help.

"I don't know half of these people," she whispered between them. "I don't think Cicely ordered enough food. There certainly isn't enough champagne for me, because to get through this, I'm going to have to be drunk."

The corners of Lisa's mouth itched to turn upward, but she refrained. "Ruby and I won't eat or drink."

Ruby sharply turned her head toward Lisa. "Bite your damn tongue. If she's drunk, I'm drunk."

That had Tina laughing through what could have been tears.

Ruby kissed Tina noisily on the cheek. "We're here, honey. We can schmooze with the aunts and cousins with the best of 'em," she said as they all saw Mindy already deep in conversation with Aaron's mother and another woman.

With that, Ruby headed toward Mindy to mingle, but Tina gripped tightly to Lisa's wrist. "Seriously consider all of this," Tina warned looking around. "This belongs to Ryan too," she said, and Lisa felt that twinge of sickness creep into her belly.

Tina looped her arm through Lisa's, and they walked toward the crowd of women who had gathered to celebrate Tina.

Lisa could feel everything inside of her clench and harden. This wasn't about her, she kept repeating to herself. And Ryan wasn't Aaron. That too, she had to remind herself. She and Ryan weren't a thing.

But yes, they were.

God, they'd had that talk. *For the record, when I do see a woman, I don't see other ones.* They were seeing each other. Damn it!

Lisa drew in a breath. God, and hadn't she been all big and wise last night when she'd teased him.

I'll let them all know you and I are going to be sleeping together, so they can forget about her, she'd said to him when they discussed his ex-girlfriend.

"You're shaking," Tina said still looking toward the crowd of women and not at Lisa.

"So are you," Lisa countered, but her voice now shook too.

"Don't you dare freak out on me."

"Kiss my ass," Lisa said through gritted teeth as they approached Tina's mother, sister, and Aaron's mother—Ryan's mother, she quickly remembered as well.

Lisa mindfully replaced any fear that might have shown on her face with a grateful smile and looked toward Cicely.

"You did a beautiful job. The venue is gorgeous," Lisa complimented.

"Thank you." Cicely pressed a hand to her chest. "It was so

much work. I really should have taken you all up on your offers to help."

Lisa saw Mindy pinch Ruby when she'd taken a breath to speak.

Aaron's mother turned toward Lisa and smiled. "Lisa, right?"

"Yes, ma'am," Lisa confirmed and reached her hand out to shake the woman's. "We've met once before."

Audrey Blair took Lisa's hand, but she held it instead of shaking it. "We have. I also subscribe to your YouTube channel. I've made some delightful things from your recipes."

And that brought the genuine smile to Lisa's face. "I'm happy to hear that."

"I told Ryan that you'd be a keeper since he likes to eat well."

Lisa felt Tina shift next to her. "Well, thank you. He's been very nice to spend time with me this week."

That comment obviously confused Audrey, which meant she had too much information already.

Before Audrey could continue the conversation further, Cicely took her sister's hand and gathered everyone to move into the other room where there was a buffet set up and bottomless mimosas were being served.

Lisa had promised herself she wouldn't partake in more than one mimosa. But when Ruby and Mindy each took one of her arms, and they followed the women into the other room, Ruby let out a low growl.

"Fuck not having enough to drink," she said, and both Lisa and Mindy shifted their wide eyes to her. "We need to be drunk for this."

CHAPTER TWENTY-SEVEN

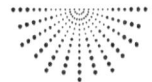

THE SMALL WHITE BALL FLEW TOWARD THE FLAG AT THE END OF the fairway. When it landed, Ryan's father judged his shot, and nodded as if he were content with it.

"I suppose with you home now, we can work on your game," Ryan's father said to him, and they picked up their clubs and started toward their balls.

Ryan's ball had shanked to the side, but both Aaron and his father's had landed close to the hole. Or at least Ryan thought it was close—much closer than his.

"When is Ryan going to have time to golf?" Aaron teased. "New job. He'll be house hunting. Oh, and he's seeing Tina's best friend."

Ryan's eyes narrowed on his brother from beneath his sunglasses.

His father let out a laugh. "Moved right on in, huh?"

"I haven't done anything," Ryan said sharply as he followed his brother and father.

"And Tina doesn't mind you dating one of her friends?" his father asked, and Ryan could see Aaron grinning.

"Lisa and I are hanging out," Ryan said.

His father slowed as they came to the green. "What does hanging out mean when you're thirty?"

"We went to a ballgame. I took her out for her birthday, and we had tacos and a beer."

"She's making him cook tomorrow," Aaron added, and that had his father turning.

"I heard she's some fancy cook. Your mom watches her on TV," his father pulled his club from the bag.

"Mom knows who she is? I mean, other than Tina's friend?" Ryan could feel his insides rolling.

"Sure. Aaron told Mom all about her."

Aaron was smiling wide, and Ryan couldn't even imagine why. Did he have a death wish? Tina surely would take it out on him before she came after Ryan, but in the end, she'd go after Lisa.

"Well, we're getting to know each other. That's all," Ryan defended himself, and his father nodded as he lined up his shot.

"Best to get to know them before you sleep with them," his father said as he made his shot, and Ryan knew right there he was going to be sick.

How was he supposed to keep his future sister-in-law's feelings intact, and accept his father saying things like that? God, he was sure he was in hell.

LISA WAS IN HELL.

Assigned seats. Who the hell assigned seats at a bridal shower?

Lisa was at one table, and Mindy and Ruby each were seated at other tables. They all shared miserable looks between them. They were the freaking wedding party. Why weren't they sitting with the bride?

This was Cicely pulling the sister card hard and keeping her sister by her side. That was acceptable, but Lisa had already had three mimosas. Thank goodness, Tina's Aunt Geraldine wasn't drinking.

Ruby was on her fourth, or so Lisa had counted as she kept raising full glasses toward them.

"So, sweetheart, which bridesmaid are you?" The older lady next to Tina's aunt asked.

"I'm Lisa."

The woman next to the lady who'd asked the question, tapped the lady's arm. "She's the one."

Lisa felt her eyes go wide.

The woman studied her. "Her?"

The other woman reached her hand across to Lisa. "I'm Ryan's aunt, Janice."

Lisa shook the woman's hand, but it didn't go unnoticed that she'd referred to herself as Ryan's aunt, and not Aaron's.

"It's nice to meet you."

Janice made eye contact with the other women at the table. "This is Ryan's girlfriend," she said, and collectively, five sets of eyes descended on Lisa. "She has her own cooking show on TV."

Lisa felt her throat begin to close.

One of the other women looked at Janice. "Ryan lives in Chicago." She turned her attention to Lisa. "You're from Chicago?"

Before Lisa could speak, another of the women said. "Of course she's from Chicago. She's been with Ryan for years. Don't you pay attention?"

There were spots in front of Lisa's eyes, and she was quite sure she was going to be sick.

As she took a breath to clear the air, the women turned their attention to Tina, who had walked up behind one of the other women at the table. She'd kissed her on the cheek and called her Auntie Dot.

"How was your lunch?" Tina asked and everyone murmured something complementary.

"It was lovely," Dot said. "We were just getting to know your fiancé's brother's girlfriend."

When Lisa's eyes lifted to Tina's, she wasn't sure which one of them was more horrified by the statement.

"Oh?" Tina finally squeaked out.

"You walked up before I could explain that I'm from Denver," Lisa said looking at Dot. "I'm not the one from Chicago."

All the women nodded slowly, their mouths formed in and O shape.

"So, you don't have a TV show?" Janice asked.

"Well," Lisa began, but Cicely drew everyone's attention to her by tapping her knife to the side of her champagne flute.

"Ladies, it's time for presents," Cicely said with a giddy mix or anticipation, tears, and jealousy. "Let's all move to the other room where Tina can open her gifts and they'll serve cake."

The women all moved their chairs back, and Lisa was all but forgotten in that moment. She was much more comfortable, and familiar, with being forgotten.

Tina helped her Auntie Dot out of her seat, but her eyes landed once more on Lisa, searing her warning through her.

As the ladies cleared out, Lisa threw back her mimosa, and the rest of Auntie Dot's too.

Ruby, with another full glass, walked to her. "I love her. I love her. I love her," she repeated over and over. "I'll still love her. I'll still love her," she said changing the chant.

Mindy walked toward them. "Those mimosas are mostly water and O.J."

"That'd explain why I'm not tipsy, and only have a stomachache from the acid in the juice," Ruby pressed her hand to her stomach.

"What's wrong with you?" Mindy put a hand on Lisa's arm.

Lisa sat in her chair, her skin flush, her cheeks hot, and her head spinning from the past few minutes.

"I just got outed."

Mindy and Ruby exchanged looks before Mindy sat down in the chair next to Lisa.

"Outed?" she asked.

"I don't think they know what they're talking about, but those old ladies have a lot of information."

Mindy looked up at Ruby, and then back at Lisa. "You're not making any sense."

"They know I'm seeing Ryan," Lisa admitted, resting her elbow to the table and then resting her forehead on her hand.

Mindy's brows drew inward. "I thought you were just hanging out."

Ruby groaned. "God, don't you pay attention? They're banging."

That had Lisa's head snapping up. "We are not. I told you we weren't."

Ruby's mouth turned up in a grin. "You're going to."

"God! What's wrong with you?" Lisa snapped out in a loud whisper.

"Girls," Cicely called from the doorway. "C'mon." She waved them toward her.

Lisa stood and Ruby quickly wrapped her arm around Lisa's shoulders and pulled her in. "Bang him. Bang him good. Tell me all about it. Get married and have babies. He's hot. You're hot. I'm lonely, and Tina will still love you," Ruby said, which warranted a snorting laugh from Mindy.

How could Lisa not laugh after that?

Arm in arm, the three of them walked to the other room.

Lisa couldn't imagine her life without her friends. But when Tina looked up in her direction from her seat of honor, her eyes full of hurt and betrayal, Lisa knew there would be no banging. In fact, there would be no getting out of bed the next morning.

CHAPTER TWENTY-EIGHT

TINA HADN'T SAID ANYTHING TO LISA THE REST OF THE DAY. EVEN when the aunts and cousins wanted to take pictures of the bridal party, and Lisa stood right next to Tina with their hands clasped or arms around one another, Tina was silent.

Guilt had made Lisa sick all night. A headache crushed her head. Sickness had swum in her belly, and she'd vomited twice. It wasn't the mimosas, orange juice, or the lack of alcohol, it was anxiety.

She'd battled it her entire life. There hadn't been a house she'd been moved into, or a school she'd started, without being violently ill the first day. Depending on the house and the family, sometimes that sickness never left.

Pressing her fingers to her eyes as she lay in her bed in the dark, she realized it wasn't always that way. When she'd lived with Mama Rose and her family, she wasn't sick a day in all the years she lived with them. She didn't start getting sick until they had left, and Lisa was on her own.

Oh, she'd saved money over the years to go visit, but something always came up and her savings were drained. Likewise, the Hughes could never afford to send for her.

Lisa pressed her hand to her chest. What she wouldn't have given to be one of the Hughes children throughout her life. But she was a Hughes child when it counted. And even though they'd been thousands of miles apart for years, she was still part of their family.

Warm tears rolled down into her hair, and she hadn't even realized she'd been crying. Drawing in deep breaths, she decided she would email Mama Rose and schedule a time to FaceTime with her. She needed her love, comfort, and wisdom right now. Lisa couldn't continue to be sick over what she was doing to Tina.

Mama Rose would be able to walk her through her feelings about ruining Tina's bridal shower.

SHE FELT ANOTHER WAVE OF SICKNESS MOVE THROUGH HER AND SHE jumped from her bed and ran to the bathroom to be sick again.

AT SOME POINT, RYAN'S LUNGS WOULD GET USED TO THE LACK OF oxygen in the air in Denver.

His morning runs had become shorter because he couldn't keep going. Filling his water bottle from the refrigerator, he kept one hand on the bottle, and the other above his head, trying to get his breath back.

When his bottle was full and he turned, he felt his heart slam in his chest at the sight of Tina sitting at the table bundled in her robe. Her eyes were covered with her hands, and her shoulders bobbed up and down.

Shit! He didn't have the tools to deal with a crying sister-in-law-to-be at six o'clock in the morning. But he figured this had something to do with him, and that was why she was in his space when no one else was.

"Are you okay?" Ryan asked walking toward the table.

Tina lifted her head, and yeah, she'd been crying for a while.

"Sit down, please."

Shit! Shit! Shit!

Ryan pulled out a chair and sat down. Then he stood, walked to the counter, and picked up the box of tissue before setting it in front of Tina and sitting back down.

Tina pulled a tissue from the box and wiped her nose.

"I'm sorry to bombard you so early in the morning," she said.

Ryan let out a nervous chuckle. "Had you been up earlier, I could have avoided running out there where there is no oxygen."

Tina let out a strained laugh, and then turned her eyes up to him.

"I know I'm petty. I know it." She wiped her robed arm over her eyes to dry them. "I can't help it. I want everything to be perfect for my wedding. I'm only going to do this once. Yesterday was a disaster."

Ryan forced himself to pick up his bottle and take a sip of water. He wasn't sure what was surging through him. Anger? Jealousy? Sympathy?

"What happened?" he asked because Lisa hadn't responded to any of his texts last night.

Tina blew out a breath. "I'll be the bigger person. I ruined it because of my feelings. But everyone was talking about you coming home and dating Lisa."

Ryan sat back in his chair, tipping up the feet as he leaned back, and then thought better of it. His mother would smack him upside the head if she saw him do that.

Leaning in on the table on his forearms, he collected his thoughts.

"Tina, I don't mean to hurt you. This thing with Lisa is…"

"Wonderful."

He knew his expression relayed his surprise at her comment.

"I was going to say it's just a friendship," he confirmed.

Tina shook her head. "No, it's more." She wiped her eyes again, and he noticed they'd gone dry. "I know you haven't slept together or anything like that. Not that that's what makes a relationship. I just know because, well, she's happy."

"And that makes you unhappy?"

"I said I was being petty." She laughed as she picked up another tissue but began to tear it into pieces instead of using it. "Let me have the next few weeks, please. Let it be all about me and Aaron. When your aunts talk, I want them to talk about us, not who you left in Chicago and who Lisa is."

Petty might have been an understatement, Ryan thought.

"So, I shouldn't see Lisa until after you're married?"

"Please."

Was it appropriate to lash out at her? Then again what the hell was three weeks?

"Okay, then you tell her. I'm supposed to go over today, and if you don't want me to be with her, then it better be you that lets her know." His voice was harsher than he'd have liked it, but he had gone from understanding to pissed.

"I'll go over and talk to her," Tina promised with a hiccup.

"Please make sure she knows it's your decision. Because what I get from her is that other people have always made the decision of who is part of her life. They come and go. I don't want to go. You make that clear," he said as he stood and picked up his bottle, leaving his future sister-in-law in a fresh wave of tears at the table.

CHAPTER TWENTY-NINE

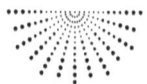

LISA HADN'T MADE IT TO BED AFTER HER LAST BOUT OF SICKNESS. Instead, she'd curled up on the couch with a blanket that Mama Rose's mother had made for her when she'd turned fourteen.

With the blanket pulled up over her head, she wept into the throw pillow under her head, and fell in and out of sleep.

Apparently, she'd been asleep again when Ruby's knock at the door had Lisa bolting straight up.

Thud! Thud! Thud! Fingernail drumroll.

"Go, away!" Lisa yelled toward the door and fell backward to the pillow.

"If you don't open this goddamned door, I'll use my key."

Lisa didn't move from the couch, and only a moment later she heard the key in the lock.

"Get up," Ruby said as she walked through the door and shut it behind her. "What in the hell have you been doing in here?" She groaned. "You need to open some windows."

"Get out!"

From under the blanket, she could hear Ruby moving through the condo. The sliding door to the patio opened. Then the window in the kitchen. A few moments later, Lisa heard the unmistakable sound of the blinds in her bedroom going up.

"Get up," she heard Ruby command one more time before the blanket that gave her shelter was ripped from her, and sunlight burned Lisa's eyes.

"Bitch!"

"Sure am," Ruby calmly replied. "Now get up."

They'd been through this before, and Lisa was sure they'd go through it again.

Ruby understood Lisa better than anyone. Not that she'd ever gone through what Lisa went through, but she just understood her.

Lisa sat up and put her feet on the ground, then buried her face in her hands, as Ruby moved to the kitchen and started a pot of coffee.

"You were up sick all night, huh?" Ruby asked. "And certainly not hung over from the mimosas. If there was even an ounce of champagne to be found within all the mimosas, I'd be surprised."

Ruby talked to keep Lisa calm. Again, it was something they'd been through.

"I can't believe your daisies are still looking nice. Even the roses from the pasta company are turning." She added water to their vases. "I see that Mama Rose sent you a card. You should FaceTime with her," Ruby suggested.

"Already emailed her to set up a time," Lisa groaned through her fingertips.

Ruby pulled down coffee mugs, and Lisa sat back against the couch and let her head drop.

When the coffee was ready, Ruby carried two steaming mugs out of the kitchen. She sat down next to Lisa on the couch and set the mugs on the coffee table.

Then, Ruby pulled Lisa to her, and let her sob.

"I didn't mean to ruin her party," Lisa said through her tears as Ruby ran her hand over Lisa's matted hair.

"You didn't. She's out of sorts right now."

"I love her. I want her to have a nice wedding."

"Screw her if she's going to treat everyone like this," Ruby said, tucking strands of hair behind Lisa's ear. "You deserve to love someone too."

"I don't love him."

"Oh, you will," Ruby pressed a kiss to Lisa's head. "God, and then you're going to have earth-shaking sex and tell me all about it."

That caused Lisa to laugh. "You're obsessed."

"I'm lonely," Ruby admitted as Lisa pulled back and wiped her hands over her wet cheeks.

"I enjoy him."

"You're dating him."

Lisa snickered. "We had that talk. You know the one where I only see one person at a time."

Ruby nudged Lisa. "You're going steady."

"Am I?"

"You're such a child. Yes. You are."

The tears rushed back. "Going steady with someone should be a happy thing. Making my friend miserable, that hurts."

"Again, screw her," Ruby said right as there was another knock on the door.

"You invited everyone to my intervention?" Lisa wiped at her eyes again.

"Nope. Solo mission. I just wanted you out of bed for your date," Ruby admitted, and Lisa felt her head spin.

Oh, yeah. Her date.

Ruby swiftly moved to the door and pulled it open without looking out first. Standing on the front step, with two large Starbucks cups, was Tina. Her eyes widened when she saw Ruby standing there.

"I didn't know you'd be here," Tina said looking down at the two cups in her hands. "I would have—"

"Someone had to get her out of bed," Ruby snapped and walked back to the couch. She picked up her coffee mug, sat on the couch, and kicked her feet up on the coffee table.

Lisa turned to look at Tina standing in the doorway. "You can come in."

Tina chewed her bottom lip as she walked into the condo and closed the door behind her. Her cheeks were bright red, and a line had formed on her brow. Lisa knew that Ruby's presence had deflated her, and at that moment, that was okay.

"I brought this for you," Tina said, handing Lisa one of the cups.

"Thank you."

Tina walked around the couch and sat down in the chair at the other end of the coffee table.

"You look like you had a rough night," Tina said, lifting her coffee to her lips.

"Full blown anxiety attack," Lisa admitted. "I much prefer a regular hangover."

Tina's eyes kept darting to Ruby, and then back to Lisa. There was something she wanted to say, and it was not coming out with Ruby there.

Was it wrong that Lisa was enjoying Tina's discomfort?

"Thank you, guys, for being at the shower and chatting among the relatives. I didn't realize Aaron had so many aunts and cousins coming. Cicely said his mom just kept adding people."

Lisa sipped her coffee and Ruby bore a firm stare into Tina.

"It was a nice party. A little light on the champagne," she teased, but there was a bite of anger to her voice.

"Yeah," Tina muttered as she took a sip from her cup. "I'm sorry if they made you uncomfortable," she said, directing the statement to Lisa. "I guess they thought you were Courtney."

Ruby shook her head. "They thought she was Ryan's girlfriend, but there wasn't a lot of time for her to explain, or accept the position, now was there?"

Lisa could see Tina's hands tremble. "Well, she's not."

"She is," Ruby defended.

Tina's eyes had gone damp, and for the first time, Lisa noticed how red they were. She'd been crying just as much as Lisa had, it was obvious.

"This is my wedding—" Tina began to cry and that had Ruby up on her feet.

"And none of us are going to be there if you keep being a bitch," Ruby laid into her. "You owe Lisa an apology. And not for the aunts that don't have all the information. You owe her an apology for treating her like shit."

Tina's eyes went wide, and tears streamed down her cheeks. "I what?"

"Yeah. You have this high and mighty attitude going on, and we're all a little sick of it."

Lisa kept her cup poised at her lips to hide any expression. She felt bad for Tina. They'd all been at the back end of one of Ruby's tirades, and when she started, there was no stopping her.

"If she's in love with Ryan, you should be excited for her. If they get married, well what an awesome opportunity for you to have a sister—one you already have," Ruby continued.

Lisa's eyes went wide when Ruby had said married. Okay, she'd only kissed the guy and known him a week, but Lisa didn't stop her.

"Lisa…" Tina said pleading.

"Look at her," Ruby pointed to Lisa. "You know what she's been through all night because of you. You know. We've sat with her like this a million times. What harm is she really causing by seeing Ryan? Huh?"

Tina was fully in a sob when she sucked in a breath. "I came over to tell you that he's not coming over. I asked him to stay away from you." The words were hardly audible through her sobbing breaths.

Ruby threw up her hands. "Why do you get to play God?"

"It's my wedding."

"And no one is upstaging you. We're right there with you. We're wearing those fucking ugly dresses, and those pointy shoes, because we love you. We love you," she reiterated.

"You think the dresses are ugly?" Tina asked, and for some reason that had Lisa bursting into a laugh.

Both sets of eyes were on her, and it made her laugh harder.

"Sorry." She covered her mouth. "Shit. I'm sorry."

Ruby shook her head, but a smile formed on her lips. "Bitch."

Tina's eyes were still wide. Ruby moved to her, pulled her to her feet, and wrapped her arms around Tina until she fell against her.

"We love you; you bitch."

Tina sharply drew in a breath, but then laughed.

Lisa watched her friends, and she knew this wasn't over. But the dialog was open. Even if the path to getting it open was a bit strained.

CHAPTER THIRTY

WITHIN AN HOUR MINDY WAS THERE WITH THEM. IT WAS reminiscent of times when Lisa's anxieties were so bad, she knew they'd hovered over her on unnecessary suicide watch. Sure, things were bad when the anxiety kicked it, but years ago, her episodes were new to her friends, but it didn't stop them from being there for her.

They came on sporadically sometimes. It could be because someone had left a nasty comment on her channel, a sponsor backed out, or because they didn't have her brand of toothpaste at the store.

Breakups would bring them on, so Lisa tried not to date. But Ryan had been different. He'd just happened.

Mindy sat on the floor with her legs tucked up under her, comfortable in a pair of yoga pants and a halter top. Her hair was pulled back, and Lisa thought she looked like a poster child for zen.

"So, where are we?" Mindy asked in a calm voice. "We love Tina? We hate Tina?"

Tina blew out a breath. "I'm right here."

"Better that way," Mindy agreed. "We wouldn't do this behind your back."

"Liar," Tina laughed through tears that still came and went.

Ruby crossed her arms in front of her. Seated on the couch in the same pose as Mindy, she didn't exude any zen.

"I want Tina to back off Lisa and Ryan," she argued.

Lisa adjusted from her seat on the couch. "I don't want this to become a—"

"Bullshit!" Now Ruby snapped at her. "You had the talk. You had the fucking talk," her voice rose.

Tina wiped at her eyes for the millionth time that morning. "What talk?"

"It's nothing," Lisa said, but Ruby shook her head.

"Basically, the going steady talk. You know, I won't bang someone if I'm banging you," Ruby laid it out.

Mindy shook her head and the zen was gone. "You are so crass."

"I'm serious," Ruby said determined. "So, they've known each other a week. If it didn't matter, would we all be in here having a morning like this? I'd rather have gone to brunch and had real mimosas."

That warranted a laugh from them all, including Tina, who laughed and then withdrew again.

"Lisa, I'm sorry about all of this," Tina hiccupped a breath as she spoke. "Truth is, it shouldn't matter. I'm so out of sorts," she admitted.

Ruby snorted a laugh. "No shit?"

Tina let that roll off her. "When I told Ryan all of this, he said I had to tell you myself. He said he knew that people always left you, and it needed to be made very clear that he didn't want to leave you."

A lightness formed in Lisa's chest. "Really?"

Tina nodded. "He really likes you."

"Well, I really like him too," Lisa said.

Mindy raised her arms. "Can we just call a truce on this? Tina, everyone met Lisa yesterday. Everyone knows Ryan is home. Now they know they're dating. And guess what? You and Aaron are still having this spectacular wedding where you're front and center. You'll be in the white dress. You'll cut the cake. You'll kiss the groom. You'll go on the honeymoon. Lisa and Ryan aren't going to ruin this."

Tina lifted her eyes to Lisa. "I'm scared."

"About me and Ryan?"

Tina shook her head. "About getting married. About living in his parents' house too long. About—shit, about all of it."

Ruby threw up her hands this time. "God, couldn't you have just had a pity party about that?"

The four of them laughed as Mindy stood, pulled Tina from the chair, and they all landed on the couch in a pile. Tears, laughter, and sisterhood intact.

Are you taking visitors? Lisa read the text four times. Each time she read it, her chest expanded just a little more.

Are you sure? She texted back.

Never been more sure about anything. Ryan replied.

Lisa let out a long, slow breath. *Yes, but you have to give me an hour.*

Why?

The simplicity of it had Lisa laughing as she pushed back from her desk and ran to the bathroom. A glance in the mirror proved to her why she needed an hour. *I'm not kidding. I need an hour.*

It's already eight-thirty.

True, and he probably had to be to work in the morning. *Okay, but I warn you, it's not pretty.*

She shouldn't have been surprised when there was a knock at the door.

"Shit!" she hollered before she picked up the mouthwash, opened it, and took a big swig. She swished it around in her mouth and then spit it out as she picked up a hair tie and pulled back her hair.

He'd seen her in her pajamas already. Her appearance shouldn't be a shock.

Lisa ran to the front door and pulled it open. And there he was leaned up against the doorjamb, a six pack of beer and a bouquet of daisies in his hand.

"For the record, you're wrong. You are so pretty."

She felt the heat rise in her cheeks as she rushed him, throwing her arms around his neck and pulling him inside.

"You're here," she whispered against his mouth as she kissed him.

"Tina feels like shit for making a big deal about it."

Her fingers wound into his hair. "Yeah, we came down pretty hard on her." She slid her tongue over his lips. "Well, Ruby did."

"I was so mad at her this morning," he said on a breath when she'd eased back for a moment. "More than interested, Lisa."

Now she pulled back so she could look him in the eye. "So am I. So am I."

CHAPTER THIRTY-ONE

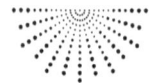

"I NEED TO PUT THESE DOWN," RYAN SAID, LISA'S MOUTH STILL hovering over his.

She laughed as she stepped back from him. "You've paid attention to more details in one week than most people have my entire life."

"You're a beer girl, and you like daisies."

"I do," she said taking the bouquet and heading toward the kitchen.

Ryan followed, appreciating the view in front of him as she reached into a cupboard and took down a vase, just as she'd done with the flowers earlier in the week.

He set the beer on the counter. "Hey, I'm sorry everything happened the way that it did."

Lisa shook her head, and loose strands of hair that hadn't been swept up into the ponytail swung around her face.

"It could have been any one of us who melted down in such a way," Lisa said.

"You all really are close, aren't you? I mean, you're not even mad, are you?"

Lisa laughed as she filled the vase with water. "Oh, I'm mad. I spent all night throwing up because of an anxiety attack."

"Are you kidding me?"

She lifted her eyes to meet his as she set the vase down. "No. It's very common for me. Well, not as common as it used to be, but…"

Ryan watched as she lifted the daisies into the vase, then he moved to her, turning her into his arms. Her arms circled his neck.

"I want to know you," he said gently, brushing those loose strands of hair from her face.

"There isn't anything to know." She swirled the hair at the nape of his neck with her fingers.

"Please."

Lisa sighed. "After the past two emotional days, I don't know if I have the nerve to share anything with you."

"Fine, just one thing."

"Okay, what do you want to know?"

Where did he start? There were so many things. How many homes had she been in? What happened to her parents? Why would she get so sick with anxiety? What were her thoughts on a relationship where someone wouldn't leave her?

"Who is Mama Rose?" he asked when the card on the counter caught his attention.

Lisa turned and looked at the card. "How did you know that name?"

"I looked at the card when I was here on Friday," he admitted. "It was standing up and displayed."

She nodded. "Mama Rose," she said the name as if it were the most important name in the world. "She and her family were my saviors."

Ryan leaned in and pressed a kiss to her lips. "Let's have a beer and you can tell me all about them."

"I'd really rather make out with you on the couch."

That caused him to laugh. It would be so much easier to get caught up in that, he thought. Hadn't he packed a bag to stay, just in case?

But he so desperately wanted to know the woman who was controlling his every waking moment. The woman whose friends protected her so dearly.

"Fine," Lisa resigned. Turning, she plucked two beers from the carrier Ryan had brought in and headed to the couch.

Ryan followed, sitting down on one end of the couch, taking the beer that Lisa held out to him. He was surprised when Lisa sat down on his lap, her legs sprawled out long on the couch.

Lisa twisted off the caps on both bottles and tapped them together. "Thanks for the beer."

Ryan licked his lips, fully aware of her body on his. "Thanks for the story."

She took a long pull from her beer and rested her head to his shoulder.

He felt her take a breath. "You know I don't have family."

"You mentioned that."

"And I assume that your brother, or Tina told you I was a foster kid."

There was a sharpness in his chest. "My brother mentioned it."

Lisa sat up and shifted off his lap. Disappointment moved through him, until she sat right next to him, so close their torsos touched.

Lisa crossed one leg over his, and to keep her close, Ryan rested his hand to her thigh.

"Mama Rose was one of my foster mothers. Her husband is John, and their sons are Jason and Ken. They were my final foster family."

"How many did you have?"

Lisa shook her head and took a sip from her beer. "You asked about Mama Rose."

Ryan chuckled and gave her thigh a squeeze. "You're right. Continue."

"Mama Rose was the first caregiver to bake cookies for me when I arrived at her house. My foster brothers were at school, so it was just us when I arrived. When the social worker left me, Rose sat down with me at the kitchen table and asked about *me,*" she said gesturing to herself with her beer bottle, "while we dunked chocolate chip cookies in milk. She showed me through the house, and to my room, and told me I was allowed to tack anything I wanted to the walls." Lisa giggled.

"That's pretty special. I wasn't allowed to do that."

"It was special." Lisa sipped her beer. "Then she let me choose which sheets and blankets I wanted to use on my bed, which we made together."

"What sheets did you pick?"

"They had pink flowers on them, and they matched the blanket."

"I like it."

"When it was time for her kids to get out of school, we walked to pick them up, and she just kept talking to me as if I mattered."

Ryan rubbed her thigh, loving how she felt against him. "You do matter."

"But I didn't back then," she said matter-of-factly. "When we got to the school, she told me that was where I would go to school. And that the next morning we would meet the principal and the teacher. Then," Lisa's eyes lit and she paused with a smile, "she asked me what part of school I liked the best."

"Like you mattered."

"Exactly. I told her art, and she promised we'd meet the art teacher too." Lisa drew in a breath and let it out slowly. "That night, my foster brothers let me choose the TV shows and what story was read before bed. Mind you, I was twelve, but no one had ever asked me to pick a bedtime story."

Ryan took a long pull from his beer. He hoped she couldn't

feel his body shaking, because her story so far had rattled him, and this was her good story.

"That night," Lisa continued, "when my brothers hugged their parents goodnight, I hugged Rose. I had never hugged anyone before that."

"Ever?"

"Yeah. I mean ever."

"And you were twelve?"

"Yep."

"That's a long time to go without hugs."

"It sure was." Lisa finished her beer. "The next day I went to school in a *new* dress, and Rose braided my hair. I had a lunch bag with my name written on it in fancy letters," she began to choke up with tears. "Inside my lunch, she'd put a note."

"My mom used to do that," Ryan admitted.

"It was the best thing that ever happened to me. I still have every note she ever put in my lunch or stuck to the mirror in my room."

Lisa's eyes welled with tears, and when one escaped, Ryan brushed it away with his thumb.

"She, and the whole family, loved me. Actually loved me," she said lovingly.

"And according to the card, they still do."

"They do."

"How long did you live with them?"

"Four years. It was a long term placement. They wanted to adopt me, but it just didn't happen in the timely manner it needed to, and there was too much red tape. Then John got a job in England, and they moved." Her voice became uneven, and Ryan felt as if he'd been socked in the gut. Even her possible forever family left her. No wonder she was so cautious.

He had so many questions, but he wouldn't ask them. He'd asked about Mama Rose, and that was the story he'd heard.

"Do they still live in England?"

Lisa nodded. "Yes. Ken is married with two kids. He's made his home and life there. Jason went into the military and became a doctor."

"You keep in touch?"

She nodded. "I talk to her once a month at the least. If they're all around, I talk to them all. They are the only true family I ever had."

"Until you met the girls?"

She smiled again, but it was different. This smile warranted a whole new story.

"My girls are my life."

And in that moment, he understood that he would come behind those girls, and Mama Rose in importance. That was okay, he thought, because in his heart, even after only a week, he knew he never wanted to leave this woman.

CHAPTER THIRTY-TWO

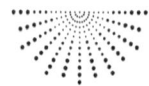

Lisa set her empty bottle on the coffee table, and then took Ryan's from his hand and did the same. He'd been quiet, and he hadn't asked more questions, though she was sure he had a million others.

Lifting herself from her position next to him, Lisa swung her leg over him and straddled him. It was obvious that she'd surprised him by the way he sharply inhaled. But as she settled down on his lap, his hands came to her waist.

"What kind of rules were you given to get to come over here?" she asked as she pulled her hair from the band that held it up, and it fell over her shoulders.

Ryan blinked hard, and his tongue flicked over his lips as he looked up at her. "Same as before. Don't hurt you."

She nodded slowly. "And is she going to come at me tomorrow with claws again?"

He chuckled beneath her, and it caused her to grind against him slightly. That did something to him, she decided, when his fingers gripped her hips a little tighter.

"There are no promises. When she came home this afternoon,

she was a wreck. She tore into me, then she tore into Aaron, and then she just fell on the couch in a heap of tears."

Lisa eased back to look at him. She didn't like hearing that.

"I thought everything was fine when she left here."

"Lisa, she's a bride-to-be. She's lost her ever loving, goddamned, mind."

Lisa laughed. "I don't ever want to be like that."

"We'll run away and get married."

She felt her mouth drop open. He'd talked of marriage more than one time that week, and it spooked her to her very core. But she let herself ease. He wasn't like her. People didn't leave him—well, not everyone left him. Marriage wasn't in her plans. It couldn't be.

His thumbs brushed against her skin now, just under the hem of her shirt.

"Hey," he drew her attention back to him. "I won't say married again."

"Why?" she asked, but her voice cracked and deceived her.

"Because whenever I do, you tense up."

"Sorry."

"Don't be," he said as his palms now grazed her sides, skin to skin. "I'm not going anywhere, Lisa. Even if this doesn't work out, I'm not going anywhere. I'm cemented into your group now."

She narrowed her eyes playfully. "We don't just pick up strays."

"Too bad. I'm going to need a pair of pajamas for the next Rom Com Movie Club night," he said as his hands moved to her back and it sent a ripple of heat through her.

"Like I said—"

"I know. No strays." His fingertips slid under the band of her bra and rubbed small circles against her sensitive skin. "I'm not a stray. I'm your other half. Let's sign cards Lisa and Ryan. Ryan and Lisa."

She swallowed hard as she let the weight of her body grow

heavier on his lap, feeling the tense muscles of his thighs working to keep himself under control.

"I'm going to freak out—a lot. I mean, I'm going to say nasty things to you. I'm going to tell you to go away. I'm going to make it so that you won't want to love me."

"Yeah, you've said that. And you hit the nail on the head there."

"What?"

"I'm going to want to love you. I know that I—"

Lisa covered his mouth with her hand. "No. Don't you dare. Don't say it. I can't hear it. Not now."

He nodded until she lowered her hand. "I'm interested, Lisa. And not just for tonight. Not just for the sex we're going to have," he said, and the corner of his mouth curled up. "I'm interested in the good and bad."

"I'm freaking out."

He shook his head. "No, you're not. You're experiencing something new. And, sweetheart, I'm going to make it worth it for you."

Her lip trembled, so she pulled it through her teeth. "Are you staying the night?"

"I want to," he said as he slid his hands down her back, and his fingertips tucked into the band of her pajama bottoms.

"You'll have to leave early then, right? To go home and get ready for work?"

He raised a brow. "I brought a bag."

Lisa couldn't help it, she let the laugh ripple through her. "You came to stay?"

"Yeah. If Tina changes her mind, it's too damn late. I want to be with you, Lisa. I didn't know why I moved home, but now I do."

Damn that lip, she thought as she bit down on it again.

Lisa let her legs widen, and it lowered her even more. Now

she was heat to heat, and she had to make the decision on which way she wanted the rest of the night to go.

She moved her hands from the back of his neck to his face, holding him in place to look her in the eye.

"Say it. Say the words, Ryan. If they're there, I want to hear them."

Both sides of his mouth curled up and it lit in his eyes first.

Mimicking her hold on him, he let go of her hips and cupped her face. "Lisa, I love you."

"Fuck," she let the word out on a low breath, and he chuckled.

"That was an intimate growl," he said winding his fingers into her hair.

"No one, no man," she corrected, "has ever said those words to me."

"I mean them. I don't just say them." He eased her toward him. "I love you, Lisa. I love you."

CHAPTER THIRTY-THREE

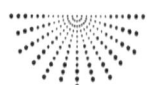

SHE'D TAKEN HOLD OF HIS WORDS, AND IT HAD DONE SOMETHING to her, Ryan noticed. Lisa's arms had wrapped around his neck again, and her mouth opened to his. In a week, they'd already had their share of kisses. The sweet ones. The testing the water ones. Even the make out ones. This kiss, oh this was different.

The heat of it made him burn through his core, and his erection was non-concealable now.

Lisa's tongue pulsed against his as she ground on his lap. God, if she kept that up, this would be over before they got started.

Ryan lifted his hands under her shirt, anxious to touch her skin. The peaks of her nipples pushed against the fabric of her bra, and when he ran the pad of his thumb over them, she moaned.

"Make your decision," he said as he scraped his teeth down her throat. "Do you want this?"

"Yes," she hummed out the word as she let her head fall back, exposing her throat to him.

"Do you want it here or on your bed?"

She lowered her head, so that her eyes met his. They were dark with need and want. "Do you have a condom with you?"

His smile was immediate. "I happen to have put two of them in my wallet."

Her cheeks pinked even more. "You came to do this?"

"No."

"Liar," she said before biting his bottom lip and giving it a tug with her teeth.

"No, but I wasn't coming unprepared. We can wait."

"I don't want to."

Ryan let out a moan of his own. "Good, because I don't want to either."

"The condoms in my drawer are probably expired and brittle," she said, running her fingers through his hair and sending a tingle of pleasure down his spine.

"You didn't go through a Costco sized box of condoms fast enough?" he teased.

Seriousness flashed in her eyes. "I don't have sex." Her voice was low, and her words straightforward.

Ryan ground his back teeth together. "You have had sex though, right?"

Lisa nodded. "Yes, but it's been a very long time."

"We can wait," he said again.

"I can't. I don't want to."

He nodded slowly. "Here or there?"

Lisa licked her lips, and Ryan's erection presented itself again.

"Two condoms?"

"Yep."

"One for here. One for there."

Ryan swallowed hard. "You're logical."

She nodded slowly as she reached for the hem of her shirt and pulled it over her head. Then, reaching behind her, she unfastened her bra, letting it drop between them. Her breasts were poised at his mouth.

With eyes filled with lust, and kiss-swollen lips, Lisa lowered her mouth to his, and hovered.

"Tomorrow I'll go to Costco. Something tells me this is the start of something," she wiggled on his lap, "big."

∾

UNTIL TWO IN THE MORNING, IT HAD BEEN HANDS, TONGUES, AND teeth. There had been moans and the unmistakable mutter of *"fuck"* whispered by both of them into the crevice of the neck of the other person.

Lisa's lips were raw from the whiskers that had not been shaved off Ryan's usually smooth face.

They each had bite marks, and he had a few scratches. There had been a lot of sex in those few late-night hours, even if there had only been need for two condoms.

He breathed deeply next to her, and Lisa watched him in the early morning light. She'd hardly slept, afraid that when she woke, he'd be gone.

It was silly to think about it that way. He'd said he wouldn't, and there he was—still.

The alarm on his phone chimed, and he rolled to reach for it on her nightstand. At one point he dropped it to his chest, and grunted, before picking it back up and shutting off the alarm.

Then, his arm still around her, Ryan scooped Lisa up against him. "Good morning," he said softly, brushing her temple with a kiss.

"Hi," she managed before she began to tremble with tears that had come from nowhere.

He'd noticed.

Maneuvering himself so that he could look at her, he studied her in the shadows. "Hey, what's wrong?"

"Nothing," she said quickly as she wiped away her tears. "I mean it. Nothing is wrong, and for that reason, I'm crying."

He chuckled lightly. "Do you want to explain that to me?"

She thought about it for a moment and then laughed. "You

know that scene in *Pretty Woman* where Vivian and Edward are lying in bed having a heart to heart?" Ryan nodded. "And Vivian tells him that it's easier to believe the bad things people say to you than the good?"

"Yeah, I remember it."

"Well, this is like that to me. You're here. Still. I mean you said you loved me last night—"

"I do."

Her breathing was ragged now. "But you're still here."

Ryan brushed her hair back from her face. "How many families did you live with?"

"It's not important."

His thumb rubbed across her lip. "It is important. To you, it's like all those people telling Vivian bad things about her."

The tears were back, and they weren't sad. He understood her. Only Rose and her friends understood her like that.

"Don't think I'm lying when I tell you, I don't know," she admitted.

His face pained. "Really?"

Lisa nodded. "I was in foster care from the time I was four. Twelve years is a long time. And the Hughes had me for four years, only because they were trying to adopt me. Otherwise, kids are in and out of houses in weeks or months."

His hand moved over her hair again. "God, Lisa. I don't know what to say."

She inched closer to him, wrapping her arms around him, feeling his skin against her skin. Their legs wound, and they pressed their foreheads together.

"You do know what to tell me. Tell me again," she requested.

Ryan placed his hand on her cheek and locked eyes with her. He sat their quietly just searching her eyes, never even blinking. He was rooting himself right there with her without saying a word.

Her fingers tightened on his hip.

"Lisa Palmer, I love you."

CHAPTER THIRTY-FOUR

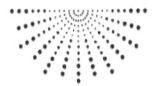

RYAN HAD BROUGHT IN HIS BAG AND WAS IN THE SHOWER WHEN Lisa's computer began to chime in her office. She sat up and contemplated the noise. Then panic shot through her. She'd forgotten about her call with Mama Rose.

As she rolled out of bed, she ran to the bathroom, pushing open the door, and nearly falling on the tile floor because she'd had so much force behind it.

"Mama Rose is calling. Don't come out wrapped in a towel. Dear God, don't do it," she yelled through the steam, grabbed a hair tie off the counter, a T-shirt out of the hamper, and ran to her office.

She slipped on the T-shirt and was still tying up her hair when she pressed the button to accept the FaceTime call.

A moment later, the face of the only woman she would ever call her mother, was large as life in front of her.

"Good morning, sweetheart," Rose's sweet voice fill the room, and as always, Lisa had to fight back tears of sheer joy.

"Morning," she said, tugging down the shirt so that her bare ass wasn't directly on the seat. Thank God Rose couldn't see all of her. "How are you?"

"Oh, happy as could be. I have some news." Rose tapped the tips of her fingers together in a clap. "Ken and Julie are having another baby."

Joy bubbled in Lisa's chest. "That is great news."

Rose pressed her fingers to her cheeks which even Lisa could see had gone pink with happiness. "It'll fill the void Jason's going to leave," she admitted, and Lisa moved closer to the screen, as if it would make her closer to Rose.

"What's wrong with Jason?" Her voice had dipped with worry over her foster brother.

"He's moving," Rose said, but a small smile curled up the corners of her lips. "Honey, he's moving home. He's headed back to Denver to work at a hospital there."

Lisa nearly jumped up off the chair, then remembered her lack of attire. "Really? No way! Really?"

Rose laughed. "It's in his heart and where he wants to be."

"He'll call me, right? I mean, he'll come see me?"

"He'd better establish regular dinner with you, and holidays when I can't be with him."

"Wow, Jason's coming home." A lightness filled Lisa, and happiness swam in her veins.

Ryan caught her eye as he leaned against the doorjamb, crossing his feet at the ankles, and his arms in front of him. He wore an enormous smile, in his blue button down that made his eyes sparkle.

"Lisa, honey? Is something wrong?"

Lisa swallowed hard as she turned back to the screen fully aware of how disheveled she looked. "I have some news too."

"Well, let me know about it."

"I'm seeing someone."

"Sweetheart, that's wonderful." Rose's voice rose in pitch, which said she was happy for her. "Who is it?"

That made Lisa chuckle. "Well, it's Tina's future-brother-in-law."

Rose lifted a brow. "And how did she take that?"

"You know."

Rose nodded. "She'll be fine. Is he there? Can I meet him?"

Lisa turned her head toward Ryan, who only grinned at her.

She held her hand out to him, and he moved toward her, taking her hand, and leaning over her so that he was visible in the camera.

"Rose, this is Ryan," Lisa made the introduction.

"Ryan," Rose sighed his name. "It's so nice to meet you."

"You as well. I've heard a lot about you."

Rose smiled, and her eyes landed on Lisa, so full of love that Lisa could feel it resonate just as if Rose had her wrapped in her arms.

"This young lady is very special to us," Rose said.

"She feels the same about you," Ryan said, resting his hand to Lisa's shoulder. "I have to head to work, so I'll leave you two lovely ladies to chat. It was wonderful to meet you," he added.

Lisa looked up at him as he moved in to press a quick and gentle kiss to her lips. "I'll see you tonight."

And with that promise he walked out of the office, and only a moment later, she heard the front door close.

Rose's grin was as wide as Lisa knew hers was.

"That was a beautiful sight, sweetheart," Rose said with her hands pressed to her chest. "Does he make you happy?"

Lisa nodded. "He does. It's new. And I mean really new. We didn't meet very long ago. And—"

"Lisa," Rose laughed. "He adores you. Enjoy this."

"I'm trying," she said as she tugged at the hem of her T-shirt. "What if—"

"Lisa," Rose stopped her again. "Enjoy it."

And just like that, Lisa knew that was what she had to do.

CHAPTER THIRTY-FIVE

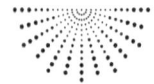

AND JUST LIKE THAT, THE WEDDING OF TINA AND AARON WAS IN Lisa's way, again.

Lisa reread the text for the third time.

I have been requested for dinner with the aunts before they fly out. I'll text you when we're done. I miss you. I love you.

She'd considered cooking the dinner she'd planned for Sunday, and they hadn't gotten to. Well, now she had all night to put the video together, and she'd keep the meal for a different time.

As she carried her lights to the kitchen, Ruby's familiar knock rapped at the door. Lisa laughed. Did she know Lisa didn't have plans, or had Ruby even given it any thought that she might not be alone?

Lisa opened the door and Ruby walked straight in, her hands in the air.

"Lost another one," she spurted out the phrase as she moved to the refrigerator and pulled out a beer.

Without another word, Ruby twisted off the top and took a long pull as Lisa watched.

When Ruby lowered the bottle, Lisa finally asked, "Lost

another what?"

"Roommate," she blurted out the word as she took another long pull.

"You had another roommate move out?"

"Middle of the day. I came home and her stuff is gone. Key was on the kitchen counter with a note that said *I'm sorry*."

"No explanation?"

"None. What the hell, Lees? What's wrong with me?"

Lisa laughed. "Nothing."

"Bullshit!" Ruby tipped up the beer until she finished it, and then let out a loud burp. "How many roommates have I had?"

Lisa shrugged. "I have no idea."

"Right, because they keep moving out."

Lisa took the empty bottle from her and dropped it into the recycle bin. "Why do you even have roommates? I mean, you don't need the extra income to pay rent."

Ruby puckered her lips, and her brows drew inward. "I like having roommates. Why have extra room without someone in it."

"Then get a smaller place."

"I like to have company around."

"Then move in with Mindy."

Ruby narrowed her gaze on Lisa. "Oh, but not you? You don't want a roommate like me either?"

"I didn't say that."

"No, you didn't, but you didn't offer and..." Ruby stopped. Her eyes widened, and then she put her hands on her cheeks and smiled. "Holy shit! Holy shit! Holy shit!"

"What?"

"You did it. Holy shit, you did it."

Lisa took a step back from Ruby. "I did what?"

"You did him."

"Now—"

"Oh, don't pull this crap on me. I'm in tune with you. I can feel it in my bones. You had sex with Tina's brother-in-law. You can't afford to have a roommate now."

Lisa pursed her lips. No, this was a conversation for after the wedding. This was between her and Ryan. God, how did she think she'd keep this from her friends?

"Listen, Ruby—"

The smile on Ruby's lips was wide. "I'm so fucking proud of you."

Lisa crinkled up her nose. "What?"

"Seriously. You went after something you wanted. It doesn't matter that Tina's been on your ass. You went after it."

"I didn't go after it. It happened."

Ruby's smile was still wide. "Yeah, it did." Ruby drummed her hands on the counter. "We should celebrate. Then, you should tell me every single detail."

"That's not going to happen."

"Why?"

"I'm not twenty-two anymore." Lisa grinned.

Ruby groaned. "I need it."

"Then go out and get it," Lisa laughed.

Ruby narrowed her gaze on Lisa. "After the wedding will you tell me? Please, just give me something," Ruby pleaded.

Lisa moved to her and pulled her to her. "It was out of this world."

"You're so lucky."

And that was what Lisa had to keep reminding herself. She was lucky. But it had only been a week, so the pessimism was strong.

She eased back from Ruby. "He met Rose."

Ruby lifted a brow. "How?"

"He was here, still, this morning when she called."

Now Ruby's face shifted into a smile that wasn't about lurid details. It was full of happiness that lifted into her eyes. "Love looks good on you, Lees."

"It does?"

Ruby nodded and reached for Lisa's hand, giving it a squeeze. "Thanks for letting me in on it. My promise to you is to not let you sabotage it. Don't let it go."

Lisa wanted to argue, but Ruby was right. Lisa was bound to do something to try and push Ryan away. It was inevitable.

She gave Ruby a nod of acceptance and turned to pick up her legal pad of notes.

"I didn't get to make dinner with him yesterday, so I'm a video behind. And he's not coming over tonight." She flipped through the pages. "Are you interested in staying and helping? I'll feed you."

Ruby nodded and moved swiftly to the hook near the refrigerator that held aprons. She took one down and slipped it on.

"I'm your girl. Feed me. It's like saying you love me to the hilt."

That made Lisa laugh. "I do."

They went about prepping the ingredients, and texting Mindy to join them, assuming Tina was busy with the aunts as well.

"I forgot to tell you, Rose had news this morning," Lisa said as they organized ramekins with fresh ingredients for filming purposes.

"Yeah, what kind of news?"

"Ken is having another baby."

"He's the married one?"

Lisa nodded. "Yeah. He's the married one with two kids."

Ruby added the measured herbs to the ramekin in front of her. "That's great."

"And there was more. Jason is moving back to Denver. He has a job at a hospital."

When Ruby turned to her, Lisa noticed the tear in her eye.

"What?" Lisa said, pulling a piece of paper towel from the roll and handing it to Ruby.

Ruby wiped her eyes. "Lees, you'll have family in town. Your brother will be here."

It squeezed in her chest as hard when Ruby said it as when Rose had. Yeah, she'd have family in town. He was her brother.

Lisa couldn't help herself. She pulled Ruby in for a hug and the two of them sobbed. A man, her girls, and her brother—Lisa's life was fuller than it had ever been.

CHAPTER THIRTY-SIX

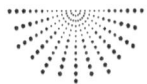

THEY FELL INTO A ROUTINE, AND LISA FOUND IT COMFORTABLE.

Ryan spent the night when he could, and Lisa had put a new toothbrush in her bathroom for him. They'd each taken a trip to Costco for condoms, so the drawer was full.

And now that she had Ryan, in the open, it hadn't gone unnoticed that she heard from Tina much less.

She was busy, Lisa reminded herself, but it stirred in her gut, that even though Tina had conceded, and *let* Lisa and Ryan continue their relationship, she still wasn't happy with it.

All the better, Lisa decided. If Tina didn't want this new relationship in her face, or interrupting her wedding, it was better if they just weren't around one another.

Mindy knocked on Lisa's door an hour before they were expected for the final fittings for their dresses.

"Extra bottles of shampoo. Cologne on the sink. Two toothbrushes. It's looking mighty cozy around here," Mindy said as she walked out of the bathroom.

Lisa grinned up at her. "Leave me alone."

Mindy laughed. "I like it. I like him. He's good for you. You're happy."

Lisa's cheeks lifted and she knew she was smiling like a fool. "I am happy."

"Tina's going to be okay," Mindy said, and that caused Lisa to draw in a breath.

"She hasn't been talking to me much."

"Well, she's been talking to me plenty," Mindy said as she hopped up on one of the stools at the counter. "She's not mad," Mindy warned as she held up a hand to block anything Lisa might say. "She's out of sorts with the wedding."

"Why hasn't she told me any of this?"

"Because she knows she'll turn it around on you. She's happy for you and Ryan. She knows what she gains if it works out between the two of you." Mindy fidgeted with her car keys. "Ryan's mom is pushing them to have kids right away and wants to help them look for a house. Her job is stressful, and Aaron's job is threatening layoffs. And then there is Cicely."

Lisa bit down on her bottom lip. "What's wrong with Cicely?"

"The spectacle that Tina was afraid you'd make with Ryan; it seems as if Cicely is making a week before her wedding."

"What did she do?"

Mindy winced. "Got engaged and made a huge deal about it on Facebook."

Lisa wondered why she hadn't seen that. She was friends with Cicely on Facebook. "Poor Tina."

"Tina will be fine. The wedding will be spectacular, and she and Aaron are going to have an amazing life."

Lisa felt tears sting her eyes when her phone buzzed on the counter, and she slid her finger across the screen to read the message.

I love you. I miss you. I can't wait until we're both home tonight. Give the girls my love.

Lisa smiled as looked down at the message.

Mindy lifted her head to look. "He's everything you never

knew you always wanted," Mindy paraphrased the line from *Fools Rush In* that always turned Lisa to mush.

"He is."

"I'm so happy for you."

TINA CRIED THROUGH HER DRESS FITTING. SHE CRIED WHEN EACH of the girls tried on their dresses. And when Cicely put on her dress, and then asked to try on a wedding dress she'd seen, Tina had lost her shit.

By the time they'd left the store, Tina was in hysterics. Her sister was in hysterics. Their mother didn't know what to think, so she scolded them both in front of everyone.

Because they were a squad, a team, a family, the girls loaded Tina into Mindy's car and they headed to Mindy's house to decompress.

Tina sobbed the entire way, and it was Lisa that held her in the backseat while she did so.

"She's such a bitch," Tina cried out. "Who does that to her sister?"

Lisa stroked her hand down Tina's hair but sat quietly.

"She's angry because you're my maid-of-honor," Tina admitted. "It should be her. But I'm closer to you," she sobbed against Lisa's shoulder, and Lisa pulled her in tighter.

Wasn't she full of guilt too for falling in love with Ryan during this time? Lisa was sure she was no better than Cicely, but she'd done everything she could to not make a scene.

Once they arrived at Mindy's, she opened a bottle of wine, and the four of them sat on the couch, squeezed close together. Mindy had turned on *That Thing You Do*, and they sat in silence and just let the movie play.

When it was over, Tina, with her head on Lisa's shoulder, sighed. "Guy Patterson."

The other's laughed.

It was Mindy who agreed with Tina's call. "God, wouldn't he be the one to capture? Talent. Romance. Ug," she let out a groan. "I want a Guy Patterson."

Ruby roared into laughter. "C'mon, you sappy twits. Tom Hanks kills it in that. I mean, it's Mr. White that gets my engine running."

All eyes turned to Ruby and the laughter grew in intensity.

Lisa picked up her wine and sipped. "You guys should do some due diligence." She bit down on her bottom lip. "IMDb that movie. You think those two are hot? Look what twenty plus years has done to Jimmy," she referenced the character's name.

Mindy had her phone in her hand first. "Oh-my-god!"

Ruby and Tina leaned in to see the more mature version of the cranky musician. His hair was fully silver and he sported a silver beard to boot.

Ruby picked up her wine and drank it all down. "That's it. I'm looking in the wrong place. I need a silver fox. Can you imagine what they could do to you in bed?" She groaned orgasmically, and again, it warranted a laugh from them all.

Mindy shook her head. "Hell no. I'm so inexperienced, that would scare the hell out of me."

Ruby held her empty glass in her hand. "They'd treat you just right."

"Then it sounds like it's what you need," Mindy countered.

CHAPTER THIRTY-SEVEN

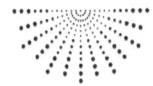

RYAN STEPPED THROUGH THE DOOR WHEN LISA OPENED IT, AND HE immediately pulled her into his arms and kicked the door closed.

"God, I've missed you," he said, pressing a kiss to Lisa's neck, drawing in the scent of her. "I know I woke up in your arms, but I think I just want to hold you like this all night."

Lisa moaned against him. "As lovely as this sounds, I made dinner."

He moved his lips to the other side of her neck and brushed soft kisses there too. "I knew I smelled something that had my mouth watering, but you smell so good. And you feel so good in my arms."

"You're staying the night?" she asked against his mouth before diving into a kiss that had him holding on to her tighter.

"Please let me."

Lisa laughed against his mouth. "Well, since you said please."

Ryan slid his hands over the curve of her ass and squeezed. "Let's eat that dinner. I want to spend the rest of the night worshipping you."

Lisa tunneled her fingers up into his hair. "You're desperate to make a dent in that pile of condoms, huh?"

A deep laugh rattled in his chest as he brushed her jaw with his lips. "I can't see letting them get old and brittle like the last ones you had," he teased. "Cleaning out that drawer was sacrilegious."

"I was just waiting for you to come into my life," she said and Ryan eased back.

"I think that's what I was waiting for too." He cupped her face in his hands, because over the past week they'd bantered like they were now, only it always ended with her telling him he could walk away when he was ready. This time, he was going to cut that off before she said it. "Therefore, I'm never going anywhere. You're stuck with me forever."

She took that breath he'd expected, so he pressed a finger to her lips.

"Forever, Lisa."

HE'D GOTTEN HIS WISH. AFTER DINNER, THEY CLEANED UP AS quickly as possible, and then their hands were on one another. Ryan understood that their relationship was new, but he wondered if they'd continue to crave each other like they did now.

As he brushed his fingers over Lisa's bare, damp shoulder, her breathing labored next to him, he was sure they would continue to crave one another. That came with love and respect.

Lisa pressed her hand to her chest as she tried to catch her breath. "If Ruby knew…" she laughed as Ryan propped himself up on his elbow, his head rested in his hand.

"If Ruby knew what?"

Lisa turned her head so that she was looking at him, and he brushed a wayward curl from her forehead.

"She always wants the details of our love lives. Like all the details," she laughed. "As she says, she lives vicariously through us."

"And in the past, you've dished about lovers?"

Her flinch didn't go unnoticed, and he wished he hadn't said anything.

"I never had anything to talk about," she admitted, and Ryan considered that he'd been the one to throw away the condoms in the drawer with expired dates on them.

Lisa tapped her fingers to her collarbone as her breath settled. "Of course, Tina is the only one who has had a love life."

"Please, whatever you do, never share those details with me."

She laughed easily at that.

Ryan reached a hand to her hip to roll her to face him. "What do you tell her about us?"

Lisa snorted out another laugh. "Nothing." Ryan raised a brow. "I'm serious," she promised.

Ryan rested his hand on her hip, kneading her skin beneath his fingertips. "You haven't told her just how amazing we are in bed?" He grinned. "How I make you roll your eyes—"

Lisa covered his mouth before he could say more. "She's never going to know that."

He kissed her fingers that were pressed to his lips.

Lisa eased against him as he rolled to his back. She rested her head on him, running her fingers through the tuft of hair on his chest.

"What are you girls doing for Tina's bachelorette party tomorrow night?" Ryan pressed a kiss to the top of her head.

"Dinner and then a dueling piano bar."

"No one is dancing on those pianos in Speedos, right?"

She laughed and it stirred a warmth inside his belly. God, he loved her.

"Tina would die." Lisa rested her hands on his chest and balanced her chin there. "We need to make it an epic night she won't forget."

"You have lots of girls going?"

"No." She pressed a kiss to his skin. "We're making it just us. Her sister is hellbent on ruining her special day."

Ryan smoothed his hand over her hair. "I thought we were ruining her special day."

Lisa let out a sigh, hinted with a laugh. "That was until her sister got engaged."

"Oh, I guess I haven't been home enough lately to pick up on that new piece of information."

"Yeah, and today at the dress fittings, she asked to try on a wedding dress she saw in the store."

"Ouch."

"Tina is a mellow gal, but I thought she was going to punch her sister."

"Well, at least I know my brother will never misstep being married to her. It sounds like she'd kick his ass."

"I can't imagine your brother misstepping enough to get that wrath."

That said a lot, he thought, and he probably owed his brother for setting Ryan up as a trustworthy person for Lisa to spend time with. And without that trust, he certainly wouldn't be sleeping in her bed already, with a toothbrush on her bathroom sink.

Lisa adjusted, draping her leg over Ryan, and then moving until she straddled him. "What are you guys doing for the bachelor party?"

He rested his hands on her hips, enjoying the view she was giving him. It took him a moment to remember their plans.

"He was specific on what he didn't want."

"Which was?" she asked, rocking against him.

God, how was he supposed to remember? "Um, no strippers or clubs. I think he said sports bar or something," but honestly, he couldn't even form sentences. "Top Golf."

Lisa laughed. "That's all?"

"No." He gripped her hips tighter as she moved on him. "God don't ask me. I can't think about my brother right now."

"Do you have something else on your mind?" She splayed her hands out on his chest.

Reaching his arm out, he managed to put his hand into the drawer of the nightstand and pull out a condom. "I think this conversation is done."

Lisa plucked the condom from his fingers. "I couldn't agree with you more."

CHAPTER THIRTY-EIGHT

THEY MADE TINA WEAR THE SASH THAT SAID BRIDE-TO-BE, AND even though Ruby protested, she wore her Bride-Crew sash that Mindy had made for all of them. Lisa gave Tina her tiara, on loan of course, to wear through the night.

Ruby had overseen dinner reservations, and when they arrived, they weren't on the list.

Lisa thought it was humorous that when Ruby was mad, she could play it multiple ways. She'd stab you in the gut when you least expected it. She'd bring a wrath down on you that you'd never forget. Or, in the case of the young maître d', she turned on the sex appeal.

"C'mon," she called from the host station as the man found them a table in the crowded restaurant.

"You ladies have a wonderful night," he said before he left the table, his eyes wide as they scanned Ruby.

She licked her lips and smiled at him. "Thanks, Ben," she said as she rested her hand on his arm.

Lisa was quite sure the man was having sex in his head, because when he came out of the trance that Ruby had put him in, his cheeks deepened in color, and he hurried off.

"And you need to live vicariously through us?" Lisa asked. "I call bullshit."

Ruby laughed as she slid into the booth next to Mindy. "Ya just know when a guy appreciates the curves."

Tina looked at her phone before sliding it back into her purse.

Lisa nudged her with her shoulder. "Everything okay?"

"My sister wants to know where she's supposed to be for the party," she said picking up her menu and scanning a look over it.

Mindy shared a panicked look between them. "We only planned for the four of us."

Tina nodded. "Yep."

"Oh, Tina, we thought that was what you wanted," Mindy's voice cracked and threatened tears.

"It is what I wanted," she said lowering the menu, a wide smile on her lips. "I'm not answering her. Tonight is mine. All mine. And Cicely can screw off."

"Hell yeah," Ruby backed up the sentiment. "Sky's the limit, girlfriend. Whatever you want, tonight it's all yours."

"You all are going to get stinking drunk, and I'm going to enjoy piano music, and then I have a surprise for all of you."

Again, they all exchanged confused looks.

Lisa picked up her menu. "I think we're supposed to be the ones who surprise you."

"I know that I haven't been easy the past few months. I've been curt, nasty, presumptuous. Well, let's say that my sister's actions have made me resign to the fact that karma is a bitch."

They all remained silent. What were they supposed to say to that?

Tina took Lisa's hand and kissed the back of it. "And I've been most nasty to you."

"I get it. You don't—"

"I love you. And the greatest gift would be if you become my sister—well, legal sister?" she laughed as she said it. "I mean, you are my sister. You all are," she said looking at each of them. "But

Ryan is a great guy who was dealt a shitty hand before. And now he found you, and it was instant. What a gift."

"It's new. It's only been a couple weeks."

"It doesn't make it any less real. I'm happy for you. He's a good guy," Tina said.

"You mean that?"

Tina nodded. "I do. I've had to work to get to it, but I mean it. He's happy. His mom is happy. You're happy. That's what matters to me. You all stuck with me through it, even when I know you had a side text going about ways to kill me."

Ruby raised her hand. "I didn't tell her," she teased, and they all shared a laugh.

Tina turned back to Lisa. "And I know you worry that he'll leave you. He's not that guy. They're not that family. Those days for you are over."

Lisa bit down on her bottom lip. "You think so?"

"I know so."

"Tina, I never meant to hurt you by seeing him," Lisa said.

"I know. You love him, right?"

Lisa swallowed hard. "I do."

"Mindy saw the toothbrushes and the boxes of condoms in the trash," Tina admitted, and Lisa felt the heat rise in her cheeks.

Ruby lifted her menu. "Bitch is holding out on me."

Mindy pressed her hand to her chest. "Sorry, I shouldn't have said anything."

Lisa laughed. "Well, it's out there. I am having sex with Ryan."

"It was out there," Ruby admitted from behind her menu. "What we don't have are details."

"I'm not giving you details," Lisa said. "Just know, it's amazing," she drew out the word and Tina rested her head to Lisa's shoulder.

"It runs in the family," Tina said, and Ruby slammed down the menu to the table.

"Gross, gross, gross. Okay, I don't want details. I don't want comparison shopping either." Ruby waved for their server. "We need to get her drunk. And if we get drunk enough, maybe I can come back here and take the guy who seated us home."

Mindy's eyes grew wide. "You wouldn't."

"I'm to the point I think I would," Ruby admitted. "I'm desperate, and you should be too," she directed the statement to Mindy.

"I'm fine."

"You need to get laid too," Ruby said. "I have a nice guy in my office."

Mindy shook her head. "No."

When the server came to the table, Ruby ordered them a bottle of wine. When the server had walked away, she leaned in toward Tina, with her arms on the table. "Maybe you should tell us what the surprise is, in case we get you too drunk."

Tina considered. "You're right." A smile turned up the corners of her mouth. "I booked us a suite at the Brown Palace. And that's all I'm going to tell you. I figured that way everyone could get drunk and land safely."

Lisa kissed the top of Tina's head. Though, she really wanted to sleep in Ryan's arms, she'd never give up a night with her girls.

CHAPTER THIRTY-NINE

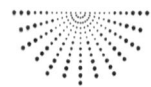

RYAN WASN'T SURE HIS GOLF GAME WAS ANY BETTER THREE STORIES high. His brother laughed when the ball didn't even get near the first target.

"We need to find you a sport, bro," Aaron teased as he lifted his beer to his lips.

"I've never been a golf guy. I'll be fine," Ryan said as he took his seat among the other guys and picked up an onion ring from the tray of appetizers.

"Are you coming home tonight or staying at Lisa's alone?" Aaron asked as he took a fried pickle, dragged it through the sauce, and popped it into his mouth.

"What do you mean alone?"

"Tina's surprising them with a suite at the Brown Palace." Aaron held out his beer to accentuate his comment. "I guess they don't know yet."

"I suppose I'll come home then," Ryan said as he picked up his beer and sipped, disappointed at the news. "Lisa only said dinner and a piano bar."

"First stops. She has a rom com wedding night planned for them."

Ryan laughed. "Those girls and their rom coms, huh?"

"They bonded over them in college. I think Lisa used the movies for therapy for years."

"They gave her happy endings," Ryan contemplated the thought.

"I suppose so."

"I met her foster mom the other day. The one she's really close to," Ryan amended, knowing that she had plenty of them.

"She lives in England, doesn't she?"

Ryan nodded. "They were FaceTiming. One of her foster brothers is moving back here."

Aaron's mouth curled into a smile. "That'll be nice for her. The girls are all she has."

"She doesn't talk about it much," Ryan said, rolling the bottle of beer between his palms. "Her life before the girls."

"Are you trying to harsh my mellow?" Aaron asked taking another beer from the bucket and opening it.

Ryan laughed. "No. God, no. Sorry."

"Tina didn't even invite her sister to go with them."

"I heard she's getting in the way."

"Yeah. Tina is pretty mad. Not like she couldn't have waited a few weeks. And the engagement is one thing. I mean, hell, it's in the air. But the stunt with the wedding dress, that pushed Tina over the edge."

"I guess I won't ask Lisa to marry me until your wedding is only a memory," Ryan laughed, but his brother's eyes grew wide.

"Are you serious?"

"I was kidding."

"I don't think you were. Dude, you're only a few weeks in. Are you that serious?"

Ryan pulled from his beer and drank until it burned in his chest. "I think I'm getting there."

"I didn't realize you had it this bad."

"She's a keeper. She's worth loving."

Aaron tapped his bottle to Ryan's. "No arguments there."

AN HOUR LATER, RYAN'S GAME HAD ONLY GOTTEN WORSE, BUT that he attributed to the number of beers and shots he'd consumed. Once they left the Top Golf, they headed to a sports bar, and from there, alcohol poured freely.

At one point, the waitresses had Aaron on top of the bar, and people were throwing money at him to buy him shots. Thankfully they had designated drivers among Aaron's friends, because, Ryan, the best man, was sloshed, and the groom was going to pass out on the bar before they could get him out of there.

Ryan heard the ringing, and it took a bit to process that each time he heard it, his pants buzzed. Finally, on a laugh, he pulled out his phone.

"Hello!" he shouted over the noise in the bar, or the noise in his head. He wasn't sure which one was louder.

"Are you drunk?" the slurred words came from Lisa.

"Are you drunk?" he countered.

There was a laugh, and God he loved that laugh.

"I'm extremely tipsy," she said, and he could hear it again in her voice. Oh, it was so cute. "Ruby is trashed. Tina is supposed to be drunk, but she's not. In fact, I don't think she's drank anything. Not that we noticed," she laughed again. "Oh, we're having the best time," she shouted over the music playing on her end of the call.

"I miss you." He'd become somber, and he wanted to be with her. Though they'd both be passed out, it just didn't matter.

"Tina got us a room. Not you and me," she clarified, and he realized she was more drunk than he'd thought.

"I heard. Be careful. No guys. Don't take any guys with you. Okay? I mean it. I don't—"

"Got it!" Then she grew quiet for a moment. "You don't have naked girls with you, do you?"

Because he couldn't see straight, he looked around. "No," he confirmed. "And I'm going to my parents' house after this. No girls in my room. That's the rule."

She snickered. "I want a combined party when we get married," her voice sang it out. "We get drunk together, okay?"

He was sobering. "You're not going to remember that in the morning," he said.

"Yes, I will. Marry you. One party. Tiny wedding. Kids."

How drunk was she?

"Okay," he said softly. "I love you."

She laughed loudly. "Get her off there," he heard her shout. "Ruby's a mess. We're going. We have a room. You can't come."

His stomach sloshed as his brain fog cleared. "I won't, unless you need me."

"I do need you," she said and then the line went quiet. He looked at his phone and realized the call had been dropped, or she'd finished it without realizing it.

His heart was hammering in his chest. *Marry you. One party. Tiny wedding. Kids.*

He leaned in on the table and rested his head in his hands. Yeah, he thought. That was exactly what he wanted too.

CHAPTER FORTY

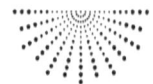

MINDY HAD AN ARM AROUND RUBY AS THEY STOOD IN THE hallway of the hotel. Lisa leaned up against the wall to steady herself.

"Okay, girls. Now the party begins," Tina said as she slipped the key card into the lock.

"Why are you sober?" Ruby hiccupped.

"Get in here before they kick us out," Tina laughed as they each passed by her.

They stepped into the suite, and Ruby stood in the middle of the room.

"Holy shit!" she said before letting out a burp, then holding still for a moment as if she didn't trust that she wasn't going to be sick.

Mindy walked to the couch where there were four plush robes. "Oh this is nice," she picked one up and noticed they had their names on them. "Ruby, this is yours."

"Well look at this," Ruby held it to her cheek.

Tina moved to the couch and picked up Lisa's. "This one is yours."

"Tina, this is awesome," Lisa said.

"You all have put up with a lot lately. I wanted to do something special."

Lisa wrapped her arm around Tina's shoulders. "We love you."

Tina blinked back tears. "There are snacks on the table, a bottle of champagne, and desserts will be up soon."

Mindy pressed her hand to her chest. "And look at this. A stack of rom coms."

"All wedding themed," Tina said. "There are pajamas on the beds for everyone too."

Lisa watched as Tina chewed her lip watching Mindy and Ruby walk into the bedroom.

Ruby held up the pajama bottoms with yellow rubber ducks on them. "Bottoms only? Am I lounging with my boobs out?"

Mindy covered her mouth, and Ruby laughed as she swayed toward the bed and finally sat down.

"I have tops for you all," Tina said, reaching for Lisa's hand. "Are you okay?"

"The world is a little tilted, but I'm good. They don't have strippers," Lisa said, and then tried to sober her thoughts. "We don't either."

Tina laughed. "I should have rethought the part where you all got drunk."

Mindy bore a sober stare at Tina. "Tipsy. I'm only tipsy."

"I'm fucking sloshed," Ruby's voice slurred as she fell back to the bed.

"Can you stay awake for five more minutes?" Tina asked, and Ruby rolled enough so she could see them all, but she didn't sit up.

"Maybe. Did you order up coffee with your champagne?"

"Yes," Tina laughed as the doorbell to the suite rang. She looked at Lisa. "Sit down so you don't fall over either."

Tina helped Lisa to the bed, and she sat down next to Mindy, who took her hand and brushed a strand of hair from Lisa's forehead.

"You're going to hurt tomorrow," Mindy teased.

"So worth it. Though I won't get laid tonight. But he's drunk," Lisa managed as she burped behind her hand, and Ruby snored, and then woke up and sat up. "I won't get laid," Lisa whispered in Mindy's ear.

"So you said."

Tina carried a large tray into the bedroom and set it on the table by the window. There was a pot of coffee, four mugs, a bottle of champagne, and three glasses.

"They dropped a glass somewhere," Mindy said.

"Nah, this is enough glasses."

Tina poured four cups of coffee. She handed two to Mindy, and carried Ruby's to her, and helped her to sit up and sip.

"This don't fucking work," Ruby spit out the words. "Can't I just pass out?"

"I need a few more minutes of you." Tina held the mug to Ruby's lips, and she sipped.

Mindy cautiously watched Lisa drink her coffee. "Tina, what's going on? Why the surprises?"

Tina took the mug from Ruby. "I hope you didn't burn your mouth," she laughed looking into the mug.

Lisa looked up, feeling her head only slightly clear, but still, she just wanted to pass out too. Only, she'd like to pass out naked on top of Ryan.

She giggled to herself.

Mindy nudged her. "What's so funny."

"Oh, it's not funny," she said seriously, but with a wide grin. "Just thinking."

Mindy rolled her eyes.

"Okay, this is going to be a mess, but maybe you'll all remember it," Tina said walking to the dresser and pulling out three wrapped packages.

She handed each of them one of the gifts wrapped in yellow tissue paper.

Ruby swayed, but Lisa thought maybe she'd sobered slightly. Then again, maybe it was Lisa that had sobered slightly.

Tina stood in front of them all scanning a look of love over them. "You three are my rock. I can't imagine how I got through anything without you all before college. I love you."

Mindy looked at each of them, and then up at Tina. "Are you okay?" Worry filled her voice.

"I'm perfect," Tina said, but she was crying.

Lisa wanted to stand and pull her in, but she knew her legs were unstable now, and worry made them more so.

"Why are you crying?" Lisa asked. "You and Aaron—"

"Aaron and I are fine. In fact, everything is fine. I love you and I'm happy for you and Ryan. Just don't you dare get engaged at my wedding."

Lisa laughed, sobered, then covered her mouth. "Never. I promise."

"I know. And my sister is out of sorts. But I don't share things with my sister like I share with the three of you. In fact," she said pressing her hand to her chest, "I don't share everything with Aaron first either."

Ruby swayed against Lisa, but her eyes were fixed on Tina. "Are you having an affair?"

Tina burst into laughter. "God, no. I love Aaron. Oh, hell, open your gifts."

"Is it a shirt to cover my boobs?" Ruby asked, which caused them all to laugh.

Lisa managed to rip the paper from her gift first and held it up.

Aunt Lisa, the shirt boasting a rubber duck said.

She lifted her eyes as Ruby pulled out her shirt and studied it. "Aunt Ruby." She curled up her lip in confusion, then read it again. "Aunt Ruby."

Ruby and Lisa turned to Mindy when she began to sob. "You're pregnant?" she asked, and Tina nodded.

Lisa reread the shirt. Oh, God! She lifted her eyes to Tina. "You didn't drink all night. I noticed you kept passing up drinks."

Tina laughed. "I haven't told a soul. You girls are first. And I mean first. I found out yesterday, and I haven't told Aaron yet."

Lisa managed to stand and pull Tina to her. "You're going to have a baby."

"I'm going to have a baby," Tina cried as the other two enveloped them in a hug. "I'm going to have a baby," she said again.

Suddenly Lisa felt sober as she held her friend. She'd been part of something big. Tina told them first. What a gift. What a gift!

Lisa eased back, forcing the other two to do the same. She rested her hand on Tina's belly. "I can't believe you haven't told Aaron yet."

"I'll tell him later. Tonight, I wanted this to be our secret. I wanted to be wrapped up with you girls. You're my family I choose. I wanted to share this with you."

Lisa cupped Tina's face in her hands. "I've never felt more honored to keep a secret in my whole life."

"You can't tell Ryan. He can't know until after the wedding."

Okay, that was going to suck, but it was doable. "I promise."

CHAPTER FORTY-ONE

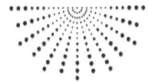

They'd slept in matching pajamas, though Tina's shirt said Mom-to-Be on it.

At some point, they'd had to take Ruby out of the bathtub, where she'd crawled after throwing up, and had fallen asleep.

Of course, they watched *She's Having a Baby*, and didn't the end of that movie always sober Lisa up? Happily ever after, but first she had to be kicked in the heart.

They just didn't make rom coms like they did in the eighties and nineties, Lisa thought as they turned off the TV.

Ruby had passed out long ago, and somehow she'd curled up to Mindy.

Lisa and Tina went out into the living room of the suite, pulling the bedroom door closed behind them

In their duck pajamas, announcement shirts, and wrapped in the lush robes with their names on them, they sat on the couch together, their feet tucked up under them.

"My head is going to kill me tomorrow," Lisa said rubbing her temples. Her drunk had subsided, but a buzz lingered.

"You had fun," Tina laughed.

"I had a blast. Who knew your bachelorette party would be so fun," Lisa nudged Tina. "I can't believe how quickly you pulled this surprise together."

Tina chewed her bottom lip. "I had to make it special."

Lisa took Tina's hand in hers. "Isn't it?"

"It is. It's just unexpected. I mean I want babies. We plan on having them, I just didn't..." her voice trailed off, and Lisa wrapped her arm around her shoulders. "It's a surprise."

"When are you going to tell him?"

"When I get home. I'm not hiding it, I just needed to celebrate it. I'm afraid where we are right now, it'll be a shock to him. With the wedding costs, and needing to move out of his mother's house, and student loans..." she drew in a breath.

"It's a lot."

"Yeah," Tina agreed.

"He's going to be happy. This is the best news. And, wow, first to get married. First to have a baby."

Tina laughed a nervous laugh. "My head is spinning."

"Mine too," Lisa teased and kissed Tina on the head.

"Okay, enough about me. You and Ryan."

Lisa pulled her lip between her teeth. "What about us?"

"Now that my priorities are shifted, you're official? You're dating? You're in love? You're just sleeping together?"

Lisa felt her cheeks grow warm. "I expect this kind of stuff from Ruby." She drew in a breath and let it out slow. "I love him. I know I haven't known him long, but I do. I love him."

Tina's eyes dampened. "That's a big step for you."

"I introduced him to Rose."

Tina smiled wide. "And how did that go?"

"She said to enjoy this. And I am, but I have to talk myself out of a meltdown every day. I don't want him to walk out on me. I don't want him to give up on me too."

Tina rested her head on Lisa's shoulder. "You tend to forget, we've never left you. And you've given us reason to reconsider that."

Lisa laughed. "I have."

"I hope it works out for you. I'd love to have you be my sister-in-law, and we can share a monster-in-law."

"Shit."

"Yeah, shit." They both laughed. "And you can be overwhelmed with aunts and cousins you didn't know existed."

They were in a good place, but there was no way Lisa was going to tell Tina that she'd told him she wanted to get married and have a small wedding. No, that was a conversation to have months from now.

It was nearly three o'clock in the afternoon when Ryan knocked on Lisa's door. When she opened it, he laughed, and then winced. She looked like he felt.

"Get in here," she said, pulling him inside and closing the door.

The blinds were all pulled, and she didn't have the lights on. He laughed when he noticed that *The Proposal* was playing on the TV, but the sound was nearly inaudible.

"Is this recovery mode?" he asked, pulling off his sunglasses.

"Don't talk so loud," she said as she walked to the kitchen, pulled down two coffee mugs, and began to brew coffee.

Ryan moved in behind her, wrapping his arms around her and pressing a kiss to her neck. "Did you have a good time?"

Lisa leaned back against him. "I did. It was wonderful."

"That's good. Tina needed a good night out."

She turned into his arms, looping her arms around his neck. "And you? No strippers?"

He grinned down at her. "Only Aaron, but they got him in the car before he embarrassed himself."

"I'm ready for the wedding to be over. Does that make me a bad friend?"

"No. You've been in on the planning much longer than I have." Ryan ran his hand over her hair. "I missed not sleeping with you last night."

Lisa laughed. "I slept on the couch. Ruby was so drunk, she took over most of the bed. But Mindy and Tina managed."

"I wish I could have seen you all."

Lisa turned to fill the coffee mugs. She handed one to Ryan.

"It can't hurt to just keep drinking it, right?" she asked as she lifted the mug to her lips.

"Last time I saw you hungover, you had Gatorade."

"This morning I need coffee first."

They each leaned a hip against the counter. "Tina didn't look hungover," Ryan said.

Lisa worried her lip. "She didn't get drunk."

"She must have known she was going to have to take care of my brother all day," he laughed and winced.

Ryan watched Lisa sip her coffee from a Harry Potter mug, and he thought about how much he'd missed her last night. As they had since she'd said them, her words kept repeating in his head. *Marry you. One party. Tiny wedding. Kids.* Had she meant them, or was she caught up in the moment of the bachelorette party?

"I was thinking we could just veg and order dinner later," he offered, watching her, assuming she had a lot on her mind. She seemed reserved, but then again, maybe it hurt them both to talk.

"I'd like that."

"Can I stay again?"

Lisa lifted her gaze to his and held it there. "Yeah."

"Good. I'm not so fond of that twin sized bed anymore." He sipped his coffee. "Okay, that's a lie. It's not the bed. It's that you're not in it."

"Move in with me," her words came out fast and worry shrouded her face the moment she'd said them.

"What?"

"I mean, if you want. Well, it's crowded at your parents' house. Tina and Aaron need some time and space. I mean, if you want."

"You said that."

"Well, answer me then," she said with her lips pursed.

Her face had flushed, and her eyes had gone wide. Was she still drunk?

"Are you sure you want me to do that?"

Lisa put her mug down on the counter and then did the same with his. "I am. I don't want you to go anywhere, and I've been pretty clear on not wanting you to leave me."

"I get it. I understand that now."

"Yeah, but if you lived here, you'd be here—always."

"Always. That's a lot. I'd be in your space."

She pushed him back and moved from under him to pace the kitchen. "If you don't want to—"

He reached for her arm and tugged her back to him. "I want it more than you'll even know. I just don't want you to think you made a mistake," because he'd heard that before, and by the look in her eye, she knew exactly when he'd heard it and it stirred anger up in her.

"No, you're no mistake. I want you here."

Ryan searched her eyes to make sure the sincerity of the sentiment was there. Telling her no, or that they'd think about it was the equivalent to him leaving, right? He'd only tell her no so she could think about it more, but really, he didn't want to tell her no.

In his entire life, nothing had ever felt as right as him and Lisa. It didn't matter how quickly they had come to the realization that they loved each other or wanted to be together.

"You're thinking about it too hard. You don't want to be that linked to me, do you?" Lisa's lips quivered. "I mean, spending the night, you can choose to come or go."

"Don't do that to me. Don't peg me to do the same thing everyone else has done to you."

"I can't help it. It's out there and—"

"And if you'd let me answer, I'd tell you I want to move in with you."

CHAPTER FORTY-TWO

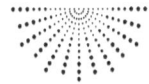

Lisa eased against Ryan, and he drew her in. Her arms lifted around his neck, and he pressed his face against hers and breathed her in.

"God, I love you," he murmured into her hair. "I want to be with you forever."

"I don't know what to do with that. It's going to take me a while to accept it."

Ryan eased back and pressed his forehead to hers. Lifting his hands to her face, he held her there. "I need to know you. I want you to tell me about your life. I have to know what walls I'm going to walk into, and how to tear them down."

Lisa squeezed her eyes shut. "I really don't want to do that."

"Then I have to learn it by mistake, or I have to ask your friends. But I'd rather hear it from you."

With his hands still cupping her face, Lisa drew in a breath. She took his hands and removed them, then she walked away from him.

Ryan watched her disappear into the room where she had her office. He didn't follow, and a moment later she returned with a box.

Lisa set it on the counter and stepped back.

Cautiously, Ryan moved to the box and looked inside. There were various notebooks, hard cover journals, and pieces of paper clipped together.

"There you go," she motioned to the box. "That's me telling you all about me," she smiled, but it strained on her lips.

"What is all of this?"

Lisa glanced at the box and swallowed hard. "When I moved in with the Hughes family, I started journaling. Rose would keep buying me journals, and I'd fill them."

"These go back to you at twelve?"

She nodded. "She saved me, Ryan. I've lived on my own since I was sixteen. I couldn't have done that without what she gave me, and that was peace of mind to keep going."

Ryan reached for her hand and linked their fingers. "You're offering these to me to read?"

Lisa nodded again. "If I sit down and tell you about me, you learn the candy-coated version. You learn what I want you to know." She looked at the box. "If I let you read those, you get the raw version. If you're the first person I'm inviting to live in my space with me, you should know the raw version."

He drew her in again and held her to him. "You have no idea what a gift you're giving me."

Lisa rested her head on his shoulder. "You can call Rose too. I'll let her know. And ask the girls anything."

Ryan eased back to look at her. "That's a big deal."

"I'm scared to death. Not of you living here, but of you learning about me."

Again, he lifted his hands to cup her face so he could look her in the eye. "I asked to know it all, Lisa. I love you. Nothing in here is going to scare me."

She bit down hard on her lip, and he knew she wasn't so sure.

. . .

THE JOURNALS WERE PUT BACK IN THE OFFICE, AND LISA GAVE HIM permission to read them whenever he wanted. Ryan had promised to read them when she wasn't around. He was considerate like that.

Later, she'd tell the girls that they were free to answer any questions he might have about her. Perhaps it was the chicken's way out of the situation, but she'd already lived the life of rejection. She wasn't wanting to live it again.

They spent the rest of the afternoon laying on the couch, wrapped around each other, and watched rom coms—one after another.

"Is there one of these movies you haven't seen?" Ryan asked as he smoothed her hair, her body rested on top of his, as they laid out on the couch.

"Probably. But I can't think of one," she chuckled. "The journals were my therapy, but so were these movies. Though, they probably gave me an unrealistic view of how to handle life."

"How so?"

"It always works out in the end."

His arms came to her back and his fingers skimmed down her spine. "It's not unrealistic anymore," he promised, and she let it simmer in her chest. "Which one is your favorite?"

Lisa let out a low hum as she thought about it. "That's hard. But I do love Hanks and Ryan, so *You've Got Mail.*"

"Shop Girl and NY152," he said, and Lisa lifted her head and grinned at him. "For the record, Gray's Papaya hot dogs aren't that good."

Lisa let out a loud laugh. "I know. We made a trip just to have them. But, God, to stand there," she let out a breath, "I was in heaven."

She studied him for a moment, and she let the look of love that resonated up from him sink into her. It was okay to be raw around him.

"You are my soulmate, aren't you?"

"I never had any doubt." Ryan laughed as he kissed her. "Roll off. I have to use the bathroom," he said, and Lisa reluctantly shifted from her comfortable position.

Ryan climbed from the couch and headed to the bathroom. When the door closed, Lisa stood and walked to the kitchen. Neither of them had felt like eating dinner, so they'd just drank their Gatorade and watched movies. But as Lisa's stomach rumbled, she pulled a bag of popcorn from the cupboard, unwrapped it, and put it in the microwave. She pushed the button marked popcorn and waited.

But just as the bag was filling up with popped kernels, Ryan walked out of the bathroom, the yellow duck shirt in his hand.

Lisa felt her mouth open as he held it up to her. The popcorn finished popping. The ding of the microwave went unanswered. The smell of burning kernels filled the air as the hot popcorn stayed sealed in the bag, but she didn't move.

"I just saw this in your hamper," he said with a raised brow. "Aunt Lisa?"

"Um," was all she could manage. *Shit! Shit!*

He continued his walk toward her. "Where did this come from?" His voice was humored. There was a smile curling up the corner of his mouth.

"It's nothing."

"What is it?"

"Just something I got at Goodwill."

Ryan shook his head. "At least I know you'll never lie to me. You're horrible at it." He held the shirt by the shoulders and gave it a little shimmy. "Tell me."

"I can't."

"Can't? Won't?"

"Just a shirt," she said, and he drew closer to her.

His smile grew wider as he came to her, then looked in the microwave. "Do you want to set that outside?" he asked, wrinkling up his nose.

Lisa looked at the bag that sat in the dark microwave. She pulled it out and hurried it toward the patio. She pulled open the doors, set the bag on the table on the deck, and closed them again before turning back to Ryan, who was still grinning.

"You have a secret, don't you?" he began again.

Lisa tucked her lips between her teeth. "I don't know what you're talking about."

"He knocked her up before the wedding?" His voice lit in humor.

Lisa shook her head.

"C'mon," he urged. "That was Tina's surprise?"

Lisa crinkled up her face and pressed her lips together so tight her jaw hurt.

Ryan's phone dinged in his pocket, and he looked down at it. "Speak of the devil," he said as he ran his finger over the screen.

A moment later he lifted his head, his brows drawn together as if in worry.

"What did he say?" she moved to him.

Ryan held out his phone.

Shit. Tina just told me she's pregnant. What the fuck? As he held it out to her, another text came through. *Meet me for a beer? I need to wrap my head around this. We can't afford this.*

Lisa felt the sting of tears rise behind her eyes, and she covered her mouth with her hand. Was that what her birth father had thought all those years ago? Was that what had led her to the life she'd led?

"Go. He needs you," she said.

"She told you first?"

"She wanted someone to be excited about it. She made it a celebration."

Ryan looked at the message. "I know he's happy about it. It's just a shock."

Lisa nodded, but the tears surfaced, and she tried like hell to bat them away. "Maybe you could convince him it's a blessing."

"It is a blessing."

"It doesn't come across that way."

Ryan reached for her hand and gave it a squeeze. "I'm going to go meet him. I'll be back."

Lisa moved from him and walked to the kitchen. She opened a cupboard, reached inside, and pulled out her spare key. She took Ryan's hand and pressed it into his palm.

"You live here now. You always have to come back," she said.

Ryan moved in close and pressed a kiss to her lips. "I'll always come back," he promised and kissed her again. "And for the record, I'd never react like this if you gave me this kind of news."

His words squeezed at her heart so hard she had to lift her hand to press it to her chest. "I love you."

Ryan kissed her one more time. "I love you, too."

CHAPTER FORTY-THREE

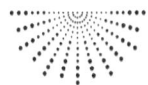

H<small>IS BROTHER WAS ALREADY AT THE BAR, BEER IN HAND, WHEN</small> R<small>YAN</small>
arrived.

Cautiously, Ryan pulled out the stool next to Aaron at the
high top.

"You okay?" he asked as the server came by for his order. He
ordered a beer, even though he wasn't sure he could stomach it.

"Shit."

Ryan couldn't believe this was his brother's reaction to news
that was wonderful. They'd planned for this. He and Aaron had
talked about it.

"I really didn't think this was how you'd react to something
like this," Ryan said as the server brought him is beer, and he
pushed it away—at least for the moment.

"I messed up. I shouldn't have gotten so worked up about it. I
mean, shit, I accused her of doing this on purpose."

Ryan winced. "You don't actually think that's what she did, do
you?"

"No," Aaron's voice was sullen. "I didn't tell her I got laid off.
She knew it was coming, but it officially happened Friday."

Perhaps that was why Aaron had tied one on so hard, Ryan decided.

"I didn't know."

"No one did," Aaron admitted. "We don't have a house. Everything is tied up in this fucking wedding. We live with Mom and Dad. And now this."

"It's special," Ryan said contemplating his beer, then still deciding he didn't want to drink it.

"It is special, and I ruined that," his brother hiccupped what Ryan considered a sob, though there were no tears. "How do I make it up to her?"

"You tell her how you really feel about the baby. That your reaction was surprise and a little shock. Tell her that you love her, and you can't wait for this new adventure."

Aaron chuckled and wiped his now moist eyes. "When did you get to be so smart about women?"

"Tried to marry one, failed. Now I'm with a good one who's afraid I'll leave her. I'm just putting together pieces, dude. But I've been around you and Tina for years. This is what you always wanted. And, hell, you can have my savings if it helps."

"It might," Aaron laughed and sat back, scrubbing his hands over his face. "She told the girls first. She didn't even tell me first."

"Maybe she knew what your reaction would be."

Aaron nodded. "She was right." He leaned in on his elbows and clasped his hands around his beer. "I need to make this right."

"Where is she now?"

Aaron pulled his phone from his pocket and searched for her location.

"She's at Lisa's."

Ryan crinkled up his nose. "You can follow her?"

"Yeah."

"Next level commitment," Ryan contemplated.

~

LISA OPENED THE DOOR TO MINDY AND RUBY. MINDY MOVED around them quickly to sit on the couch next to a sobbing Tina.

"I can't believe he reacted like that," Ruby whispered.

Lisa shrugged and they both walked to Tina, sitting themselves on the edge of the coffee table and facing her.

"This is useless. I don't even know why I want to get married," Tina sobbed.

Mindy rubbed Tina's shoulder. "Because you love him."

"Who reacts like that?"

"It's a life changing piece of information," Mindy soothed her, just as Mindy was good at. "With the wedding, and living in his parents' house, I suppose it's a lot for him."

"He lost his job," Tina sobbed. "Friday. He didn't even tell me until I told him about the baby."

Mindy took Tina's hands in hers. "Honey, you didn't tell him about the baby first either."

Though it was true, it sent Tina into another fit of sobs. "See? We hide things from each other."

Mindy pulled Tina in again and held her. "No, you don't. This is just bad timing on all ends. You love him. You've always loved him. And he loves you. It's a bit sickening how much he loves you," Mindy said, and it was Ruby who laughed first.

"Sickening is true," Ruby reiterated, and Tina lifted. She looked toward Ruby and giggled.

"We are a bit gross about it," Tina said wiping her tears.

"Uh, yeah," Ruby moved to sit next to Tina and pulled her in to hug her. "It gives us all hope. Give him some time to process. I'm still processing."

"Yeah, but you're hung over," Tina muttered against Ruby's shoulder.

"I am. You know if I'm here, and I'm hugging you, I'm in pain."

They all laughed at that.

"I'll make some coffee," Lisa said, standing and walking to the kitchen.

She looked back at her three dearest friends in the world. This was how it had been since that night they'd wandered into that coffee shop. Not everyone walked away from her.

Lisa turned toward the coffee maker and batted her eyes. This wasn't about her. Not today, but she couldn't fight it off. The Hughes family wouldn't have left her either if they'd had a choice, she thought. And now she had Ryan.

She chuckled to herself when she thought of him. *She had Ryan.* He wanted a forever with her, and he already knew that. She'd handed over her journals to him. Those were raw and ugly feelings written on those pages. She'd asked him to move in.

Lisa gripped the counter. *And for the record, I'd never react like this if you gave me this kind of news.* His words were in her head.

At the moment, it was Lisa who had the most stable relationship in the group. Well, that had never happened before.

She shook off the thought as she made the coffee. No, Tina and Aaron were fine. This was the kind of thing that would happen in a marriage. They'd work through it.

They all exchanged looks when they heard the front door unlock, and a moment later it pushed open. Aaron and Ryan cautiously walked in. They didn't seem all that surprised to find everyone in the living room.

Ryan looked at Lisa and gave her a thin-lipped smile before closing the door behind them. Aaron moved right to Tina, and Ruby and Mindy stood.

"I want to talk to you," he said softly, sitting on the coffee table so he could face Tina.

"We'll give you two some alone time," Mindy offered, and Aaron reached for her hand and stopped her.

"No, you all can stay."

Mindy nodded, patted Aaron's hand, and then she and Ruby walked to the kitchen as well.

Ryan moved in next to Lisa, wrapping his arms around her as she leaned back against his chest.

"Tina, I didn't respond right. I mean, I didn't respond with my heart. We've talked about this. We've planned for it. I've always wanted kids with you."

She wasn't looking up at him, so he lifted her chin with his finger.

"You're my whole world, sweetheart. And now we're going to have a baby." Aaron's mouth curled up into a wide smile, and it was genuine.

"You're sure you're okay with this? I didn't do it on purpose."

Aaron moved to sit next to her, pulling her to him. "I know you didn't. Those were stress words, and I didn't believe them when I said them. And now that I've calmed down, I have to consider that the universe knows more than we do. It's saying, we need this baby."

Tina wrapped her arms around Aaron and sobbed into his shoulder. "I love you."

"I love you, too. This is all going to be okay." He kissed the top of her head and eased back to look her in the eye again. "But I'm going to want one of those duck shirts for myself," he said, and that had everyone laughing.

CHAPTER FORTY-FOUR

Ryan adjusted his tie, loosening it, since he didn't see why he had to wear a suit for a dinner on Friday night. He looked up at the motion that had caught his attention.

Lisa walked out of the bedroom, her fingers at her ears clasping her earring. She was just moving through her space, but he had to stop and take it all in.

Her blonde curls fell over her shoulders, which were sculpted from mid-day yoga, he'd come to learn. Her sundress dipped low enough to hit at the swells of her breasts, tender and sweet.

The bright, flowery dress grazed her beautiful curves, ending just above her knees. She had on low heels and brightly polished toes.

She was a vision of absolute beauty, and she was his.

"What's wrong with my dress?" she asked looking at him.

"Tell me my face doesn't actually register that something is wrong. I was taking in the sight of you, and wow."

Her mouth curled into a smile, painted pink. "Thank you. You clean up nice too," she said, moving to him and giving the lapels of his sports jacket a tug.

"Ya know, Mom said I had to look nice."

Lisa laughed as she slid up to him, pressing her thigh to his already attentive crotch. "I guess dressing up does something for us."

"Thinking about taking that dress off you is doing it."

She laughed in his ear. "Okay, when we get home," she promised, her breath hot on his skin.

Ryan adjusted himself as she moved from him to gather her purse.

"How long do rehearsal dinners last?" he asked, his voice strained.

"We have to rehearse too."

"Right. That can't take long, right? We walk down the aisle, they say *Yep!*, and I get to have you on my arm walking back down the aisle."

Her face shifted, and he couldn't read her.

"Yeah," her word was strained.

"What's wrong?"

"We're going to walk down the aisle together. I just got choked up about it."

"Because you think about it? I mean with us?" he asked, because he thought about it a lot.

"Yeah," she said on a sigh. "I never thought about that before with anyone."

"That's a compliment I'll take with me the rest of my life."

She flashed him a smile as she picked up her tiny purse from the counter, opened it, checked its contents, and tucked it under her arm.

"Let's go look like the power couple we are," she said, and it warmed him.

When Courtney told him he was a waste of time, he didn't think this would be his life a few months later. It was fate, he thought. Fate that Courtney made a mistake so big he didn't even consider going back. Fate that he walked into that Rom Com

Movie Club night and saw Lisa with that green mask covering her beautiful face.

With his hand on the small of Lisa's back, they walked into the church. Needing to keep her close, he moved in closer to wrap his arm around her waist.

"I feel the need to ask you to keep an open mind," he said softly.

"Why?"

"Like the bridal shower, I just realized you're now going to be spending time with my family, only this time I'm here. I don't know how they're going to react to me or you."

"I think we'll be fine," she said leaning into him. "You're not judging me on lack of family. I won't judge you on your family."

That landed heavy in his chest. He understood the trauma of her not having family and having been moved around. But he hadn't given much thought to the fact that there were two people out there who created the woman he loved.

They approached his parents, and his mother reached out her hands to cup his face and kiss him. "There's my son," she said lovingly. "The one who doesn't live in my house, but left all of his stuff," she joked, but he knew that was a fight coming his way.

His father placed his hand on Ryan's shoulder, as a sign of solidarity, without a word.

Ryan's mother took Lisa's hand. "Lisa, it's nice to see you," she said, managing to maneuver her away.

"I would like the garage back," Ryan's father joked.

"I'll get to that after the wedding. I promise."

"Things are good with you two?"

They were both looking toward Ryan's mother and Lisa, huddled with his grandmothers.

"They are," Ryan said.

"I guess I should start saving for another wedding," his father teased, but Ryan heard the strain in his voice.

"I don't think Lisa and I will be having a wedding like this."

"So, you are talking about it?"

"It's new, Dad, and I've already moved in. I need to give her some time to make sure she still likes me before I propose."

His father wrapped his arm around Ryan's shoulders. "Tina loves her, and Tina has good taste in people."

He watched her smile at his grandmother who was holding her hands and telling her a story. "Yeah, she does."

EVERY NERVE IN LISA'S BODY WAS FIRING. GRANDPARENTS. AUNTS and uncles. Cousins and spouses. When did wedding rehearsals include every single member of the extended family?

Tina moved people from place to place with ease, and Lisa was happy to see her enjoying herself. Someone must have had a talk with Cicely, because Lisa was sure she hadn't even muttered one word all night.

The nicest part of the rehearsal was walking down the aisle arm in arm with Ryan.

"Do you know what the best part of Sunday morning will be?" Ryan whispered in her ear.

"What?"

"All of this will be over."

Lisa rested her head on his shoulder. Not only would it be over, but they'd wake up together.

CHAPTER FORTY-FIVE

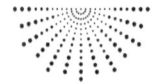

Lisa's dress hung in its bag on the door to her office. Ryan's tux hung on the coat closet door. They were expected for brunch at his parents' house at ten.

Ryan leaned against the counter drinking his second cup of coffee, absorbing it all. Weddings were a lot of work, and it wasn't even his wedding, he humored.

Lisa crossed from the bedroom to the bathroom, and just the slight glimpse of her in her robe, her hair up in curlers, set off the warmth though his body. They'd just been moving through life, each day getting them to his brother's wedding. After today, it would be their own adventure.

Ryan sipped his coffee. He'd yet to read any of her journals. A part of him wondered if he even should. Maybe it was better just to know who she was now. Would digging into her past really make him understand her more? He knew he loved her, and in a few short weeks, he'd moved in with her and made forever kinds of promises. So, they were already cemented in the now, why look back?

Lisa walked out of the bathroom and headed to the kitchen. "I swear I'm going to throw up," she said.

"Why?"

"I'm nervous. I want this to all go off without a hitch for Tina. I mean she's the first one to get married. She's been so stressed the past few weeks."

Ryan set his coffee on the counter, reached for her, and pulled her to him. "I wish I had friends like Tina does," he said gazing into those blue eyes that sent sparks through him. "What you all have is enviable. I'm not sure I'm even as close to my brother as you are with those girls."

Lisa pressed her forehead to his. "I think Aaron is happy to have you home."

"No doubt. Maybe we'll be closer now," he said reaching for the ties on her robe and untying the knot.

"What are you doing?"

Ryan let the robe open, and then he ran his hands under the fabric over her soft skin. "Just appreciating."

"We don't have time for this," she argued without moving from his touch.

"I know. This is all I'm doing. A short twelve hours from now, I can have you under me, and I don't have any plans on moving tomorrow."

THE HOUSE WAS FILLED WITH PEOPLE AND RYAN WONDERED WHY his mother had volunteered to take on something like a brunch a few hours before the wedding. Not only was his family, local and from out of town, milling around the kitchen and dining room, but all of Tina's family was there too.

He heard the door open to the garage and was happy to find that it was Lisa walking through the boxes toward him.

"Is this your secret club house?" she asked as she skirted Aaron's couch to walk toward him and sit down on his couch beside him.

She curled up next to him.

"Not much of a secret anymore," he teased, pressing a kiss to the top of her head.

"How much of this stuff is yours?"

"This couch and this side of the garage."

Lisa let out a hum. "I guess we're going to need to do some fancy configuring."

Ryan laughed. "Yeah, my father did mention he'd like his garage back."

"I guess a storage unit for now?"

Ryan shrugged. "Considering there's repeat items, like a bed, bedding, kitchen stuff, I figure I could sell most of it."

"We can combine. You don't have to get rid of all your things just to live with me."

Ryan cupped her cheek and moved them so that she was looking up at him. "Most of this is from a life I'd like to forget. When we decide to start brand new, then you and I can pick out all of this stuff again."

She licked her lips. "I didn't really consider that you've combined households before."

"This is the last time," he promised, because he'd seen her eyes go sad.

"Your grandmother must not have known about your past living arrangement. No matter how many times your mother or I say that I didn't live with you in Chicago, she doesn't believe us."

Ryan chuckled. "She's a bit senile."

"She's delightful."

"Can I ask you something?"

Lisa bit down on her lip, as if she anticipated that he'd ask her something she didn't want to talk about but would. "What?"

"Did you ever know any of your real family? I mean, did you know your grandparents?"

She drew in a soft breath. "I knew Rose's mother. She was a peach of a woman who loved me as much as she loved the boys."

"I mean your biological family."

Now she swallowed hard. "I knew what you meant," she said and readjusted on the couch. "I knew my mother's mother. She was the one who had me pulled away from my parents. She had custody of me from the time I was two. Then, she fatally overdosed while I was in the house when I was four, and the rest is history."

Her cheeks had flushed under the beautiful makeup.

"Thank you," he said pressing his forehead to hers.

"For what?"

"Sharing that with me."

Lisa pressed a gentle kiss on his lips. "Thank you for sharing your grandmothers with me."

"Grandma Alice, the senile one, bakes the best pies. Grandma Dorothy makes handmade birthday cards and sends two-dollar bills."

Lisa laughed. "Rose's mother made me the blanket on the back of my sofa."

Happy memories, he thought. She had some. He couldn't wait to meet Rose and her family. They'd provided her with those memories. And now he knew it was up to him, and her friends, to continue to create happy times for the woman he loved.

CHAPTER FORTY-SIX

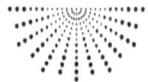

Tina had thrown up three times already, and because her hands shook, Mindy worked to fix her makeup.

"I'm going to trip and fall out there," Tina choked out as Lisa handed her a bottle of water with a straw in in.

"You're going to do just fine," Lisa said. "You are the most beautiful bride I've ever seen."

Tina smiled up at her as she sipped from the water. "Thank you," she said, handing Lisa the water. "Don't let my craziness steer you away from all of this."

Lisa thought it was the most forward-thinking thing Tina had said in months. "Oh, I'm quite sure I don't want any of this." She laughed. "This is about you. Not me."

"Okay, you look perfect," Mindy said, stepping back and looking at Tina as if she'd just painted a portrait.

Ruby nodded. "Yeah, perfect." She reached for Tina's hand and gave it a squeeze.

"I was thinking, when you get home from your honeymoon, let's meet at my house for rom com night," Mindy offered.

They all nodded in agreement.

"I'd really like that," Tina said as her father walked into the bridal suite.

"They're ready, sweetheart."

Tina's face went white again, and Lisa leaned in. "Almost there, honey. Go marry that amazing man who loves you. We'll be right beside you."

Tina nodded as each of them hugged her and headed toward the hallway, collecting their bouquets as they went.

Ryan had escorted his grandmothers to their seats. Behind him, his brother walked their parents to their seats. He kissed each of them, and when he met Ryan at the altar, he hugged him.

"Here we go," Aaron whispered.

"You're a lucky man. She's wonderful," Ryan said, and Aaron smiled as he turned toward the back of the church.

Tina's young cousins were the ring bearer and the flower girl. The ring bearer helped his little sister walk down the aisle and sprinkle flowers. But when she was done with that, halfway down the aisle, she traded him the pillow for the basket.

That received a laugh from the guests.

When the kids reached their mother, who was seated near the front, the little girl jumped into her lap. The little boy sat next to her, retrieving the pillow from his sister so that he could do his job when it was time.

Ruby was the first of Tina's friends to head toward the altar. Her red hair was styled just as Lisa's had been, with ringlets framing her face. Ruby had a unique take on being the center of attention. She made eye contact with everyone she passed. Ryan thought it was a stark contrast to Mindy who walked behind her. Her dark hair in the same style, but her eyes were focused on the runner in front of her, as if she were afraid to look at anyone. He wondered if she would realize she wasn't even smiling.

Then there was Lisa. She wasn't the bride. And she'd been

right, those dresses they wore were hideous. But when Ryan saw her, his heart rate quickened. Blonde ringlets accented her beautiful face. Those bright blue eyes sparkled at him from the back of the church, and they were on him. He only saw her, and he knew, as she walked toward them, she only saw him.

She was mesmerizing, breathtaking, and absolutely the most beautiful woman that had ever walked the planet. In just a few short weeks they'd become a happy couple. He briefly thought about the ultimatums that Tina had handed out weeks ago. God had any of that stuck, they'd only now be getting the chance to be together.

Oh, they may never have a big wedding, but he was okay with that. Hell, they may never be more than roommates, but that didn't matter. They were together, and she made him happier than he'd ever been in his life.

The closer she got to the altar, the wider he knew his smile grew. Surely, everyone who was there to witness his brother's marriage to Tina now knew what he felt for the maid-of-honor. It had to be obvious to everyone.

As she stood next to Mindy and Ruby, Lisa locked eyes with him. She was feeling everything he was. It radiated in her, and he couldn't wish this wedding to go fast enough.

Then, his attention was drawn away from her as the wedding guests stood.

Tina and her father stood at the back of the church, and now his brother's smile was as wide as Ryan's had been.

"She's gorgeous," Aaron said, seeing his bride for the first time in her dress.

"I'm happy for you," Ryan said, patting his brother's shoulder.

Tina's eyes were on his brother as they walked toward them.

They'd been brought up in a house of love, trust, and compassion. Aaron and Tina would carry that on in their marriage.

Ryan shifted his gaze to Lisa, whose eyes were damp as she watched her dear friend walk toward them.

Lisa might not have had that same upbringing, or at least not always, but he knew she had it in her to provide that kind a stability to their own marriage and to kids born of it. They'd get to that, he thought. They had a lot of learning to do about one another, but he was more than willing to put in the time.

When Tina's father kissed her on the cheek, and then hugged his brother, Ryan choked up. Then, the look of admiration between Aaron and Tina squeezed at his chest. They'd been together so long, he'd long ago forgotten there was a spark between them, but it shone brightly in that moment. Only those who stood with them knew what was in store for them, that a baby was on the way.

As the minister began the wedding, Ryan worked to control his emotions. He absolutely hadn't expected to be shaken like that.

CHAPTER FORTY-SEVEN

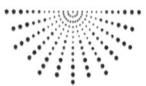

"I DO," TINA SAID WITH A VOICE FULL OF CONFIDENCE, AND LISA noticed Mindy sob.

She couldn't help but hold in her humor about Tina suddenly being so strong in the moment, and Mindy crying. But it had been a group effort to get to that point. Even Cicely was crying and dabbing her eyes.

The minister announced them as husband and wife, and when Aaron wrapped his arms around his new wife, and dipped her into a warm and romantic kiss, the church exploded into applause. It was then, Lisa felt her tears.

Tina was headed into her happily ever after. This was the last scene in every romance. This was only the beginning of wonderful memories to be made.

When Lisa looked up from Aaron and Tina, she saw that Ryan was smiling at her.

Through her smile, she let out a breath. And he was Lisa's happily ever after.

. . .

RYAN LAUGHED WHEN THE KISS HIS BROTHER LAID ON TINA WAS SO long, the minister tapped his shoulder. There was a mix of laughter and applause.

Aaron took his wife's hand, and they started down the aisle.

Then, Ryan took Lisa's hand. She gave his a squeeze, and he thought his heart could explode at that moment, it was full of love for her. And he knew it wasn't just being caught up in the moment. He loved her.

They started down the aisle, and it was the first time he looked out at the sea of guests. He didn't know anyone from Tina's side of the family. On his brother's side, there were cousins, longtime friends, aunts and uncles he couldn't even call by name. It wasn't until one of the guests waved in his direction that his heart slammed in his chest.

Courtney sat among his brother's guests. The ring he'd left in their apartment, the one he was going to propose with, sparkling on her finger. He'd noticed, because after she'd waved at him, she'd turned her hand over to show it to him.

"Are you okay?" Lisa asked softly in his ear.

He quickly worked to gain his composure as they got to the back of the church. "Yeah. I'm fine. I think I just need some water."

"I'll get you one. Maybe you had your knees locked up there."

"Right. That must have been it."

Lisa had hurried off to find him water, and his mother was the next one to approach him. But he'd been so worked up, he jumped when she touched his arm.

"Are you okay, honey?" she asked as his father moved in beside his mother.

"I'm fine. I'm fine," he repeated. "Why? Don't I look fine?"

His mother shook her head slowly. "No. You don't. You're sweating and pacing."

That was because someone had let Courtney into the church. Why was she even there?

Lisa returned with his water. "Here, maybe this will help." She looked up at his parents. "I think he locked his knees up there or something."

His mother nodded. "That's probably it." She patted Lisa's arm before they walked off.

"After they are done receiving their guests, we'll take pictures," Lisa said, but that didn't calm him.

"Do we have to receive guests?"

A smile curled up the corner of her mouth. "She asked that none of us be part of it. One, I think she wants all the attention. Two, it keeps her sister from hanging around, too. Three, I think she'd being kind to me because she knows my anxiety is at an all-time high."

Ryan studied her. "You don't look anxious."

"If I think about it, I think I could be sick," she said with an upbeat tone and it caused him to laugh.

"Good. Can we hide out until it's time for pictures?"

Lisa watched him, and he could feel the sweat on his brow. "You seem more out of sorts than I do. What's going on?"

"Let's just say I saw some guests I didn't think should be mixed in with the family."

Lisa raised a brow. "Really?"

"Yeah. As in I can't believe they'd show their faces."

She let out a low hum. "I didn't think your family had any black sheep."

Fine, he'd let her think that. That was easier. "A few. Let's just go back to the room where we got ready. They'll find us when they're ready."

Her eyes lightened. "I'm not fooling around with you in a church."

Even though every muscle in his body ached from being so tense, he laughed at that.

.   .   .

THE GUESTS HAD MOVED ON WITHIN A HALF HOUR. THEN THE wedding party was taken to the church where they took wedding photos for the next hour.

"You know, that's the first picture of us," Lisa said as she sat on Ryan's lap on the front pew.

"We haven't selfied?"

"I'm not twelve."

"I am. Why haven't we done that?" he asked as he pulled his cell phone from his pocket, held it up to them, and snapped the picture.

"If that shows up anywhere, I'll hurt you," Lisa said.

"You're a knockout."

"This dress is seriously a crime. I have a reputation on social media to uphold."

He tucked his phone back into his pocket. "I'll keep it in my secret Lisa folder."

Her eyes went wide. "You'd better not have one of those folders."

Ryan only grinned and took the sucker punch to the arm when she gave it.

CHAPTER FORTY-EIGHT

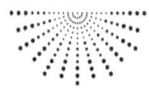

Luckily wedding receptions had protocol. The couple was ushered into the reception hall. Meals were served. Champagne was poured.

It was then Ryan realized he was going to have to speak.

"I didn't prepare anything," he leaned into Lisa.

"You didn't know you were going to be doing this?"

"No. He didn't mention it," Ryan said through gritted teeth as he stood and held up his champagne glass.

His heart was racing, and he didn't know if it was because he wasn't prepared, or if it was the number of people looking up at him in the dim reception hall.

"Where do I start? Aaron and Tina, I have to think back a long way to remember a time when the two names weren't synonymous. Tina, I remember when my brother first met you at college. He'd transferred back from the east coast, and was *not* excited to be in state," Ryan teased. "But a few weeks later, the complaints stopped, and everything was about this girl he met in math class."

Tina leaned in closer to Aaron, who draped his arm around her.

"The name Tina was in every sentence. And collectively, we knew you were the one. No one talks that much about someone, unless they're all in."

From the side of his eye, he could see Lisa dab her hers. Okay, maybe he wasn't sucking at this.

"Brother, you're a lucky man. And I know that going forth, this is going to be one of those marriages that's envied by everyone. You will be poster children for hashtag couple goals."

There was a rippling laugher that came from the crowd.

Ryan held up his glass. "To my brother, and my new sister, may you only have happiness the rest of your life. Congratulations."

The room of people applauded and both Tina and Aaron moved to him and hugged him.

Lisa wiped at her eyes again and drew in a deep breath as she stood. Her hands shook, and Ryan noticed she didn't lift her glass.

"The definition of a meet cute is when the characters of a movie or TV show meet for the first time. I wasn't there for your meet cute, but I heard all about it. That afternoon, Tina walked into the coffee shop, where I worked, and she tripped over the rug at the front door." That had drawn laughs from the guest.

"Not only had she tripped," Lisa continued, "she hit her head on one of the tables as she tried to get up." Again, more laughter.

"I remember running to her to help her up. I was genuinely concerned for my friend. But when she looked up at me, she was grinning from ear to ear. It was then I'd noticed the soda stain on her shirt."

Lovingly, Lisa looked at Tina, who smiled up at her, still wrapped in Aaron's arm.

"She'd come to tell me of this guy she'd met in math class. They had both moved in to take the same seat, and his Big Gulp Pepsi became something of a distraction between them when they ran right into each other, the Big Gulp spilling on them."

The apples of Lisa's cheeks were pink as she recalled the story. Ryan smiled up at her. He'd never known that Tina had had the same reaction as his brother, because Ryan had received a phone call with similar details.

"Usually, Tina isn't one for messes or embarrassing situations. I mean, who really is?" Lisa laughed. "I knew that day, when she was a mess of a person, so insanely excited about a boy she'd met in class, that he must be the one."

Picking up her glass, she held it out. "Tina and Aaron, I know that forever is cemented now. And I agree with Ryan, you are hashtag couple goals, and we should all be so lucky."

Everyone stood from their seats and raised their glasses. Ryan wrapped his arm around Lisa and pressed a kiss to the top of her head as everyone saluted his brother and sister-in-law.

"Meet cute?" he said in her ear as his brother and Tina were whisked off to dance their first dance.

"Yup."

"We have a meet cute too, then?" he asked.

The corner of her mouth curled up. "We do."

Ryan nodded as he scanned a look over her beautiful face, contemplating what their meet cute would be. "Rom Com Movie Club. UCLA T-shirt. Avocado mask. Pink Lemonade polish on your toes."

She inhaled as if his recollection of it had moved her. "Total meet cute, Mr. I'm-Thirty-and-Forward."

Not wanting even the chance that he'd upstage his brother by kissing Lisa, he took her hand and gave it a squeeze.

"Meet cute. Who knew?"

When the song ended, the wedding party was called to the dance floor to dance. Ryan's parents, Tina's parents, he and Lisa, and humorously Ruby and Mindy, walked to the dance floor.

He decided it was the duty of the best man to change out partners every few spins. Lisa laughed as he spun from her to

Mindy, whose face had gone instantly red. But when he spun to Ruby, he was no longer leading. Who knew she was a force to be reckon with on a dance floor? Well, now he did. He'd have to remember that if he ever needed to sign up for a competition.

CHAPTER FORTY-NINE

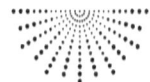

WHEN ALL THE TRADITIONAL PARTS OF THE RECEPTION WERE DONE and the cake had been cut and served, it was time to celebrate, eat, and dance.

Lisa had been dreaming of wedding cake, and when she took her first bite, it was the most delightful thing she'd tasted in a very long time.

"I assume it'll be your wedding cake we eat next," Mindy said as she stuck her fork into the slice of cake in front of her.

"I'll do wedding cake, but you can guarantee I will never, ever, have a wedding reception like this."

"He must have a hundred of his own relatives here. How do you get out of that?"

"Trust me," Lisa said as she looked out at the dance floor where Ryan danced with his mother.

He looked up at her, just as his father moved in to take his mother from him. Then, motioned to her with his crooked finger to join him on the dance floor.

"I guess I'm being summoned," she said laughing and pushing back from the table.

She joined Ryan on the dance floor, his hand moving directly to her waist as he held her hand in his.

"My mother loves you," he said, and Lisa felt her heart begin to hammer in her chest.

"She does?"

"Yep. She wanted me to know that you are delightful, beautiful, and she's envious of Tina and all her friends."

Lisa eased in even closer. "Well, that makes me feel wonderful. Rose was the only mom who ever thought those things about me."

A hand came to Ryan's shoulder, a large diamond on the ring finger. His feet stopped moving, and he looked at the brunette beside them.

"Do you mind if I cut in?" she asked, and Lisa took a step back.

"Sure," she said, realizing that everyone there knew him. She couldn't monopolize him.

Lisa sat back down at the table next to Mindy.

"Who was that?" Mindy asked.

"I don't know. Maybe a cousin or something."

"Yeah, well, I don't think so."

Lisa lifted her head to see the leggy brunette leading Ryan from the dance floor by the hand and heading out of the reception.

RYAN FOLLOWED BEHIND COURTNEY, BUT THE MOMENT THEY'D cleared the door, he yanked his hand back.

"What in the hell are you doing here?" he blasted the question in her direction so forcefully, she winced.

"I was invited."

"Are you kidding me?" Ryan ran his hand over his hair. "Who in the hell invited you?"

Her brows drew inward. "Who? Tina and Aaron. What kind of question is—"

"A very legit one. Don't you think that since we aren't together, it would have been wise to have refused the invite?" His words were sharp as he paced in front of her.

He watched as she wiped a tear from her eye, and he grabbed her hand. "And why do you have this on?" he asked looking down at the ring he'd bought for her, but never gave her.

Courtney pulled her hand back and adjusted the ring. "You left it when you took everything from our apartment."

"I forgot it."

She batted her eyes. "I thought you wanted me to have it, and that was why you left it."

"Give me a fucking break, won't you?"

"I mean it," she was sobbing now. "Ryan, I made a mistake."

"You think?" He shoved his hands into his pockets and continued to pace back and forth. "I've been moved out for months. So don't you think that if I wanted you to find the ring, I would have been waiting for you, or you might have called me?"

"I have called you. Obviously, you've blocked me, because my phone calls don't go anywhere. And when you left your last company, your email disconnected, and," she emphasized, "I don't see you on social media anymore. And I know you certainly didn't disappear from everyone."

Ryan bit down on his lip, hard. "So you thought you'd show up to my brother's wedding wearing an engagement ring, that I *didn't* give you?"

Courtney reached for him, gripping his wrist. "Ryan, please give me a chance. I'm begging for your forgiveness."

"You don't deserve my forgiveness," he hissed through gritted teeth.

"Oh, Ryan," his aunt's voice came from behind him. "I don't think I can dance anymore." She laughed as she placed her hand on his arm, just above where Courtney held him. "What is this?"

His aunt took Courtney's hand and examined the ring.

"Ryan, so this is the girl? The one from Chicago?"

Courtney looked at him, and then directly at his aunt. "Yes, ma'am."

Ryan bore a stare into her. What the hell was she doing?

"What a wonderful treat to get to meet you. There was some confusion as to which one you were," his aunt laughed.

Ryan took hold of Courtney's hand. "Auntie, I hope you'll excuse us. I need to get her to her car."

"Of course, honey."

Ryan pulled Courtney by the hand to the parking lot. "Where is your car?"

"Right over here." She pointed to her rental car.

"Well, it's time for you to go home. You shouldn't have come."

"Ryan, let's just talk," she said stepping to him, her hand on his chest.

"I can't think of anything I'd like less." He took her hand and pulled the ring from her finger. "You don't deserve this."

"I love you," she sobbed so near he could feel the heat of her breath on his skin.

"Go home."

As he turned, Courtney reached for his hand again. She pulled him to her and pressed her mouth to his.

LISA STOOD AT THE CURB AND WATCHED THE MAN SHE LOVED KISS the woman she'd learned was the same woman he'd left in Chicago. Certainly, that cake and champagne were about to come back up.

"Aren't they sweet," a voice said next to her, and Lisa hadn't even noticed the woman smoking the cigarette. "I'm his auntie Bridget," she said, but Lisa wasn't listening. Her eyes were stinging with tears and her hands shook.

Ruby rushed up next to her and her arms wrapped around her and turned her away.

"Go back inside," Ruby said.

"I want to go home."

"Go inside and get your purse. Tina is getting ready to go in the limo. The minute she heads out, I'll take you home."

Lisa took Ruby's hand. "Your home. I can't go to mine."

Ruby gave Lisa's hand a squeeze. "For as long as you need."

CHAPTER FIFTY

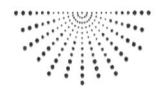

Ryan pushed back from Courtney, gripping the ring in his hand. "I don't ever want to see you again."

He turned from her as she sobbed, scrubbing his hand over his face. When he looked up, he saw Ruby standing next to his aunt. His aunt was smiling, but Ruby stood in a defensive stance with her fists on her hips.

God, had she seen all of that?

As he neared her, Ruby turned and started back toward the building.

"Ruby. Ruby!" he called after her.

Ruby stopped and turned. "Don't even think about talking to her." She pointed her finger toward him.

"This was all a misunderstanding."

"I'm sure when Lisa was watching you kiss that woman, that's what she was thinking too." Ruby turned to walk back inside, but Ryan caught her arm and spun her back.

"What do you mean when Lisa was watching?"

"It's fine," Ruby argued as she pulled from him. "She doesn't really know you. This short-term thing—"

"It's not short-term."

Ruby shook her head. "It is now."

RYAN WAS CAUGHT UP IN THE MOVEMENT WHEN HE MADE IT INSIDE. All of the guests were filing out as his brother and Tina started toward the limo that waited out front. His mother caught him, looping her arm through his.

"C'mon. We have to see them off," she said.

Ryan scanned the crowd throwing birdseed toward the newlyweds. Mindy was at the limo, holding open the door. Ruby threw birdseed in the air, but he didn't see Lisa anywhere.

Maybe she was in the bathroom, or still seated inside.

The moment the limo pulled from the curb, Mindy and Ruby hurried down the sidewalk to the parking lot. Before he could free himself from his mother, and then his grandmother, he saw a car with Ruby driving peel out of the parking lot. He couldn't tell if Lisa was in the car or not, and he had no idea where Ruby lived.

All he could do was go home and see if she'd be there, and to wait her out. He'd done nothing wrong, so if she did see it, as Ruby had said, he'd fix it.

LISA SOBBED ON MINDY'S COUCH. AS THEY'D DRIVEN AWAY FROM the reception hall, she was sure to turn off her phone. Ryan was the only person who would try to call her.

In true form, the anxiety from what she'd seen had her throwing up champagne and wedding cake. Her friends had gotten her out of the wedding reception without Tina even noticing she was missing for the sendoff.

Mindy held Lisa to her chest and stroked her hand over her hair, while Ruby made mugs of tea.

"There's an explanation," Mindy said softly. "You just need to talk."

"I'm an idiot. That's the explanation. God, who thinks they fall in love in three weeks and let's a man move into their house?" Lisa sobbed. "I'm so stupid."

Ruby walked out to the living room with three mugs balanced on a serving tray. "I can't decide if it's disturbing that you kept all of your grandmother's serving items, or if it's cute."

Mindy shook her head. "Now is not the time for that."

"Sure it is. We're going to hole up here for days and take care of our girl. Don't think I'm not going to get a few jabs in otherwise."

The banter made Lisa chuckle before another sob broke through.

Mindy readjusted to keep her protective hold on Lisa.

Ruby set the tray on the end table, and then plopped down on the ottoman, facing Lisa and Mindy.

"Who was she anyway?" Ruby asked.

"Courtney, his ex," Mindy answered, and Lisa sucked in a breath so hard she choked.

As she coughed, leaning forward with her hands on her knees, Mindy patted her back.

"Nice job," Ruby scolded.

"Shut up," Mindy returned. "Tina mentioned it when she saw her among the guests."

Lisa shook her head when she'd composed herself. "Why did they invite her? Did Tina do that to me on purpose?"

Mindy shook her head. "No."

"Then why? And have I just been some idiot falling into this? Seriously, what bad timing. I could have made a scene. I could have ruined their wedding. I could have—"

"You wouldn't have," Mindy said. "I don't think Tina, or Aaron, set you up to fall."

Lisa fell back against the couch. "God, this is a disaster. Who did I think I was for this to work out?"

"Shut up," Ruby said, earning glares from them both. "What? You've primed yourself for this. Is there a rom com you haven't seen, or that you can't quote? Your entire life is thinking that romances just happen, and men sweep women off their feet and carry them away."

"I do not."

Mindy shrugged. "You kind of do."

Lisa stood and paced a small circle. "This is all proof that I'm not worthy of love. I knew this would happen. I knew he'd leave me."

"He didn't leave you," Mindy argued.

"He was kissing another woman," Ruby replied. "His ex."

"Was he? Was he really kissing her?"

Ruby and Lisa exchanged looks.

Lisa threw her hands in the air. "She had on a ring. She was sure to make me see it when she cut in on our dance. Of course, I didn't know who she was when she did that. Then, the next time I looked up, she was holding his hand and they were walking out of the reception."

Mindy shook her head. "Listen, I'm not saying you're not right, I just think you should mellow out and then talk to him."

"I think that's a horrible idea. Maybe one of you should go to my place and change the locks."

Ruby reached into her hair and took out the first set of pins that held it in place. "How about we spend the rest of the weekend here. Then, when you know he's at work on Monday, you can go change your locks. Just lay low for a few days." She took out more pins. "When Tina gets back, then we can ask her about the woman."

Lisa held her fingers to her eyes. Did she want to know about Courtney? Truthfully, she just wanted to forget it all. She'd known better than to let his charms work on her, but they had.

From their meet cute, to their first kiss, to the first time they slept together, it had been a whirlwind that was bound to crash. If Lisa had learned anything from all the movies she watched, she knew romance didn't always win. *La La Land, Ghost, My Best Friend's Wedding, (500) Days of Summer, Shakespeare in Love*—she stopped thinking about it. God, they were right. She thought of life as a rom com, because they'd always made her feel better about her situation. But not everything ended in a happily ever after, and that included her and Ryan.

CHAPTER FIFTY-ONE

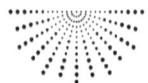

THERE HAD BEEN NO ESCAPING THE RECEPTION FOR RYAN, AS THE girls had. His grandmother took hold of his hand as they'd walked back into the hall. She'd taken time to stop and commiserate with other relatives he didn't even know.

When his grandmother had finally let go of him, his mother found him.

"We need to load up all the gifts and take them home. They'll want to open them on Monday night before they fly out," she'd said.

Irritated at the entire situation, he nodded. "I'll load them in my truck."

She scanned a look over him. "What's gotten into you?"

"I just need to get out of here."

"I see no one stuck around to help. Where did the girls go? Where is Lisa?"

Ryan bit down on the inside of his cheek. "Whose idea was it to invite Courtney?" he bit out the words.

His mother's eyes narrowed and then a line formed between her brows. "Honey, why would we invite her?"

"That's what I'd like to know."

"When you said you'd broken up and you were moving home, I took her invitation out of the box. Besides, Tina's mother kept adding people, so I just kept taking out the extra people I'd added. I didn't invite her, sweetheart."

He ran his fingers over his hair. "She showed up. And she was wearing this," he said pulling the ring from his pocket.

"What is that?"

"The engagement ring I bought for her and forgot in the apartment when I left."

"Ryan, why would she do that?"

"She was apologizing."

"For what?"

God, he hadn't shared all the details with his mother because it had just seemed like a bad idea at the time. And now, it seemed like a worse idea. But what choice did he have?

"I caught her cheating on me. I moved out a few weeks later and moved home. A buddy had put me up, and then they laid me off. It all just lined up."

"Why didn't you tell me all of this?"

"You were busy planning a wedding. No one needed my sob stories. But now, I need to make Lisa understand that—"

"Where did Lisa go?"

Ryan shrugged as he dropped the ring back into his pocket. "I don't know. The girls took off with her. She saw me and Courtney together."

"Well, if she saw you, then she knows there is nothing between you."

Ryan ran his hand over the back of his neck. "Leave it to Courtney to screw that up. She kissed me, and that's when Lisa saw us."

"Oh, Ryan," his mother sighed and pressed her hand to her chest. "Surely she'll be at home when you get there."

"I'm sure she won't be. Those girls aren't going to let me near her."

"Call them."

"I don't have their numbers."

"I'm sure Tina—"

"I'm not going to do that to Tina." Ryan let out a long hard breath. "I'm not going anywhere. At some point, she's going to have to talk to me."

His mother lifted her hand to his cheek. "I really like her Ryan. I hope she understands that there was a misunderstanding."

He did too.

RYAN WASN'T TOO SURPRISED THAT LISA WASN'T AT THE CONDO. She'd turned off her phone right after she'd left the reception. His calls went directly to voicemail and his texts hadn't been delivered.

For the next few hours, he paced through the house, stopping frequently at her office door, wondering if there was something inside that would tell him where she was.

No, he'd give her that space.

There was no doubt in his mind that she was with Ruby and Mindy.

Ryan sat down on the couch in the silence. He clasped his hands and pressed them to his forehead. The ring he'd bought for Courtney was on his pinkie. Now Ryan wished he'd gone back after it when he'd realized it had been left in the apartment. But in that moment, he hadn't thought about anything other than getting as far away from Courtney as possible.

Surely his mother could help him sell it. He needed it out of his life.

Ryan decided to settle in. He knew Lisa wasn't coming home. And though, in their situation, he worried about her. There was never a time when he wanted her sad and miserable, but he knew she was with people who would coddle her and take care of her.

In that moment, he was envious of the relationship that the girls had.

Ryan picked up the remote, kicked his feet up on the coffee table, and turned on the TV. No surprise, Lisa had a rom com paused.

He pressed play and watched Meg Ryan standing in the middle of the road in Seattle watching Tom Hanks and Rita Wilson hug.

Sitting up straighter, he watched Meg Ryan's character, Anne, process what she was seeing, when Hanks starts toward her. He'd always thought *Sleepless in Seattle* was one of the strangest romances he'd ever seen, but in that moment, he felt as if it had been cued up for him to process his situation.

Courtney had kissed him. That much was true. But he hadn't kissed her back. As far as he'd been concerned, Courtney had been removed from his life.

Laying the remote to his side on the couch, he watched Meg Ryan fly back to Baltimore and reconsider her life.

Much like the romance in the movie, his romance with Lisa wasn't over. He wasn't going to walk away, and Ruby and Mindy couldn't keep Lisa from him forever. He could be patient. But in the end, Ryan wanted his happily ever after and he wanted it with Lisa.

CHAPTER FIFTY-TWO

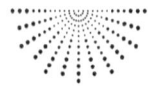

Lisa pushed open the door to her condo on Monday morning and stood with the sun behind her, looking into the dark space.

He'd been there. She could smell his cologne and the faint scent of coffee.

Everything was tidy, more so than when they'd run out of the house Saturday morning for the breakfast at Ryan's parents' house.

Lisa slid her keys back into her purse and closed the door behind her. She walked slowly, as if she were awaiting him to walk out of the bedroom, or something. It was then she saw the large bouquet of daisies.

She swallowed hard as she walked toward them. There was a folded note on the counter and her hands shook as she reached for it.

"Don't you think daisies are the friendliest flower?" Lisa's lip trembled, and tears pooled in her eyes. He'd quoted *You've Got Mail*.

When she'd batted back the tears, she read the rest of the note.

Everything went wrong on Saturday, and I just need a few minutes to explain it to you. Tonight, when you're at my parents' house watching them open their gifts, I only ask for a few minutes. If what I have to say doesn't change your feelings about me, well, at least I got to tell you my side. I need to talk to you. No matter what you think, you need to know I love you.

Lisa had forgotten about them going to Ryan's parents' house to watch Tina and Aaron open their presents.

She couldn't do it. Already she felt sick, so she'd just call it in.

Besides, Tina didn't need the drama. It would resonate hard, and Lisa couldn't have Tina's upcoming honeymoon ruined by her tainted love life.

Lisa pulled her phone from her pocket. It had been off since she'd left the reception. Even if she turned it on to text the girls that she couldn't make it to the gift opening, she'd surely see the many texts and voicemails Ryan left. She just wasn't where she could deal with that.

Okay, maybe she'd just no show.

When there was a knock at the door, Lisa jumped, and her hand went directly to her heart, which now thudded rapidly.

Logic had her standing there, in the dimly lit condo hoping whoever it was would go away.

They knocked again.

"Lisa?" she heard the male voice, but didn't right away recognize it. "Hon, are you home? I tried calling."

The voice had deepened over time, and now held the slightest inflection of a British accent.

Lisa hurried to the door and pulled it open.

There on the other side, all grown up, a full beard, with those dark and kind eyes, stood Jason Hughes—Mama Rose's son.

"Oh my God!" Lisa lunged herself at him, wrapping her arms around him.

Jason picked her up and squeezed her. "Hey, squirt."

She laughed. Oh, it felt good to laugh.

"You're here," she said looking him over after he'd set her back down. "I mean, you're on my doorstep. I could have picked you up from the airport."

Jason chuckled, and it was deep, and all grown up. "I've been calling you for days. I just figured mom had the wrong phone number."

Her shoulders dropped and she bit down on her bottom lip.

Jason studied her. "And I don't have the wrong number, something is wrong."

Lisa batted her eyes to ward off any tears. "It's nothing. Come in."

When they turned to walk into the condo, she realized just how dark it was. She hurried to the patio doors and opened the blinds. Then she opened the blinds over the sink.

"Can I make you some coffee?" she turned toward the coffee maker as Jason sat down on one of the stools at the counter.

"Sure. And then you can tell me why you're so fidgety."

"Am I?" she let out a little laugh as she began filling the filter with grounds.

"Yes, and I'm going to guess it's over that man that Mom told me about."

Lisa pressed her hands flat to the counter. "I really don't want to talk about it."

"That's too bad," Jason said, leaning in on his forearms on the counter. "I'm family and I think under law you're required to spill all details to your family."

Lisa's chest hurt when he said that. She covered her mouth, because a sob would certainly escape if she didn't. She was still turned away from him, but when his hands came to her shoulders, she knew she hadn't hidden it well.

Jason turned her to face him and wiped away the tears that rolled over her cheeks with his thumbs.

"Go sit on the couch, I'll finish this. And then I want to hear all about him."

"There's nothing to tell."

"If there wasn't, you wouldn't be crying."

Lisa took his hands in hers and gave them a squeeze. "No one else in the world has ever said that they were my family," she let the sob shake her breath. "My friends are my family, and you all have been too."

"But we left." He pressed his forehead to hers. "It took Mom years to recover from leaving you here."

"Really?"

"We all love you, Lisa. You have no idea what a hole it put in our lives to not have you with us. But," his voice rose in a happier pitch, "you found those girls and you've made quite a life for yourself. We're all so proud of you."

A laugh broke through the sob. "Really?"

"Go sit down. Do you have to go anywhere today?"

Lisa worried her bottom lip. "Tina and her husband are opening their presents tonight before they go on their honeymoon."

"Great. I'm tagging along. I need to meet these girls."

"Oh, you don't—"

"Lisa, go sit down. Because until we leave for that, we're going to catch up. I've missed my big sister and I want to know everything that you've done since I got dragged away from you."

He kissed her forehead, turned her around, and gave her a small shove toward the couch.

CHAPTER FIFTY-THREE

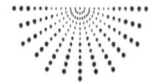

RYAN WIPED UP THE COFFEE HE'D SPILLED ON HIS PANTS IN THE board meeting. His head wasn't in the game this morning, and everyone who had to deal with him knew it.

He'd checked his phone no less than fifty times that morning, but his messages hadn't been delivered, and Lisa hadn't reached out.

The daisies were a long shot, but all he could do now was hope she'd give him time to talk.

Anger pulsed through his veins even days later, because if he lost Lisa over Courtney's little stunt—well, somehow, there'd be hell to pay.

There was a tapping at his office door, and when he looked up, his boss was standing there, his hand braced on the doorjamb.

"Ryan, do you have a minute?"

Ryan tossed the paper towel into the trash. "Yeah."

His boss walked in and closed the door behind him. "You seem a little off kilter this morning. I just want to make sure everything is okay."

God, had he really made such a scene? "I'm fine. It's the Mondayest of Mondays."

His boss chuckled. "Coffee on khakis is never good."

"Very much so."

"Well, if you need to take a personal day, you let me know."

Ryan nodded. "I do appreciate that. I think I have it under control," he said and knew it was an absolute lie.

"You're a great asset to have here. Our clients have been really pleased with what you're giving them."

That seemed to boost his mood a bit. "I'm glad to hear that."

His boss opened the door. "But if you need anything, just let me know."

"Thanks."

Ryan watched his boss walk out, casual in his own khakis and a button-down shirt rolled at the sleeves. Ryan didn't peg his boss to even be as old as he was, but he got the respect he deserved. Maybe it was because he cared enough about his employees to take a moment to be sure they were okay.

Lillian from accounting, and the woman with the office next to Ryan's peeked her head through his door.

"Dude, are you really seeing that Lisa gal from *Lisa Does Dishes* on YouTube?"

Ryan raised his brows. "You know her?"

"I know her show. I saw your face on her last video."

"Seriously?" There was a lightness in his voice that he hadn't expected.

"Yes, seriously. Didn't you know she was making a video of you?"

They'd made a simple dinner one night, spaghetti and meatballs, but she'd walked him through it and had three different lights with recording devices going.

"I guess I did. I just didn't know it posted."

Lillian laughed. "You're internet famous now," she said.

"Whatever," Ryan humored as he typed YouTube into his browser.

"It has a million views already, and the comments want to know who the sexy guy with her is."

He could feel his face go warm. "It says that?"

"Yes," she laughed again. "I think if you ever break up with her and put a personal video on YouTube, you'll be fine in the dating department."

"Well, if I have anything to say about it, I won't ever be breaking up with her."

"Serious thing, huh?"

"I'd sure like to think so," he said as the video came up on Lisa's channel and Lillian walked away.

The comments were in his favor he realized as he watched them cooking in her kitchen, but the happiness didn't come from the outpouring of internet love. The happiness the video brought was hearing her voice and seeing her smile. It had only been a few days, but he felt as if his heart had been ripped from his chest and stomped on.

They were all meeting at his parents' house at six-thirty. If he left work a few minutes early, he could stop by her house, say his piece, and they could go together. Because once she finally talked to him, she'd understand, right? Seriously, how stupid was it to be worked up over what happened?

He turned off the video.

Why would he have tried to sabotage what he and Lisa had, at his brother's wedding of all places, by giving his ex-girlfriend a ring and kissing her. The whole thing sounded like it had been written for one of Lisa's rom coms.

With that in mind, he had to consider that even all of those rom coms, always had a huge misunderstanding that eventually was rectified.

Okay, he thought as he refocused on his work. He'd just assume that rectification of this horrible misunderstanding was coming.

CHAPTER FIFTY-FOUR

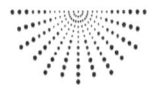

Jason sat next to Lisa on the couch, and she couldn't help but stare at him. When they'd left for England, Jason was twelve. Now he sat on her couch, a man of almost thirty, with a full beard, and deep manly voice.

"You look really good, by the way," he said as he sipped his coffee. "Mom watches you all the time on YouTube. She's made everything you've posted, and she boasts about you to everyone she knows. *That's my girl,* she says."

Lisa was grateful that the smile she wore was so wide that it nearly hurt. Rose loved her. The entire Hughes family loved her.

"You have no idea how happy that makes me," Lisa said.

"Yeah, I do. You should see your smile. And Mom told me she met your man too. That's big news, Lees."

She felt the smile fade. "Well, I don't know where that stands now."

Jason raised a brow. "Why?"

"It's really not important."

"Bullshit," he said, and Lisa couldn't help but feign a bit of shock by his language. "Yeah, I'm not twelve anymore," he said as if he knew what she'd been thinking. "Tell me about him."

Lisa chewed the inside of her cheek giving it some thought. "Ryan is Aaron's brother. Aaron married Tina."

"Okay. I'm going to need a notepad, aren't I?"

She had to laugh at that. "He lost his job in Chicago, the company downsized. His girlfriend was sleeping with someone else."

"Ouch."

"And he moved home. He came over during rom com night and we just really hit it off."

"Mom said the two of you looked smitten. And she said it was early when she called you, and he was here."

Again, the heat rose in Lisa's cheeks. "I know I'm old enough to have men sleep over, but I really feel dirty about your mom saying that."

Jason shrugged. "She's so giddy over my brother having another baby, she doesn't think about those kinds of things being bad anymore."

Lisa shook her head. "Good. I never want to fall out of her good graces."

"I can't imagine there is anything you could do to make that happen." He nudged her knee with his. "Keep going. I'm not going to let you skip around this."

That was too bad, she thought. "There's not much more to it than that. We started seeing each other almost immediately. We fell in love and I asked him to move in."

"Nice and tidy."

"Sure."

"And yet he's not here for me to meet him."

Lisa rubbed her fingers over her forehead. "At the wedding I saw him kissing his ex-girlfriend."

Jason's face contorted in a confused look, but she thought he should have been angrier.

"His ex-girlfriend, whom he dated in Chicago?"

"Yes."

"She lives here now?"

"I don't think so," Lisa admitted.

"Why was she here?"

"Well, I don't know. All I know is she cut in when we were dancing. I thought she was a cousin or something, but she was flashing a big diamond. Anyway, they left the dance floor holding hands, and when I went out to the parking lot, he was kissing her."

Jason put down his coffee. "And you, who has every screwy romantic movie ever made memorized, don't think this all sounds a little screwy too?"

"Are you defending him?"

Jason held up a hand. "I'm saying, it all sounds a bit contrived. I mean he's with you. The ex shows up with a ring and kisses him? C'mon, Lees. Why would he do that at his brother's wedding?"

Her mouth went dry. "Because men are stupid."

He frowned. "Not all of us are. I mean, I guess if he hates his brother and his brother's new wife, then yeah, screw up their wedding."

Lisa pulled her lip between her teeth to keep it from trembling. "You think she just planned that?"

Now he smiled. "If you wanted to make an impression where no one was going to make a big scene, sure. God, seriously, isn't there a movie about this that would prove it to you?"

Probably. Maybe. Well, now she wasn't thinking about movies with happily ever afters. She was wondering if her brother was talking foolishly or maybe he had some real thought on the matter.

"Listen, Lees, all I know is you should talk to the man. Have you done that?"

"No."

"You left the wedding. Turned off your phone, which also stopped me from getting in touch with you," his brows rose again, "and you just assume that what you saw is the truth and he's one more person to upset your balance and leave you."

She took a breath to speak, but nothing came out. Lisa stood, and Jason stood too. A move she knew was to intimidate her with sheer height.

"Go tonight and talk to him. You owe this to yourself. And, since I've been on the other end of many of your fights, I know what you'll give him. So do some listening too. If it's over, then there's that. If it's not, I'd hate to see you miss out on something amazing."

Lisa moved into Jason and wrapped her arms around him. "Twelve-year-olds are really smart."

He laughed. "Yeah, we're going to have to fix your perception of me."

"I know. You have a beard."

"Mom doesn't care for it."

She looked up at his face and gave the beard a tug. "I like it."

"It gives me some age," he admitted. "I guess if it doesn't work out with the two of you, I could move in and be your roommate."

Lisa puckered her lips. "My spare is my office."

"That's a shame. This is a nice place."

Running her tongue over her teeth, Lisa looked him over again. "I think I know of a place you could stay until you get settled."

"Really?"

"My friend Ruby is currently roommateless."

"Oh yeah?"

"Now, here's my big sister warning."

"I'm all ears."

"She's often roommateless."

Jason considered. "As in there's something wrong with her?"

Lisa shrugged.

"Will she be there tonight?" he asked.

"She should be."

"Point her out. I'll see if it feels right or not. Then you can make that happen—or not."

Lisa rested her head on Jason's chest and squeezed her arms around him tightly. "I'm so glad you're here now. I'm going to love having family around."

CHAPTER FIFTY-FIVE

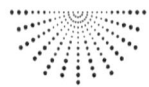

Traffic getting out of downtown had been a pain in the ass. So much for leaving early, it sure hadn't helped.

When Ryan pulled up in front of the condo complex, he noticed that the parking lot appeared to be full. Seriously, was someone having a party?

His eyes went directly to Lisa's door as he slowly drove past. He watched as it opened, and at that moment, he saw a parking space open on the street and he pulled in.

Just as he put the truck in park and opened the door, he watched a man walk out of Lisa's place, and she followed, locking the door behind her.

He stayed seated in the truck, watching as the man waited for her, and when she caught up to him, she tucked her arm in to his and they walked toward her car.

Ryan set his jaw. Seriously, she hadn't talked to him in days because of Courtney, and here she was on the arm of some bearded man who made her smile.

He slammed the door to his truck and sped off. It looked as if he'd be spending his evening on his couch in his parents' garage. No need to make any kind of appearance for the night, but maybe just knowing he was in the house would make Lisa horribly uncomfortable.

TINA PULLED OPEN THE DOOR WITH A SQUEAL. SHE PULLED LISA into her arms. "Wasn't it beautiful? It turned out to be the perfect day, didn't it?"

Lisa hugged her friend. "It was beautiful."

"We're going to make our big announcement tonight," she whispered into Lisa's ear.

"That'll be perfect."

Tina eased back as she looked beyond Lisa. "Who is this?"

Lisa reached back for Jason's hand. "Tina, this is my brother Jason."

Tina's eyes went wide. "No kidding? Hughes?" Lisa nodded, and Tina pushed past her and hugged Jason. "Oh, my gosh, it's so nice to meet you."

"You as well," he said as Tina eased back. "I hope you don't mind that I tagged along."

"Of course not," Tina said as she waved Aaron over. "This is Lisa's brother, Jason."

Lisa noticed Aaron's face flash confusion, but he recovered and shook Jason's hand. "I'm Aaron, Tina's husband. It's nice to meet you."

"You too. And congratulations on getting married."

"Thanks. I'm so glad it's over," Aaron laughed, and Tina elbowed him in the ribs. "Can I get you a beer?"

"I'd like that."

Jason followed Aaron and Tina laced her arm through Lisa's. "Where is Ryan?"

Lisa stopped walking and Tina looked up at her. "His truck is out front. I assume he's here somewhere. I have no idea."

Tina managed to move them into the hallway away from the

family members that had gathered in the house. "Something's wrong. What's going on?"

"Tina, it's not important."

"Don't give me that," she scolded. "You don't have to protect my feelings anymore."

"You're still in wedding mode. I'm not going to discuss this with you. You're going to open your gifts, go on your honeymoon—"

"And worry about you the entire time?" Tina interrupted. "Now tell me what the hell happened."

Lisa drew in a deep breath and told Tina what had occurred. But instead of Tina growing angry at Ryan for what had happened, she folded her arms in front of her. "We didn't invite her," Tina said sternly. "I saw her there but didn't think she'd cause issues."

"If you didn't invite her, why was she there?"

Tina puckered her lips. "I'm going to find out, but if you throw away what you and Ryan have over some tart's public show, you're stupid."

Lisa stood staring at her friend. Was she seriously calling Lisa out on this? This was not her fault. But she supposed if it was Courtney putting on a show, then it wasn't Ryan's fault either.

Well, shit.

Ryan heard voices as the door to the garage opened. He'd been hoping to hide out all night, so knowing his space was going to be invaded had his mood plummet even more.

"We have all our shit out here," he heard his brother's voice. "So we made ourselves a little man cave."

Someone else laughed from behind his brother as Aaron cleared the boxes and then jumped back seeing Ryan seated on the couch.

"Shit, bro. I didn't even know you were here," Aaron said.

"Looks like this is where I am. What are you doing out here? I thought you had gifts to open."

"I was getting Jason a beer," his brother walked out from the boxes, and the man that had been in Lisa's house followed Aaron.

Ryan kept his feet crossed on top of the cooler. "There are beers in the house."

"What is up your ass?"

Ryan shifted his look to Jason, who obviously felt the burn of it, because the man took a step back.

"Just go back in the house and leave me the hell alone."

Aaron kicked Ryan's feet off the cooler and that had him standing up, nose to nose with his brother.

"I should punch you." Aaron squared up. "Lisa's inside, maybe I should get her to straighten your ass out."

"Fuck you," Ryan spit out the words. "Why would she give a shit about me out here when she's got him?" He pointed to the man lingering by the boxes.

The man's eyes went wide. "I think I'll go back inside. I didn't mean to cause any problems." He turned and headed back into the house. At least she picked one with some brains.

Ryan should have kept his attention on his brother, because he was totally unprepared for the slap he received to the back of his head.

"Way to make an impression, asshole," Aaron said, his stance ready to smack Ryan again.

"What the hell do I care what kind of impression I make? Two days of shutting me out of her life, and she's got that guy in her house."

Aaron shook his head. "I don't have a goddamned idea what you're talking about, but that guy should have free access to her and her house at any time."

"Wow, way to back me up, bro."

"You are a freaking moron. That's her brother."

CHAPTER FIFTY-SIX

RYAN RAKED HIS FINGERS THROUGH HIS HAIR. *HER BROTHER.*

"As in Rose's kid? The doctor?" he asked, keeping his fingers in his hair and gripping.

"I don't know. They said her brother. What the hell are you talking about she's shut you out?"

Ryan moved his hands to the back of his neck and gripped them there. "Courtney was at your wedding, wearing the ring I had bought to give her when I proposed."

"You proposed to someone at my wedding that wasn't Lisa?"

Ryan dropped his hands. "Are you even listening to me? Courtney is my ex. You've met her plenty of times."

"Right. Okay."

"I left the ring in the apartment when I moved. And you guys invited her to the wedding."

"We did?"

"Someone did," he said as the door to the garage opened again.

Tina appeared from between the boxes, her cheeks red, her hands fisted on her hips.

"You kissed her?" she shot out the accusation and Aaron slowly turned his attention from his wife back to Ryan.

Ryan set his jaw. "No. She kissed me. Lisa saw that."

"Oh, yeah she did."

"I was trying to get Courtney out of there."

"Well, she shouldn't have been there," Tina said, slipping her hand into Aaron's as if to steady herself.

"I didn't ask her to be there," Ryan said. "I don't know what the hell she was thinking."

Tina gripped Aaron's arm with her free hand, as if to keep him close. "The invitation went out by mistake." Her lips flattened and her jaw tightened. "Your mom took her invitation out of the box when you broke up and put it in the pile of *don't send out.* But I took the box home with me, and my mother sent them out." She bit down on her bottom lip. "Ryan, I'm so sorry."

"Yeah, well, Lisa hasn't talked to me since then. She didn't go home. She didn't reach out. She just cut me off." He plopped back down onto the couch. "You two should go back inside and open your gifts."

Tina moved from Aaron and sat down next to Ryan on the couch. "We want you inside. We're going to announce the pregnancy too."

"I'm better off in here. I don't think I can see her and know she hates me."

"I don't hate you," Lisa's voice came from between the boxes before she appeared.

Tina stood and reached for Aaron's hand. "We'll go in. We'll wait for you two."

TINA REACHED OUT FOR LISA'S HAND AND GAVE IT A SQUEEZE AS they passed by her. Her heart hammered in her chest looking at Ryan on the couch in his parents' garage.

She wrapped her arms around herself.

Ryan shifted his gaze to her. "Are you just going to stand there?"

"I'm not sure what to say," Lisa said stepping into the clearing behind Aaron's couch.

"Well, something would be nice. You've shut me out for the past few days, so anything would be a start."

A million things ran through her head. Everything that had happened in the past three days was all about her. Not once had she thought about Ryan and what he'd been going through.

Now she knew how the invitation got into Courtney's hands, and she just had to ask the questions to get the rest of her answers.

"If you're not going to say anything, I don't see any reason for you to just stand there and—"

"Why did you kiss her?" Lisa blurted out the question before he dismissed her.

Ryan scrubbed his hands over his face. "I didn't kiss her."

"I saw you."

"You saw her kiss me. I guess you didn't notice I wasn't embracing her. You didn't notice me push her away, trying to get her into that damn car so she'd leave. No, you saw what you wanted to see, and then you held it over me."

"What was I supposed to think?"

"That something didn't seem right." He stood as his voice rose in pitch. "I fucking moved in with you and told you I love you. You think I'd make sure my ex, who, let me remind you, cheated on me in my own bed, was at the wedding? Yep," he threw his hands in the air, "that sounds like a hell of a story. You know, I think I'll ruin everything my brother has put into this wedding. I'm going to date and fall in love with one of the bridesmaids, and then, I'll send for my ex, give her a fucking ring, and kiss her in front of the woman I *want* to marry. Yeah, that's a solid plan right there, Lisa."

Her jaw trembled and there was no holding back the tears

that fell from her eyes. But Ryan didn't move toward her. He stood with his hands on his hips still defensive, and she couldn't blame him.

"I know they sent out the invitation by mistake."

"Well, at least you're getting some of the story now."

"I just assumed—"

"You just assumed I was like everyone else in your life. I was going to turn you away. Well, here I am. I'm not the one that turned you away. You turned me away."

Lisa wiped frantically at her cheeks. "What else was I supposed to think?"

"You were supposed to believe in me enough to ask questions."

"You walked out of the hall holding her hand," she reminded him.

His jaw twitched. "She pulled me from the hall, and I thought that was the best idea. I wasn't there to ruin my brother's wedding," he shouted.

"The ring?"

"I left it in the apartment in my haste to get out."

Lisa blinked hard. "You don't love her?"

Ryan threw his hands up. "I love you. God, how many times do I—"

"You don't." Lisa moved to him, almost afraid to touch him. "You still love me?"

"I've never stopped. And if you walk out of this garage, and leave me and my shit for good, I'll still love you. I didn't do anything to hurt you—not on purpose."

With her entire body shaking, Lisa stepped to him, pressing her hands to his ridged chest. "Did you really think I'd come here with another man?"

He rose a brow. "You did come here with another man."

Lisa chuckled and felt the muscles under her fingertips soften slightly. "I did." Lifting her arms to circle his neck, she wondered if he'd touch her, but he still didn't move. "Jason showed up at my door this morning. It appears I've had my phone off, so he couldn't tell me he was coming."

"You knew he would be here," Ryan reminded her.

"I didn't know when," she admitted. "And for the record, he thinks I'm a little crazy for how I've handled this."

Now his hands came to her hips. "I think your brother is a smart man."

"He's a doctor you know," she lifted her eyes to meet his as she smiled.

"I had heard." Ryan lowered his head so that their foreheads pressed together. "I don't love her. Courtney," he added. "I'm not sure I ever did."

"It's okay."

"I mean it. Nothing has ever felt like it does with you. No matter the length of time we've been together, I just know with you, it's different."

His hands moved to the small of her back and he pulled her closer. As their chests pressed together, she knew she'd been foolish for thinking such things, but it had been hard when she'd seen them with her own eyes.

"This is going to happen again." Lisa lifted her head to look him in the eye. "I mean, it's wired into me."

"And forever is wired into me."

She let out a long, unsteady breath. "Are you really willing to go through this again? I don't know what will ever set it off."

"At your lowest, you had those girls right by your side. I know that if this happens again, where you feel unworthy, unloved, or just out of control, you'll go to them. But from here on out, I'm in that loop, okay? You can sleep on Ruby's couch for a month, as long as I know you're safe and where you are."

Lisa wrapped herself around Ryan again, tighter this time. "I promise."

They heard the door from the house open. "Are the two of

you coming in here or not?" Tina's voice rang through the stacks of boxes. "This baby will be here before I get to announce it."

Lisa laughed as she buried her face into Ryan's chest. "We'll be right there," Lisa said.

"You guys are okay? You figured it out?"

"We'll be right there," Ryan answered this time. "We just need to clean up the blood spatter on the walls."

"Jeez," they heard Tina sigh out the word before the door closed.

Ryan brought his hands to her cheeks and eased her back so that their eyes met. "It's only you, baby. I don't want anyone else. I don't want to live anywhere else. And I don't want anyone else wearing my old college T-shirts to movie night."

Lisa chuckled. "I'm so sorry."

He kissed her forehead. "We're moving on. Don't be sorry." He wiped away the traces of tears with the pads of his thumbs. "I'm going to need you to introduce me to your brother again. I don't think I made the right first impression."

CHAPTER FIFTY-SEVEN

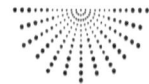

ROM COM MOVIE CLUB HAD STARTED BACK UP A MONTH AFTER Tina got married.

After they had watched *While You Were Sleeping*, that fateful night Lisa had met Ryan with her face full of avocado mask, it had moved on to Ruby's house in July.

Ruby had chosen *Crazy, Stupid, Love*. She had a hard crush on Steve Carell, though she was all in with his older look. Mindy argued that no one really had abs like Ryan Gosling, and Lisa mouthed the words to the entire silly rom com. Tina sat with her feet kicked up on the ottoman rubbing her still flat stomach, but no one commented.

In August, Mindy hosted movie night, but she'd pulled out all the stops and set up the gazebo with pillows, snacks, and a projection screen. Twinkling lights encircled the gazebo and draped across the little back yard. Lisa was damn sure she could live happily ever after in that very spot. Maybe if she and Ryan did ever decide to get married, they could get married right there. Small. Intimate. Special.

Mindy chose *Fifty First Dates*, and though comic genius, they all knew it so well, they managed to plan Tina's baby shower while the movie played.

Tina and Aaron opened their new house to movie night in September, and it was the first time they allowed the guys to join them, including Jason. Tina chose rom com gold with *When Harry Met Sally*.

"I couldn't have been your friend," Ryan whispered in Lisa's ear as they cuddled together in their pajamas and NYU T-shirts on the oversized chair.

Lisa tipped her face toward Ryan's. "You wouldn't have been my friend?"

"I said couldn't have been. I found you too irresistible the minute I saw you."

"I know what I looked like when you met me."

"Point still stands." He kissed the top of her head. "I guess that's why I dragged you to bed so quickly," he whispered.

"I guess you're right. We couldn't have been friends."

October's movie night was Lisa's to host. She'd spent the morning cleaning and preparing special treats. Now she fussed with the final details before her friends arrived.

"When are you leaving?" she called through the condo to Ryan.

"They're picking me up," he called back as there was a knock on the door.

Lisa tightened her ponytail and opened the door. Ruby and Mindy walked through, each with a tray of desserts.

"You brought brownies and cookies?" Lisa took the trays.

Ruby shrugged. "I'm PMSing, I need sugar."

Mindy shook her head. "We're all going to gain ten pounds tonight. I feel as if we've been helping Tina gain her baby weight."

Lisa laughed. "I can't think of a better reason to gain weight."

Ryan finally emerged from the bedroom. He was going out

with Jason and Aaron, but he was dressed in a button down, a nice pair of slacks, and shined shoes.

"Where are you guys going?" she asked as he walked toward her, kissed her, and then took a brownie from the tray in her hand.

"No idea."

Lisa set the trays on the counter. "Well, you look like you're going to some fancy restaurant."

He shrugged. "I guess we'll see," he said as the door opened and Aaron and Tina walked through.

Aaron wasn't dressed quite as nice as Ryan, and when Jason walked in behind them, he too was casual. She wasn't sure why he wanted to spend a Saturday night dressed as if he were going to work, but she did like looking at him like that.

"Okay, we're out of here," Ryan said as he moved in and wrapped his arms around Lisa. "Get those toes painted and those masks on." He winked.

"If you'd get out of here, we would."

"I enjoyed staying last month. My skin has never felt better and I still have red on my toes."

She shook her head and laughed. "That was a one-time deal. Now go."

He pressed one more kiss to her lips before they disappeared.

Tina held her hands on her now slightly swollen belly. "Aaron was acting funny on the way over here. Do you think they're going to a strip club or something?"

Ruby let out a snort of a laugh. "Oh, that's funny. We should put on our masks and follow them. Wouldn't that be the worst thing ever if the women followed the men into a strip club looking like we do?"

Mindy looked at Ruby, and her face had gone pale. "You're kidding, right?"

Ruby scooped up a handful of M&Ms and popped a few in her mouth. "Girl, loosen up."

Before they poured their wine, or started the movie, they applied their facial masks and painted their nails.

"What are we watching?" Tina asked as they all squeezed in on the couch.

"*Sweet Home Alabama.*"

"God, I love this one," Ruby wiggled beside Lisa and Tina.

Lisa picked up the remote and started the movie. After the opening credits, the scene jumped to the moment the lights turned on in Tiffany's and Patrick Dempsey's character told Reese Witherspoon's character to choose a ring.

"What the?" Lisa picked up the remote again, but before she could restart the movie, it cut to Sandra Bullock on her knee in front of Ryan Reynolds when she asked him to marry her in *The Proposal*. Again, it jumped.

Bill Pullman was sliding a ring through the coin drop to Sandra Bullock asking her if he could ask her a question in *While You Were Sleeping*, and then there was Billy Crystal telling Meg Ryan that as soon as he realized he wanted to be with her he wanted that time to start right now in *When Harry Met Sally*.

"I don't know what happened here," Lisa said holding the remote toward the TV, when the door opened.

All four of the women turned their charcoal covered faces to the door.

A smiling trio of men walked through, and Ryan immediately dropped to his knee and opened a ring box.

Ruby reached for her phone and began to record the moment.

"Don't you dare," Lisa shot the words at her.

"Screw you. I'm capturing this!"

Lisa stood and walked around the couch. "What are you doing?"

"I thought my little video would tell you."

Lisa looked at the TV, now stuck on Richard Gere climbing the fire escape toward Julia Roberts at the end of *Pretty Woman*.

"You did that?"

He was grinning up at her. "Yes. So?"

"Are you seriously proposing to me while I look like this?"

Ryan nodded. "You looked like that when I fell in love with you. I thought it was only appropriate to ask you to be my wife looking that way."

Tears began to roll over her cheeks and into the mask.

"Really? You want to marry me?"

"Yes. So?"

Lisa dropped down in front of him, but she didn't look at the ring. The ring just didn't matter.

"I'm a lot to handle," she said.

"Look around you. We've got your back." He took the ring from the box, set the box on the ground, and took her hand. "Tell me you'll marry me. You'll wear my T-shirts to movie night. You'll let me love you forever."

Lisa hiccupped a breath as she nodded her head. "Yes. Yes, I will do all those things."

Ryan slid the ring on her finger. "Quick love," he said. "Our trope?"

"You're learning."

EPILOGUE

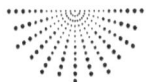

Colorado was always iffy when it came to weather, especially in November. But when Lisa had mentioned getting married in Mindy's back yard on the gazebo, Ryan knew it had to happen.

They'd rented outdoor heaters and white folding chairs for the yard. Though the day had been unseasonably warm, the afternoon could grow rather cold. Mindy already had the twinkling lights draped across the yard, and she'd set up the dining room for a small reception after.

Lisa hadn't wanted anything big. Small was more her style. But the girls had persuaded her to go dress shopping, which she'd agreed to. And when she'd found a dress, which was much nicer than she'd ever thought she'd wanted, she'd refused to let Ryan see. That was fine by him. He liked surprises too, but it would be nothing compared to the one he had planned for Lisa.

Lisa sat in front of Mindy's make-up vanity and put on her earrings, which Ryan had bought her.

When he'd walked through her door last May, she had teased

that she was going to make him Mr. Palmer, but now she laughed. She hadn't seriously thought this was where she'd end up.

"I think everyone is ready when you are," Tina said, wearing a dress that accentuated her small swollen tummy.

"I'm ready."

"Okay, well, Ryan has something for you before you walk down the aisle. He wants you to have it now," Tina said as Mindy opened the bedroom door and Rose and John Hughes walked into the room.

There were no words as she ran to Rose and wrapped her arms around her.

"Oh, honey, look at you," Rose said over her shoulder. "You've grown into a beautiful woman."

Lisa eased back, sure that her makeup was ruined now. "I can't believe you're here. Both of you," she said reaching for John's hand.

"We'd like to walk you down the aisle and give you away. It's what parents do for their daughters, and you've always been ours, sweetheart."

Lisa fell into their arms again and felt the love that they had always given her.

RYAN STOOD IN THE COOL NIGHT, THE TWINKLING LIGHTS illuminating the back yard. His parents and grandmothers sat on chairs wrapped in blankets. His brother and Jason stood next to him. He'd heard the squeals when his surprise had been received. One thing had always been for sure, Mama Rose and John had to be there when they got married. Ryan wouldn't have had it any other way.

Mindy, Ruby, and Tina stood across from them and wore happy grins.

Then, he saw her. On the arms of the of the only people she'd ever considered her parents, she walked toward him in a white dress, simple and elegant.

When he'd left everything in Chicago, he didn't think that this was where he'd end up. But, the moment he'd seen Lisa, he knew where his heart was headed.

As Mr. And Mrs. Hughes brought Lisa to him, Rose reached her hands to his cheeks and kissed them. "She's very important to us. Take good care of her," she said to him.

"I promise."

John shook his hand and then turned to kiss Lisa on the cheek before sitting with his wife.

As Ryan led Lisa up the steps, her hand trembled in his. "I can't believe you brought them out for this," she whispered.

"I wouldn't have let them miss it. I want you to know how loved you are. What was your past, isn't your future."

"I know that now. I'm so very glad you're my future."

"I'll be here for all of it. I promise."

Lisa lifted on her toes and pressed a gentle kiss to his lips. "I promise too."

Ruby cleared her throat. "Seriously, you two. Get on with it."

Lisa laughed as she pressed her head to his shoulder, and before the November evening turned frigid, she'd promised again to be his wife and love him forever. And in that moment, Ryan knew they had their happily ever after.

THE ROM COM MOVIE CLUB - BOOK TWO

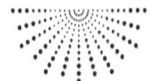

We hope you have enjoyed *The Rom Com Movie Club - Book One*. Here is an excerpt from *The Rom Com Movie Club - Book Two*, available December 1, 2022.

THE ROM COM MOVIE CLUB - BOOK TWO

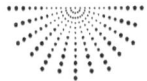

YES, SHE'D PUT PINE-SCENTED FLOATING CANDLES IN THE CLAW foot bathtub, because Lisa always thought it was a nice touch.

Yes, she'd made ice cubes out of punch for Tina to put in her sugar-free, caffeine-free, color-free soda.

Yes, she'd made the special peppermint candy cookies her grandmother used to make, just for Ruby.

In lieu of the usual college T-shirts which they would always wear with pajama pants for rom com movie night, Mindy had a box for each of the girls under the Christmas tree with a sweater to wear with their pajama pants. Of course they were ugly sweaters, and she couldn't wait until the girls saw them.

Mindy had chosen *Bridget Jones' Diary* as the holiday movie, and it seemed appropriate to have uglier sweaters than even the ones depicted in the movie.

She had real gifts for each of her friends as well, because this would not only be their Christmas Rom Com Movie Club night, but it would be their time to celebrate each other before the holiday.

Now that both Lisa and Tina were married, they'd have family to be with at Christmas. Ruby had already told everyone she was going to Hawaii with mother for Christmas, and they weren't going to celebrate at all, which was no surprise. Ruby could be a Scrooge, but her mother could be a bigger one.

Mindy would end up at her parents' house with her sister and her family. Her grandmother would be there, and probably an aunt and uncle or two. She would endure the many questions. *Why aren't you married? Why don't you date more? I know a nice guy, would you like to meet him?*

She didn't want any of it, but she was a rule follower and the keeper of any tradition, so she'd put up with it, even if she'd rather fly to Hawaii and be Scroogy with Ruby and her mother.

As she pulled a tray of chocolate chip cookies from the oven, the doorbell rang. Right one time, she thought as she set the tray on the top of the stove and hurried to answer the door.

Her three dearest friends stood together on the porch, each with boxes and bags in hand.

"Come in. Come in," Mindy said stepping back from the cold.

"How Lisa got married outdoors a month ago, and today I have on long underwear under my pajama bottoms, a sweatshirt, a coat, scarf, hat, and gloves amazes me," Ruby complained as she handed Mindy her stack of gifts to hold while she toed off her boots.

"Yes, and next week there are two days predicted to be in the sixties," Tina said, setting her bags on the ground and slipping out of her coat.

"Why would we want to live anywhere else? Colorado gives us all four seasons every day of the year. We're lucky," Lisa added her optimistic view.

Ruby growled as she pulled off her coat and hung it on the rack by the door. "Bite me. I want seventy every day of the year."

Lisa shook her head. "Boring."

Once everyone was free from their winter wear, they moved to the living room where they tucked their gifts under the Christmas tree.

Tina shook her head. "Seriously, Mindy, you should go into professional holiday decorating. People pay good money for perfect trees and lights like this."

Mindy laughed. "I had help with the lights."

"Still, I've never seen a more curated tree."

"You should see my mother's house. She has a tree in each room, each with a theme."

Ruby shook her head. "Your mother has a tree filled with porcelain dolls."

Mindy laughed at that. "And she curated that tree after you freaked out about her doll collection. So, Rube, that's your tree."

The four of them laughed as Mindy pulled the three boxes from under the tree and handed them each one.

"Okay, this goes with our movie night," she said.

The three women sat down on the sofa in the formal living room. Due to the many comments, mostly from Ruby, Mindy had taken the plastic cover off the couch. Yes, it was something her grandmother had left, and Mindy had found hard to remove, but it had been time.

Tina pulled her sweater from the box first, and wrinkled her nose. *"Bridget Jones' Diary*, huh?"

"You got that from the ugly sweater?" Mindy asked.

"You have your tells, Mind."

"Oh, hell no," Ruby held her sweater up which had an elf hat and legs that protruded from the sweater itself. "Are you kidding me?"

Mindy held up a hand. "For the record, I wrapped them all, walked away, mixed up the boxes, and then put a name on them. I didn't choose one certain sweater for any one person."

"Liar," Ruby snorted.

Each of the women pulled their sweater out of the box and slipped it on while they laughed.

Then Lisa, with her blinking Christmas tree sweater on, looked at Mindy. "If you don't have one, I'm taking this off."

Mindy grinned. "I'll go get it. And tonight I have a pink champagne face mask, and a sparkling red nail polish."

Tina was the first to stand. "I'm ready for a facial. Let's start there."

As was tradition, they'd all come bare faced and they put on the pink facial masks that tingled. Then, they polished their toenails and fingernails and started the movie. Glam came before drinks and snacks.

Crowded onto the sofa in the family room of the little home, they watched as Bridget Jones pulled up to her mother's house and proceeded to walk through a crowd of guests, while her "uncle" grabbed her butt.

"I had an uncle like that," Ruby said, tight-lipped because the mask had hardened. "He never tried anything, but he was—bleh."

"He's dead now, right?" Lisa asked. "I mean, I would think if he tried that on you now, you'd stab him."

"Damn right I would. Knee to the balls, and a knife in the heart while I looked him in the eye," Ruby said with confidence.

Mindy felt her cheeks heat under the facial mask she wore. Ruby could always take it that inch too far that made Mindy uncomfortable. But, that was some of her charm. Ruby was raw and uncensored, and sometimes Mindy wished she were more like that herself.

When the doorbell rang, the four of them exchanged looks.

Tina held up her hands. "I don't live with my mother-in-law anymore, so I know she didn't send her boys over here to deliver anything," she said referring to the night Aaron, her husband, and Ryan, Lisa's husband, brought over cookies while the women were all masked up as they were now.

Mindy stood, hobbled to the door on her heels, so as to not mess up her wet toenail polish, and looked out the peephole of the door. The man on the step was turned around as if he were looking at the lights on the trees outside. Hesitantly, Mindy opened the door just a crack.

"Can I help you?" she asked.

When the man turned, her heart caught in her throat. It was dark on the porch, and green and red lights shadowed his face, but it didn't matter, because she could see that he was heavenly perfect.

Dark eyes smiled at the same time his perfect mouth did. "Hi," he said with a hint of humor. "I think I caught you at a bad time."

"We're good."

"Mindy, right?"

She stared at him, studying him. "I'm sorry, do I know you?"

"Victor Hayes," he said the name as if she were supposed to know it. "My grandmother was Victoria Hanson, she owned the house next door."

"Vic?"

His smile widened. "You remember me?"

"I remember you being ten," she said, her lips held tight by the constriction of the mask.

When he laughed, it was deep, just like his voice, and it surged through her. "And that's how I remember you, too." He leaned in. "Remember when we played married couple in the treehouse across the street at Mr. Smith's?"

Mindy swallowed hard and nearly choked. "*You* remember that?"

"My first kiss."

Holy shit!

"So what are you doing here?" Mindy asked, now fully aware of how she looked with her mask on and the reindeer with the blinking nose on her sweater.

"I just moved into my grandma's house. I'm going to renovate it."

"It's been empty for years."

"Yeah, I have my work cut out for me. But I locked myself out. My phone is in there too. Can I use your phone to call my mom?"

It sounded childlike when he said it.

"Um, sure," Mindy said as she stepped back and let him in.

He eyed the pile of shoes at the door. "I've interrupted a party. I can go ask Mr. Smith to let me use his phone."

"It's dark out. Mr. Smith will have already barricaded himself in his house. But, no laughing when you see us."

"You all look like this?" he asked, scanning a look over her.

"Yep," she said and wondered what kind of impression she possibly could have made on the handsome man she'd once kissed in childhood.

PLEASE REVIEW

We hope you enjoyed *The Rom Com Movie Club - Book One* by Bernadette Marie. If you did, we would ask that you please rate and review this title. Every review helps our authors.

Rate and Review: The Rom Com Movie Club - Book One

MEET THE AUTHOR

Bestselling Author Bernadette Marie is known for building families readers want to be part of. Her series The Keller Family has graced bestseller charts since its release in 2011. Since then she has authored and published over fifty-five books. The married mother of five sons promises romances with a Happily Ever After always...and says she can write it because she lives it.

Obsessed with the art of writing and the business of publishing, chronic entrepreneur Bernadette Marie established her own publishing house, 5 Prince Publishing, in 2011 to bring her own work to market as well as offer an opportunity for fresh voices in fiction to find a home as well.

When not immersed in the writing/publishing world, Bernadette Marie can be found spending time with her family, traveling (mostly to Disney parks), and running multiple businesses. An avid martial artist, Bernadette Marie is a second degree black belt in Tang Soo Do, and loves Tai Chi. She is a retired hockey mom, a lover of a good stout craft beer, and might have an unhealthy addiction to chocolate.

PUBLISHER ACKNOWLEDGEMENTS

The team at 5 Prince Publishing would like to give special thanks to the following people for helping make The Rom Com Movie Club - Book One the best that it can be:

Bernadette Soehner, Cate Byers, Marianne Nowicki, Sophie Jefferson, Cayla Rusielewicz, Megan Hammond, Lindsey Haggerty, Daisy Salgado Pham, and Carrie Winfield. We would also like to thank our Brand Ambassadors, touring companies, bloggers, and influencers that help to promote the work of Bernadette Marie.

OTHER TITLES FROM 5 PRINCE PUBLISHING

Kennedy Devereaux *Bernadette Marie*
The Seven Spires *Russell Archey*
At Last *Bernadette Marie*
Masterpiece *Bernadette Marie*
A Tropical Christmas *Bernadette Marie*
Corporate Christmas *Bernadette Marie*
Faith Through Falling Snow *Sandy Sinnett*
Walker Defense *Bernadette Marie*
Clash of the Cheerleaders *April Marcom*
Stevie-Girl and the Phantom of Forever *Ann Swann*
The Last Goodbye *Bernadette Marie*
The Gingerbread Curse *April Marcom*

www.ingramcontent.com/pod-product-compliance
Lightning Source LLC
Chambersburg PA
CBHW030648020726
47493CB00006B/1925